FROM INTERNATIONAL BESTSELLING AUTHOR

DAVID B. LYONS

THE FOOTAGE THAT SHOOK AMERICA

Print ISBN: 978-1-7398552-1-5

❀ Created with Vellum

PRAISE FOR DAVID B. LYONS

"A masterpiece"
– The Book Magnet

"Best book of the year"
– BooksFromDuskTillDawn

"A devastating twist in its tail"
- Irish Independent

"Powerful"
– The Book Literati

For Margaret

—AMERICA PRESENT—

Power attracts the corruptible…
Suspect anyone who seeks it.

1

SHE HAD FORGOTTEN TO BREATHE. WHICH WAS UNUSUAL. CERTAINLY unusual for her—for somebody regarded by the nation specifically for her level of composure. When the tightening across her chest became unbearable, she exhaled with a panic that instantly transitioned to relief. Then she flicked her eyes across the length of the desk before immediately glancing down at her notes as soon as she feared her guest's eyes might meet hers. She consciously tried to steady her breathing; to ensure she wouldn't have to repeat exhaling in a panic again.

Once her breaths steadied, she swiped up the cards from her desk and then began to shift her hips awkwardly in her famous chair—the same twenty-thousand-dollar black leather chair she had first sat in for her debut show way back in 1997. As her hips were shifting, she glanced up to notice the heads of the silhouettes in the shadows swiveling—all looking toward each other.

"Y'okay, SJ?" her earpiece croaked.

She fingered her ear, glanced up to the large-windowed gantry above and beyond the swiveling heads in the shadows of the studio, and subtly nodded.

"Never better," she whispered.

"You sure?" Her earpiece crackled again. "You look like you're nervous. S'not like you. First half of the interview went great. No need to be feeling antsy.... Forget about the viewing figures—"

"I couldn't give two shits about the viewing figures," she whisper-shouted.

Her guest snapped a stare across her long desk at her, and Sarah-Jane felt a need to push out an uneasy laugh as an instinctive response.

"Sorry, Meghan," she said tip-tapping one of her pointed fingernails against the plastic piece in her ear. "Just talking to my god."

Meghan offered a sterile smile before glancing over her shoulder at her team of four suits huddled into an unlit corner of the studio. When one of her team — a middle-aged, bald man sporting an overly-groomed hipster beard — noticed Meghan glancing back at them, he offered her a wink and two thumbs up. He had been somewhat buoyed by how the first half of the interview had gone. It certainly hadn't been as pressing as his worst-case scenario. In fact, it hadn't even come close. Sarah-Jane Zdanski may have held a reputation for being bi-partisan in her politics, which both riled and seduced America's population in equal measure, but the majority of the country were pretty much in agreement that her questioning, while notoriously tough, was *always* fair. And *always* balanced. She had built her reputation on it. Guests may have been intimidated by appearing on *The Zdanski Show* for fear of the notoriously tough line of questioning, but they simply couldn't help themselves. Zdanski had been the most watched evening show on US television for over two decades. Celebrities and politicians benefited tremendously from a surge in reputation once they appeared on it, unless, of course, they crumbled under the heavy questioning. Despite the risk, however, it was seen as a badge of honor to sit on the opposite side of Sarah-Jane's sausage-shaped desk. Which is why Meghan Markle was now sitting across from her—hoping to benefit from that badge of honor. Ten million Americans were projected to be watching live tonight in what was being dubbed "2022's must-watch TV interview"—the highest viewership number *The Zdanski Show* had amassed since the turn of the century.

"Twenty seconds!" a high-pitched voice shouted out.

Then a brush appeared on Sarah-Jane's brow, and as was by now a regular tic of hers, she stiffened the muscles in her face to allow the bristles to sweep down her nose. While her face was being cleared of the glean from the strong white lights sizzling above her, she poked an index finger at the screen of her iPhone. Another tap of that finger brought her straight into her Twitter feed.

She picked the phone up as her makeup artist swept herself back into the shadows of the studio, finger typed "S," and quicker than a blink, "SJZ" showed up as an option in the search bar. She tapped at her own initials and began to gnaw at the excess skin on the back of her thumb while she read what America was thinking about her in real-time.

SJZ is letting the Duchess off the hook here. This ain't date night. Ask some tough questions, bitch! #tellCSNsheispastit

Sarah-Jane scrolled.

SJZ is handling the Meghan interview with the same grace she's always carried through her illustrious career #SJZ&Meghan #TheZdanskiShow

Scroll.

Who lux more fuckable 2nite? SJZ or Meghan? #ImagineBothAtThe-SameTime

"We're back in ten," the voice in Sarah-Jane's ear squeaked.

The floor manager — a young woman with scraggly, unkempt dry hair who looked as if she was being swallowed by the oversized pale gray hoodie she had chosen to wear that day — took a step toward Sarah-Jane's sausage-shaped desk and then sneezed into her elbow.

"Don't worry. It's not COVID," she said, straight-faced. Then she rubbed a circular pattern into the nub of her nose with her palm, creating an ugly squelch sound just as the studio had fallen suitably still and silent in anticipation of the countdown.

Sarah-Jane and Meghan both squinted at her as they soaked in the few final silent seconds of quiet, then the floor manager lifted a tiny hand out of the oversized sleeve of her gray hoodie to show three of her fingers… then two… and then just the one. As soon as she stepped backward, camera one's red light blinked on and then it wheeled forward, creating a cool whoosh.

"Welcome back to the show," Sarah-Jane beamed down the lens before swiveling in her famous leather chair to face her guest. "Meghan, we spoke in the first half of this interview about your acting career, before moving on to the time you met and fell in love with Harry. But I just want to go off-script and return to something you mentioned before the commercial break, if you don't mind." Sarah-Jane noticed the bald, hipster-bearded suit snap a stare at her over her guest's shoulder. "You said — and I hope I am quoting verbatim here — that once you had moved to London and attempted to settle into life as a royal, you began to feel 'an enormous mental strain,' is that the correct phrase you used?"

Meghan creased her bottom lip into a grimace, then clasped her hands across the naval of her midnight-blue Victoria Beckham dress suit, all while continuing to maintain her ruler-straight posture.

"You quoted me correctly, yes. Although to label it a 'mental strain' is somewhat underplaying how I was feeling back then," she said, softly.

"You mean it was *more* than mental strain?"

"Oh, it was much more. I suffered mentally. I am on record as saying this publicly before. My mental health was really struggling around this period of my life."

"*Where you going with this?*" the voice in Sarah-Jane's ear squeaked.

The host tilted her head at her guest and offered a half-smile.

"Really?" she said. "I know this is subjective, but you're surely one of the most attractive women I've ever laid my eyes on. You had just married a prince. You were living in a castle. You were experiencing a life all little girls can only ever dream about. Every girl is filled with the fairy tale of becoming a princess from... what, aged three?"

Meghan's marble brown eyes narrowed, and she leaned her forearms onto the sausage-shaped desk, rounding her perfect-posture spine for the first time since the interview had begun.

"Sarah-Jane," she said, "you are showing quite a level of naivety with regards who mental health struggles can and cannot affect."

"*Where the fuck are you going, SJ?*" the voice in the anchor's ear spat.

Sarah-Jane pinched two fingernails into her ear, took the plastic piece between them, and then laid it down carefully next to her glass of water—noticing that even the water was rippling.

"I don't believe you," she said.

In the stunned silence that followed, Sarah-Jane could hear the vibration of frustration sizzling from the earpiece lying in front of her.

"Sorry... sorry, you don't believe what?" Meghan asked, wrinkling the freckles on the bridge of her nose.

Sarah-Jane pressed her lips together, then glanced sideways at camera number one before darting her eyes around the shadows of the studio, noticing that her executive producer Phil had his palm slapped to his mouth. Her team of three other producers were all huddled into such a dark corner behind him that Sarah-Jane couldn't quite make out how high their eyebrows had raised. "Tell me... tell the nation, Sarah-Jane," Meghan said, her brown eyes glistening even more than usual, a look of bewilderment washing over the tiny features of her beautiful face. "What don't you believe?"

Sarah-Jane lightly drummed her pointed fingernails against her desk, before glaring at her guest.

"I don't believe *you*, Meghan," she said. "I don't believe for one second that you were suffering from a mental illness."

NATE BENNETT

I suck a sharp breath in through the gaps in my teeth, then stab a finger to my cheek. It burns. So, I reach for the tissue paper and snap a sheet off with a flick of my hand.

"You an old man, Nate," I say to my reflection as I ball the tissue up before pressing it against the bubble of blood.

It ain't no surprise I keep cutting myself shaving. Not with the amount of lines on my face. I've always blamed the cheap-ass razors for these cuts, and not the wedges cut deep into my skin. Maybe Abigail is right. Maybe I do enjoy lying to myself.

I'm already running late, so I'll have to get dressed while I've still got the tissue pressed to my cheek. I head to the bedroom and throw my arms into the short sleeves of my navy shirt before smelling the shoulders of it. It smells okay, even though I haven't worn it in months. Then I step into my navy pants, wondering if they'll be a little loose 'cause I'm sure I've lost weight since I've last worn 'em. But when I pull up the zipper, they seem to fit as snug as they ever have.

I turn to the mirror in the bedroom and begin to pat the blood with the tissue. It stings like hell. So, I suck on my finger, then stab the tip of it against the cut and hold it there while I stare at the reflection of my heavy-ass eyes.

In the silence between my huffs, I hear a key turn in my hall door.

What the fuck does she want? She only ever stops by when she's looking for something.

I kicked her outta here last year. Or she left. Depending on whose side of the story you wanna believe. She still has a key 'cause technically it is still *our* house, even though it's my wages that have always paid the big-ass mortgage on it. I hear her running up the stairs without entering the living room, probably because she saw our bedroom light on, and she knows I'm up here.

"What the fuck?" she says as soon as she sees me. She looks terrible. "They're letting you back on the streets?" I look down myself while she puffs out her cheeks and when I stare back up at her, she is shaking her head. "They truly do not give a shit, do they?" Then she holds her hand up. "Sorry," she says. That's unusual. She never apologizes. "I shouldn't be talking trash 'bout you 'cause I, ah... I need some money. I'm all out and—"

"The guy you're fucking not got no money?" I say.

"How many times do I hafta tell ya, Nate?" she says. "There's never been another guy. Can't you just accept I left you because... well, because of you?"

"Fuck off, Abigail!" I snap, just as I begin to thread my leather belt through the loops of my navy pants.

"Look, Nate," she says. "I just need a couple hundred bucks. I'm late paying a small debt and—"

"To your drug dealer?"

She holds her hands to her hips and tilts her head in disappointment. I already feel like an idiot. She hasn't even been here one minute, and I've already thrown three insults at her.

"No. Of course not a fuckin' drug dealer. A neighbor of mine. She was selling these air fryer things on a stupid pyramid scheme, and I bought one. But today's the day I'm supposed to pay her for it and well... I just don't have the money. And I... I... I..."

While she's stuttering, I reach for the jeans I wore yesterday that I had left in a ball next to my bed so I can snatch my wallet from the back pocket.

"Here," I say, pulling out three fifty-dollar bills and tossing them to the bed we both used to have sex on. "'S'all I have."

"Thank you," she says sweeping them up. And then she pats me on the shoulder, spins on her heels and leaves our bedroom to skip down the stairs.

"Y'cut your face again, Nate… must be those cheap-ass razors, huh?"

The front door slams shut, and the house goes all silent again. I hate this fuckin' silence.

"Bitch," I snarl into the mirror. I hate calling her a bitch. But sometimes I can't help myself.

I suck on my finger and stab it against the bubble of blood again before sucking in another sharp inhale through the gaps in my teeth.

Fuck it. I gotta go. Else I'm gonna be late. And being late won't go down well with Costello. Not on my first day back.

I grab my wallet, stuff it into the back pocket of my navy pants, then jog down the stairs where I sweep my keys up from the hall table before opening up the front door just in time to see her Audi screeching away with my hundred and fifty bucks sitting pretty in her pocket.

"Fuck me!" a voice shouts from my neighbor's front yard. "They're not putting you back on the streets, are they?"

AIMEE STREET

I thought wearing a microphone that curls over my ear and wraps around my cheek would make me look more professional, more legitimate. But it's actually making me feel a bit self-conscious up here; like a bit of a tit. Mainly 'cause I don't know what to do with my hands. I keep shifting them from the pockets of my trousers, to holding my fingers in a diamond shape around my abdomen, to pinching at the small, bubbled microphone hanging on the side of my cheek. But I can't let my flailing hands get inside my head. I have to nail this. I just have to….

I squint at the group gathered in front of me as they continue to watch the screen behind me. I count forty heads. Definitely the largest group I've ever pitched to.

When the video stops playing and the light overhead turns back on, an applause ripples around the small room and as it does, I walk to the center of the stage, offer the group a purse of my lips and then shove my hands immediately back into my pockets because I don't know what else to fucking do with them.

"Thank you," I say, bowing a little. As if I've just won an Oscar. I cough, self-consciously. Then purse my lips again. "As it astonishingly says in that video, over two thousand children will die from cancer in America this year. One child every week is dying in our state of Connecticut alone. *One. Every. Week*! In St Bernard's Hospital right now," I say, pointing at the name tag pinned to my collar, "we have one hundred cancer patients under the age of eighteen in our beds. This, I'm proud to say, is down ten percent from this time last year. But it is still way too big a number. Waaaay too big. The reason the number has been decreasing, however, is down to kind and generous folks just like you; the everyday people of Connecticut who support the work we do at St Bernard's Hospital." Another round of applause ripples. But I don't pause. I go on, my confidence reigniting. "The more research we can do on this subject, the more cancer patients we can support. The more funding our hospital receives, the more cancer patients we can support."

I cough lightly into my hand, to clear my dry throat, and then I step back to pick up the bottle of water I'd left standing on the stool in the center of the stage. All choreographed. While I take a sip, I convince myself that despite my nervous start, the pitch is going as well as I could've expected by this stage; that I've delivered most of my lines just as confidently as I delivered them to the mirror over and over last night. After I place the bottle back down on the stool, I reach for the remote control and press the arrowed button. There's a pause, before an image of a bald five-year-old me blinks up on the screen over my shoulder.

"I know first-hand just how much the funding at St Bernard's Hospital helps young patients of cancer. This is me—age five. As bald as Kojak. As sick as a dog. At one point, a surgeon told my mother that I may only live another two years...." I pause, to touch the bridge of my nose, pushing it ever so slightly downward so that it helps the first tear to fall. Then I lick across my crooked teeth before taking my hands from my pockets and forming my fingers into a diamond around my abdomen again. "But here I am, twenty-one years old and as healthy as the healthiest person in this room. I am cancer free. And have been since I was eight years old. In fact, it was when I was eight years old that I told my mom and dad that when I grew up, I wanted to work at St Bernard's Hospital; that I wanted to be just like one of those grown-ups who helped me when I was sick. And, ladies and gentlemen, I stand in front of you today as a proud, elected member of the St Bernard's Hospital Cancer Trust."

A ripple of applause, louder this time, makes its way toward me from the back of the room. And as I practiced, I hold my hands out wide, nodding my head, and encouraging the applause to rise in volume. When it eventually dies down, that's when I thumb away the tear that's been clinging to my cheek. All choreographed.

"So today, I am asking you to be a hero to the children I work with every day; to play your part as honorably as you possibly can. I have a bowl here for those who would like to donate using cash… everybody remember cash?" I say, pushing a laugh into the microphone. But the joke I practiced in the mirror over and over again last night doesn't go over as well as I'd hoped it would. Maybe it's because they're all still numbed by the photo of a bald five-year-old me glowing on the screen over my shoulder. "And I also have a card reader here that accepts all major credit and debit cards as well as Apple Pay…. Thank you for spending your time with me this morning."

I step back, soak in the light smattering of applause, and almost immediately a swarm of folk rush to the edge of the tiny stage. As I lose count of the notes and coins being dropped into the bowl, an elderly woman with her debit card held aloft cocks her head, inviting me toward her.

"I wanna donate twenty dollars," she says. "The job you people do is incredible."

I hand her the card machine and watch her punch in her donation amount. As she does, a line forms behind her. Goddamn. I think this is gonna be my biggest take ever.

I stand awkwardly by the edge of the stage, trying not to give away my excitement as the card machine gets passed back down the line, then I glance over at the bowl to see it filling with notes. To stop my palms from sweating, I shove them into my pockets again. That's when a man, dressed in a sharp three-piece suit, catches my eye. He approaches me, gripping my card machine.

"I, ah… I hate to ask," he says, "because you were wonderful, but can you show me your credentials? I know you have a name tag, and the pitch was awesome, really touching I have to say, but we don't feel comfortable donating until we know for certain…."

"Sure thing," I say.

I clear my dry throat as I spin away from him, then I reach into my bag, slide out the A4 sheet I printed at the hotel office earlier this morning, and turn back to him, holding it out proudly.

"Here you go," I say, "confirmation that I work for St Bernard's Hospital."

He darts his eyes across the words on the page as I form another diamond with my fingers around my abdomen. And when he looks up at me, he nods... much to my relief.

"I work for the Governor," he says.

"Oh," I reply, nodding too, a wave of excitement rippling in my stomach. I sure didn't think anyone from the Governor's office would show up.

"We'll have to keep an eye on you," he says. "You really are doing marvelous work at St Bernard's."

He grins, handsomely, then punches numbers into the keypad before holding his card against the machine until it beeps.

"A generous donation from the Governor," he says. "With our best wishes."

Holy. Fucking. Shit.

MAGGIE ZUCHA

I toss the ball of rubber bands I've spent the past three weeks adding to from one hand to the other. Again. Then I kinda like yawn one of them huge I'm bored-outta-ma-fudge-pocket-type of yawns; like a hippo yawns.

"Late night, sweet cheeks?" Boris says.

"Always thought you were a dirty up-all-nighter," Wilson says.

Everyone sitting around us laughs. I glance over at Karen to see if she's laughing. She is. So, I kinda laugh too. 'Cause that's how it goes around here.

"Good one," I say.

Then I throw the ball of rubber bands back onto my desk and pick up my sausage roll. I begin unwrapping it 'cause, like, although I brought this in for lunch I kinda wanna eat it now 'cause these things are so yummy. And I ain't got nothing much else to do anyway. I buy these down in that British grocery store on Connolly Avenue. Three dollars. But they're so worth it. Don't know why it took me until I was twenty-four to find out that these mouthgasms exist. Brits sure do know how to make food better than we do over here. A hot dog ain't got nothing on these bad boys.

I fold the paper wrapping back and take a nibble off the corner of the dry pastry before placing it back down on my desk. Then I push my hands against the arm rests of my seat so I can lift my short ass a little higher and look around.

"Who you spying on, sweet cheeks?" Boris says.

My ass lands back down on the chair and I stare straight ahead at my blank computer screen.

"No one… I, uh… I was just, uh, I guess I was just wondering if there were, like, any sauces in the canteen area?"

"Sauces?" he says, laughing. "I'll pump you full of my sauce."

And then everyone laughs. Again. Even Karen. She looks at me this time while she's laughing—as if she's laughing in my face. So, I laugh, too. Just 'cause that's how it goes around here.

"Good one," I say again before I lean forward and begin tapping at my mouse so I can wake my computer screen up.

When it falls all quiet around me, I pick up the mouthgasm and gnaw at another corner of the pastry. Flakes from it fall onto my crisp navy shirt and, just as I'm about to brush them off, I can see him in the reflection of my computer screen, standing tall behind me.

"Zucha," he says.

"Sir, yes sir, yes sir," I say, standing to attention, before quickly trying to brush the pastry flakes away from my chest.

When I spin around, he is squinting at me for, like, way too long. And it begins to feel like I'm in high school again.

"Follow me," he barks.

Then he turns on his heels and marches off.

I stand still, not knowing what to do at first. I stare at the sausage roll in my hand, before snapping back to attention and tossing it onto my desk. Then I begin to skip-walk after him.

NATE BENNETT

All of the heads look up from their computer screens to stare at me as I walk down the corridor. Some of 'em mutter a "Hey Nate," but most don't bother their lazy asses. I just nod back at the ones who do, even though none of 'em bother to get outta their chairs to come shake my hand like proper men do. Fuck 'em. Fuck 'em all. I honestly couldn't give a shit.

I make it all the way to Costello's office without being stopped for a chat like I used to back in the good old days, and after pausing with my eyes closed, I finally rap my knuckles against his door.

"C'min," he shouts.

When I snatch the door open, I offer him my widest grin.

"Great to have you back, Nate," he says.

He stretches over his desk to offer me a fist to bump. The world's changed so fucking much in the past couple years. These days even your oldest buddies won't shake your hand no more.

"Thank you, Chief," I say as I'm bumping my knuckles against his. "I know you did your best to get me back in uniform and you've always looked out for me, so uh… thanks." Costello nods, and points his whole hand to the chair on the opposite side of his desk.

"I fought to bring you back for a specific job," he says. "And I need you to nail it. And nail it as soon as you can, you hear me?"

"No better man, Chief."

"Listen," he says, standing up before walking over to the window that looks out on to the parking lot. "Anybody here asks you about your suspension, just tell 'em to go fuck 'emselves. You served your time. And you don't need to answer to nobody."

"They can all take a hike, Chief," I say.

"Well…" he stares back over his shoulder at me, "taking you back has raised some eyebrows 'round here. Some of the guys are glad to have you back. Some saying you should never be seen wearing that uniform again. But in the wider world, I think we got away with it. You being reinstated only made it into one of the local newspapers. Nobody reads *The Daily Connecticut* anyway. So, all looks kosher. But I need you to nail the job you'll be given today. And I need you to do it keeping your nose clean, you hear me?"

"Whatever you say, Chief."

"S'why I'm giving you a partner."

"A fuckin' partner?" I say, gripping the arms of the chair. He never said nothin' to me about no partner when he called last night telling me he got me back on the job. "Why the hell do I need a partner?"

Knuckles rap against his office door before he has time to answer me.

"C'min," Costello shouts.

The door pushes slowly open, and I turn around to see who the hell my new partner is. I know the face as soon as I see it. Tall. Good lookin', I guess. At least the ladies think he's good looking. Abigail certainly does. She voted for him 'cause he's good looking. I didn't. I voted for him 'cause Trump said we needed to vote for him.

"Governor Rex Haversham," I say. Then I twist around to face the chief again. "He's my new partner?"

The chief tuts.

"Shut up, you dumb shit," he says. "He's here cos he asked me to get my best guy on this job. My best guy happened to be suspended. So, you've been brought back under Governor Haversham's orders…. Just don't tell anybody that."

I nod to take the compliment. Then, from behind Haversham, a tall guy with wide shoulders and a round stubby nose like a bulldog, walks in—dressed in a neat gray suit. Only the neat suit doesn't make sense. Not for him. Not when his face looks like a mess, with tufts of hair growing randomly from his bald head, from his ears, his nose.... This ugly fuck must be Haversham's heavy—his bodyguard.

"Nate Bennet," Governor Haversham says, walking toward me with his fist clenched. I bump my knuckles against his and then sit back and stare at him as he leans his elbow on top of the filing cabinet. "I've been assured you will complete the case Chief Costello is about to give you. I cannot stress how important this job is any more than for me to turn up here this morning in person and look you straight in the eye."

I nod again, impressed not just with the trust these guys are putting in me, but mostly with how good lookin' this guy is up close. He looks like a movie star. A proper old-time movie star like Clark Gable or Gregory Peck or something, not one of these stupid surfer dudes they call leading men these days. He has a perfect head of thick black hair all swept to one side, and a razor-sharp stubbled chin with a dimple in it.

"Make no mistake about it, Governor," Costello says. "Nate won't let you down. Right, Nate?"

"I don't let no one down," I say. That's a lie. Abigail goes on and on about how I *always* let her down; about how I let everyone down—even myself. But I guess her opinion don't count no more. She left me... so I don't need to care what she says to me. I swivel around in the chair, to look back at the chief, finally peeling my eyes away from the Governor's chiseled jaw. "Tell me," I say, "who's this new partner you're giving me?"

MAGGIE ZUCHA

I brush the flakes of pastry from my chest as I skip after him, trying to catch up.

He's so scary. Or at least I think he is anyway. Everybody else who sits around me say he's a kinda super cool boss or something. But I'm not sure they know what cool means. Or... maybe it's me who doesn't know what it means?

He pushes his office door wide open, and I immediately see a familiar face as I get closer and my stomach sort of, like, swallows itself. He's just as handsome as he looks on TV.

"Morning, Governor," I say, almost bowing as I step inside the chief's office for the very first time.

The Governor nods back at me, without saying anything. So, I flick my eyes to the big guy with the rough face behind him, dressed in a gray suit. He doesn't bother to say hello to me either. He doesn't say anything. Not even a small nod like the Governor did. Then Chief Costello points his hand behind me and I spin to see a gruff-looking cop slouched in the chair at his desk.

"Maggie Zucha, this is Nate Bennett. One of Connecticut's finest," Chief Costello says, while shutting his office door.

"How ya doing, Nate?" I say offering him my sweating hand and a big old smile, even though he looks like the kinda guy who'd never smile back. He just has one of them faces. Stern. Gruff. Ugly.

"Ahhh," he says, gripping my hand tight... too tight. "Somebody who's not afraid to shake somebody's fucking hand anymore. Fuck COVID, am I right, Zucha?"

He laughs, kinda like there's smashed glass in his throat. So, I laugh too. Just as I've trained myself to laugh at the jokes the men make around this place.

"How've you settled in, Zucha?" Chief Costello asks.

"Fine, sir, yes sir, fine sir."

Nate raises his eyebrows at me. I know why. It's 'cause I keep using too many "sirs." I always use too many "sirs". I can't help myself.

"Wait, hold on," Governor Haversham says, "She's new?"

"Governor," Chief Costello says, sitting into his oversized leather chair. "This is a balancing act. Trust me. Nate here, and Zucha together... they'll solve this. I'm partnering them up because it'll calm him down. He's got the responsibility to look after her, so I know he won't do anything too crazy... nothing like what got him suspended in the first place. Right Nate?" I stare at Nate, wondering why the hell he was suspended in the first place. "I promised I'd get to the bottom of this for you, Governor if you signed the paperwork to get Nate back in uniform. I've thought this all through. This is the best way to approach this matter. We have our most forceful officer here... and I'm teaming him up with a newbie, just so he doesn't get too forceful that he goes over the top again."

I feel like a schoolgirl again. The girl everyone is talking about. Not with.

"Okay... just make sure this gets fucking done," the Governor says. And I almost gasp. He, like, *never* cusses when he's on TV...

"Listen up, you two," Chief Costello says, leaning back in his leather chair and clasping his fingers behind his head. "This investigation has to be kept between us five folks, and these four walls. Understood?"

Nate nods while I shout, "Sir, yes, sir," again. And I immediately feel like an idiot. I need to cut out all the "sirs." I'm not at training camp no more.

"I cannot stress how important this investigation is," Costello continues. "It's so important, I can't even tell you about it." He sniffs, and sits more upright, leaning his forearms onto his desk. "Very sensitive footage has been brought to our attention. So sensitive, it'd shock the entirety of America to its very fucking core if it ever leaked out. Thing is... the folks who have this footage, we're not sure they know how valuable it is. Or, if they've even seen it. You need to get this footage from them and bring it back here as soon as possible. It should be straightforward, but we'll need to play this a bit forcefully to make sure it's done, Nate. We've no warrant. We can't apply for one because we need this to remain just between the five of us. Understood?"

"Understood," Nate says, before grinning.

"Understood Zucha?" Chief Costello says to me.

I take my eyes away from the nasty cut on Nate's cheek.

"Sir, yes sir, yes sir," I say.

And even though I'm cringing again, I'm actually starting to feel a bit excited and nervous all at the same time: My first day out on the streets. I can't wait!

AIMEE STREET

A police car whooshes by, wailing its sirens, as soon I step outside the hotel lobby. The sound of it causes me to clutch at my chest and take one large step back. Then I laugh at myself as I watch its wheels screech onto Tirconnell Avenue and out of sight—its wail dimming as it speeds off into the distance.

I step back outside and fill my lungs with cool, crisp fresh air. It sure is cold today—way too cold for this flimsy blazer and blouse. After looking up and down the street, I jog across it to reach the alleyway that runs away from the hotel. I've already done my due diligence. I know there are two massive black bins down here. So, I peel the ID sticker from my collar as I go, before tossing it into the first bin. Then I lift the wig gently from my head —because I learned during my practice run last night that if I pull at this thing too quickly it can yank some hairs out. And that hurts like fucking hell.

I stare down at the wig when it reaches the bottom of the bin; splayed out like a run-over cat. Ginger hair suited my pale-ass face—which is unusual. Nothing seems to suit my face. Not really. I've always thought that if I was prettier then I'd definitely be able to bring in more money. Folks are gullible enough as it is, but certainly so when it comes to pretty chicks. If I *was* pretty, with my brains, the money wouldn't stop rolling in. But I had to come to terms by third grade that I'll never be pretty. Not with these crooked teeth and this crooked-ass nose. I broke my nose when I was just seven. It still annoys me nobody ever thought to bring me to a hospital to have it set back in place. I've had to live my life ever since with a nose that looks as if it's trying to run away from my face.

I suck in a deep inhale before giddily taking the card machine out of my bag while bouncing up and down like a kid at Christmas. Then I thumb the buttons before closing my eyes—just so I can surprise myself with the total figure when I finally open them again. As I squeeze my eyes closed, I mentally picture the gullible idiots who held their cards against this machine back at the hotel.

"Fuck me!" I say as soon as my eyes flick open.

Seven hundred and fifty-three dollars. By far my biggest take. Kids with cancer, huh... why didn't I think of this before?

I begin to scroll through the donations on the machine, noting that one was for three hundred bucks alone. That must be from the Governor's office! Thank you very fucking much.

I roughly counted seventy dollars in cash that I spilled into my bag from the bowl earlier. That means I've taken in over eight hundred in total. Eight fucking hundred! That's a huge takeaway for a scam that only cost me around one hundred and fifty dollars to put together. And one hundred of that was spent on renting the conference room from the hotel for an hour. The rest of it... the name badge, the printouts, the editing of the video, the Photoshopping of the photograph of five-year-old me, the email invites I sent out to over five hundred people—that all cost me more time than it did money.

I place the machine back into the largest pocket inside my bag then look up and down the alleyway before throwing the strap of the bag back over my shoulder and beginning my long walk back to the bus station.

I scroll through the screen of my iPhone as I walk. Just to see the time. I'm supposed to have a class later this morning, but I'm not pushing myself to go. In fact, I haven't pushed myself to go for ages. I've barely shown up for any of the lectures since the beginning of the year. I think I've lost my hunger for journalism. Well, not journalism per se... but the media industry as a whole.

Besides, what's the point in me doing all this studying just to land a job at some newspaper that pays peanuts—especially when I can earn eight hundred bucks for just a couple hours of standing on a small stage in front of gullible idiots.

I let a scream screech from the back of my throat, then I begin bouncing up and down on the spot again. Eight hundred dollars. I can't believe it!

As soon as I turn left out of the town, to walk along the long road that leads straight to the old bus station, a silver SUV with blacked-out windows rolls past me and stops me in my tracks. I'm certain that's the same car I thought was following me this morning. But I always think I'm being followed. So, it's nothing new. I guess paranoia is a side effect of being a con woman. It's certainly a side effect of smoking weed every damn day. I should actually run by HQ on the way home to pick myself up an eighth of something I haven't tried before. I guess I owe it to myself. A little celebration.

I stop pacing to stare into a shop window at the mannequins draped in the latest fashion trends straight from last fall's runways, wondering if I should treat myself to something new other than weed. I'm not one for latest fashion—never have been. Could never really afford to keep up with the Joneses, whoever the fuck the Joneses are. But I guess we all do have to wear clothes every damn day anyway, so I may as well treat myself to something nice for a change. As I'm licking across my crooked teeth, wondering if that pale jump suit would suit me, I see it again. In the reflection of the window. A fucking silver SUV with blacked-out windows rolling slowly behind me.

BENJI WAYDE

I liked the wind blowing in my face. That's why I was up there. I wasn't going to jump. I never want to die. I'd stay alive forever if God would allow me to. But He won't allow me to. Cuz he doesn't allow anybody to stay alive forever. Just like He didn't allow Grandpa to stay alive forever. And He won't allow Grandma to stay alive forever either. I hate that she will die, too. So, I try not to think about it. I try not to think about being left all on my own. Grandma's seventy-three on her next birthday. She prob'ly don't have too many years left. She'll prob'ly only live till she's seventy-five like Grandpa did. Then it'll be just me. All on my own.

"Hey you, lazy Boy," she shouts. She still calls me "Boy", even though I'm a adult now. I turned twenty-one in January. That was the last birthday cake Grandpa was here to see me to blow out the candles for. "Get up here and help. Whatcha doin' just lookin' at that darn screen all the time? You'll go blind, Boy."

She makes me laugh. Nobody makes me laugh like Grandma. But I prob'ly shouldn't be laughing. I should be sad. So, I put my tablet down on the carpet in my bedroom and then I sneak out onto the small landing and look all the way up the top of the ladder, to the black square hole Grandma is shouting down at me from.

I'm a little scared to walk up the ladder. But I do anyway. Cuz if Grandma can do it. Then I can do it, too. Especially now that I'm a adult.

When I reach the top, I see her sitting on the far side of the attic, her legs with her wrinkly tights all stretched out in front of her. She's got a black dress on. Again. She's worn black every day since Grandpa died. Ten days in a row that is. I wonder if she'll still be wearing black after tomorrow—after we finally put Grandpa in the ground.

"Lots of dust up here," I say. I wave my hand in front of my face coz all of the dust is coming toward my mouth and my nose.

Grandma looks up at me. Her eyes are different. They've been different over the past few days. As if they're heavier. Yellowier.

"Go have a rummage in that box over there, Boy." She points to the darkest corner. "God knows what Grandpa kept in it."

Grandma's clearing out the attic cuz the landlord is making us move. We're moving into the front row of flats to flat number seven. Seven is supposed to be a lucky number. But it doesn't feel lucky. Cuz the flat's a lot smaller than this house. But we have to move to a smaller place cuz there's just two of us now. I think it's bad that the landlord, Mr. Pale, is making us move today—the day before Grandpa's funeral, but he told Grandma he couldn't wait till it was over. He wouldn't listen. Grandma says he wouldn't care even if he did listen. I wanted to phone Mr. Pale up and speak to him myself. And not have Grandma do it. But she wouldn't let me even though I've been a fully grown adult since the start of this year. And I have a moustache. I've been growing it since I was eighteen. And now it's a fully-grown adult moustache —right across the top of my top lip. Even though I have a moustache I don't think Grandma sees me as a adult. But that's okay. Cuz I love Grandma no matter what she thinks. I will always love her, hopefully for lots and lots and lots more years. She doesn't think I'm a adult cuz the doctor told her when I was fourteen that I had a mental age of somebody half my age. I'm not sure if that means I will always have the mental age of somebody half my age. If I do, that means I have a mental age of a ten-and-a-half-year-old now. But I dunno if that is right, cuz me and Grandma never talk about it. When I tried to talk about it once, after we visited that doctor when I was fourteen, Grandma said, "Oh, Boy, don't mind what that doctor say. He don't know what he's talkin' about. Yes, you're unique, Benji. But everybody is unique. That's what makes the world so wonderful." I remember her saying those words cuz I repeat them over and over inside my head when I feel sad if somebody looks at me all funny. I don't feel sad lots of times. Just some of the times. And I wasn't feeling sad last night. I just wanted to be alone. I wanted to feel the wind in my face. It was like I was up there with Grandpa when I was feeling the wind in my face. And it made me feel happy for a few minutes. Until the security guard grabbed me. Then he called the police and told them I was up there cuz I was gonna jump. He was lying. I told him lots of times before the police came that he was wrong. That I was just trying to feel the wind in my face. But he didn't believe me. I don't not like people. Grandma teached me that. But I really wanted to not like the security guard when he wouldn't believe me. He was making my hands curl up into balls and I digged my fingernails into my hands as hard as I could. It was sore. Really sore. But I still digged them in anyway. One of the policemen who came was nice though. She brought me to the hospital in the police car. And she stayed with me until a nurse came over and shined a light in my eyes. They both talked to me and said that I should speak to a therapist about suicide. I told them that they were wrong. That I wasn't going to jump. That I want to live. That I like living. Even if I am really sad cuz Grandpa died. But they didn't believe me. They didn't believe that I just wanted to feel the wind in my face.

Grandma believed me, though. And that's all that counts, I guess. When I phoned her and told her I was in the hospital, she got a cab right away even though I know that would cost her a lot of her money. I asked her how much the cab cost but she wouldn't tell me. I bet it was more than twenty dollars. I'll pay her back one day, whenever I get a job. I've been applying for jobs since I turned twenty-one. But I'm not good at interviews cuz I get nervous and fidgety with my fingers. I thought I was going to get the job in the Laundorama a few weeks back cuz the woman interviewing me was really nice and kept saying what a lovely man I was. But I didn't get it. Some old woman got it instead. Maybe she deserved it. I think I'm getting better at interviews, though. Even though I'm still fidgety and nervous I think I am answering the questions better than I did when I first started going to interviews in January. Maybe I'll get the next job, whenever one comes up in Birmingham. Grandma said I can have a job, as long as it's in Birmingham and I don't have to travel too far. Sometimes it can be a long time before a job comes up in the local newspaper. But right now, I think I need to be at home and not out working somewhere. Cuz Grandma needs me. She'd be so lonely if I was out most of the day working somewhere.

I slap at her foot when I crawl by her and she looks over her little round glasses at me.

"Oi, you," she says. And then she smiles. Her glasses move up on her face when she smiles. Her cheeks make them move, I think. That's the first time I've seen her glasses move up over the past ten days. I hope she's only sad today cuz Grandpa died. And not because she thinks I was going to jump off the roof of the North-farm Shopping Mall last night. I wasn't. I just wanted to feel the wind in my face. I wanted to feel closer to Grandpa.

"You written that eulogy yet, Boy?" she asks as I'm crawling across the attic boards.

I never heard the word eulogy till last week. Now she says it to me every day. Lots of times every day. A eulogy is a grown-up speech I have to do at Grandpa's funeral. But every time I pick up my pencil to write, I can't write any words. I don't know why. I'm a good writer. I think I am anyway. Miss Moriarty told me I was a good writer when I was in tenth grade. I never forgot that. She said, "Ooh, this is very good, Benji. You're good at writing, huh?" It was one of the best things anybody outside of house number forty-nine ever said to me.

"Not yet, Grandma."

"Well," she says, "your deadline is near ending. You better write it today. Otherwise, you'll have no words to say when you stand on that altar tomorrow, Boy."

"I will, Grandma," I say. "I'll write it today. I promise."

I don't think I ever saw this box before. I ain't ever been in this attic before. Not since I was eight years old, and I climbed up the ladder one time. Grandpa caught me and shouted at me. He said I wasn't to do that. That I wasn't to go up to the attic. He said sorry later for shouting so loud. But he thought I might fall and have to go to the hospital. That's why he was so angry. I told him I loved him and it didn't matter that he shouted at me and that I will never go up to the attic again. And I didn't. Not until just now.

I blow at the dust on the lid of the box and the dust all sprays backward into my face. And some of it even goes into my mouth. When I look back at Grandma to laugh because my face is covered in dust, she isn't looking up at me. She's reading some letter with her eyes turning really yellowy again. I hate that she's sad. I hate everything about dying. Dying is stupid. Even if we do get to go to Heaven after we die. I'd rather stay here in house number forty-nine. This is my Heaven. This is where I'm happy. I wish we were all here forever. Me, Grandma and Grandpa forever. Just the three of us. Watching TV.

I wipe the dust from my face with my sleeve even though Grandma says I should never do that, and when I think the dust is gone, I open the lid of the box. It's dark inside, but I can see four white eyes staring up at me; white eyes on small black boxes. Two white eyes on two black boxes. I lift one out and turn around to Grandma.

"What's this, Grandma?"

She looks up over round glasses again. Her eyes are yellowier than they were when I last looked at them. Really, really yellowy.

"Oh," she says. "That's one of your grandpa's old VHS tapes."

2

THE CONFERENCE ROOM HAD OFTEN SEEMED NEEDLESSLY LEVIATHAN-like to Sarah-Jane, but right now she felt as if a whole ocean was washing over her. While she sat at the head of the long-varnished conference table, with Phil by her side brushing his thick fingertips against the top of her thigh, at the other end — twenty feet away — Michael Jambon — the network owner — was flanked by two of the network's most senior lawyers, Davide Mohammed and Patricia Clarkson. Jambon had been the CEO of CSN for six years, ever since Walter Fellowes — who had run the network for almost four decades — got called out in the midst of the MeToo movement and was subsequently canceled from the television industry having been accused by fourteen separate women of, at the very least, sexual harassment, at the worst, rape. Sarah-Jane wasn't one of the fourteen to come forward, even though she had been a victim of Fellowes in some guise. He had tried it on with her when she first walked into the studios of CSN back in 1997, but she palmed him off with a level of distraction that was a league above his own and in doing so managed to retain a career at the network that didn't involve regular trips to the CEO's offices on the top floor for casual role play. When Fellowes got ousted in the MeToo movement, Sarah-Jane opted to stay out of the story; choosing to protect her sacred brand rather than make public Fellowes's attempt of sexually abusing her. Sarah-Jane's sole focus has always been her brand. Her bottom line is to protect her own legacy. Besides, Sarah-Jane wasn't overly happy that Fellowes had undergone such a cancelation. She had his number. She had control over him. Once Jambon arrived in situ, Sarah-Jane immediately felt the power she had held at the network somewhat subside.

"Just fuckin' apologize," Jambon ordered, slapping a flat palm onto the varnished conference table.

Sarah-Jane, with her arms folded, and twenty feet away — shook her head slowly while Phil's fingers continued to brush lightly up and down her thigh.

"I won't apologize. I am entitled to my opinion. I was hired for my opinion. You know what the First Amendment says about that, right?"

"The First Amendment says nothing about accusing somebody suffering with depression of just making it up!"

Sarah-Jane scoffed. Then she glanced at the jowly face of her exec producer. To Phil, she looked as sexy as ever. He actually thought fifty-year-old Sarah-Jane Zdanski was a lot hotter than the twenty-five-year-old who had been hired by CSN way back in 1997. The sharp blonde bob that she now sported worked as a perfect frame for her sculpted face. And the lines that had formed over the years that webbed from the corner of her light-green eyes actually accentuated her prettiest assets. The natural aging process looked good on Sarah-Jane's face, mainly because she had those enviable bright-green eyes that seemed to glow into the lens of a camera to light up the homes of the average American. Phil, on the other hand, had barely changed over that same quarter of a century, save for perhaps the growing of one extra chin. The bags under his eyes weren't the result of aging. They had literally been present for most of his adulthood. When Phil Meredith was thirty, he looked almost sixty. And now that he was approaching sixty, his bullish face was finally befitting of his years.

"What Mr. Jambon is saying," Davide said, to fill the awkward silence, "is that the network, at some point, has to draw a moral line across the First Amendment, Sarah-Jane. You know this. You're the finest anchor in America. You know there has to be a line drawn when it comes to Freedom of Speech. You simply can't go around saying things about people that aren't true."

"You don't know what I said isn't true," Sarah-Jane spat out. "Nobody does."

"Sarah-Jane," Jambon sighed, rubbing a hand over his face. "Stop playing with us. You will apologize on air next Wednesday, and that's it. That'll end the drama. We can deal with the waves of discontent on social media in the short-term. But if we advertise next week's show by saying you are going to apologize to the Duchess, then we can dilute the backlash and—"

"Are we still calling her a Duchess?" Sarah-Jane said, scoffing.

Jambon folded his forearms on the conference table before leaning his forehead on top of them and sighing loudly from the back of his throat.

"Sarah-Jane," Patricia, the elderly, bespectacled lawyer, said, deciding to speak for the very first time since they sat around the overly large conference room table some twenty minutes prior. "I'm afraid the board at CSN have left you no choice. I have it here in writing." She impressively swept a single sheet of paper the entire length of the varnished table, but when it skidded to a stop against Sarah-Jane's clasped hands, America's most-watched TV anchor didn't even bother to glance down at it. "The network has taken a stance. You either apologize to the Duchess live on air next Wednesday, or you're out...."

Sarah-Jane scoffed.

"Out? Me? I've been getting the highest figures for this network for a quarter of a century."

"We don't care," Jambon said, lifting his head from his forearms. "You crossed the line. Patricia is not making this up. The board of directors has voted. You either apologize, or we cancel your show."

Phil's fingers swept their way to the top crease of Sarah-Jane's thigh, making her subtly swallow.

"We're gonna need time to discuss this," Phil said gruffly. "Give us ten minutes."

The lines on Jambon's forehead straightened and he rose from his seat, sweeping up the paperwork in front of him, almost confidently—as if he felt Sarah-Jane was certain to agree to the apology. Then the two lawyers followed him as he exited the conference room, before the door was slammed shut and the negative energy that had been troubling Sarah-Jane instantly evaporated from the needlessly large conference room.

Phil immediately stood up, walked the length of the conference table toward the door and then, as quietly as he could, turned the lock on it. Then he spun around and grinned at America's most-watched face before jogging back. When he reached Sarah-Jane he ducked his head toward hers and took her bottom lip between his. He loved when they kissed. Her, not so much. If she could fuck Phil without any of the heavy petting, she would. But she's never wanted to hurt his feelings, so she has always gone along with his snogging as a snap attempt at foreplay before she lets him do to her what she really liked him to do to her. Their rendezvouses weren't overly frequent — only when Sarah-Jane's mood took her — but they were always spontaneous, and always swift. Like two minutes swift. She pants while he thrusts behind her like an overexcited dog. But, she never orgasms. In her own time, with her own toys, yes. But not with Phil. Even though they've been doing it for more than twenty-five years. They first started fucking in the back of the van they used to travel the streets of Northern Kansas in way back when they worked for their local PBS channel. Now they do it in the posh offices of the CSN studios, or — Phil's favorite — on the cream-colored leather sofa in Sarah-Jane's dressing room just before she goes live on air. Six hundred and fifty million eyebrows would raise if America found out the hottest news anchor in the country was regularly allowing her scruffy, overweight, blotchy-faced producer to have his way with her. But not one eyebrow has ever raised in that regard. Simply because nobody in America has ever entertained the notion that these two could be doing it. They've kept their affair a secret all these years. And in all that time, they've only ever made one error—a few years into their contract at CSN when the pill Sarah-Jane was taking to ensure she never fell pregnant failed her. She was almost five months in by the time she learned of her pregnancy, having gone to the doctors to inquire as to why she looked bloated every time she looked in the mirror. She was furious once she learned the reason. But once she got her head around her reality, she pushed Walter Fellowes into allowing her to take some extended time away from the show and then she and Phil lived out the rest of their pregnancy in total secrecy. Which certainly helped Sarah-Jane to get over the ordeal. She was cold and calculated through the whole pregnancy, anyway. As soon as she gave birth, she waved away the opportunity of embracing the crying bundle, and the baby — wrapped in a white blanket — was whisked away from her to find a new family. At the time, Sarah-Jane's only concern were the two stitches she was about to receive in her perineum. She didn't give two shits about that baby. She still doesn't. In fact, she's barely given the whole pregnancy ordeal a second thought since she re-started at CSN some six weeks later—her stomach as taut and thin as America liked it.

Sarah-Jane exhaled a satisfied sigh though her perfect teeth, then turned around to offer Phil a wide grin just as he was trying to stuff himself back inside his boxer shorts.

"When they come back in," he grunted, "just tell them that you're Sarah-Jane fucking Zdanski, and you don't apologize to no one!"

"I think that's a double negative, Phil but uh…" Sarah-Jane said as she dragged her knickers back up under her skirt, "don't worry. I know what I'm doing."

Sarah-Jane used the sleeve of her designer suit to wipe away the smudges her hands had left on the conference table while Phil was taking her from behind, then they both sat back down and waited on Jambon and his two lawyers to reappear. While they waited, she picked up her cell phone and chewed on her bottom lip as she typed her own initials into the Twitter search bar.

SJZ shouldn't be fired. She should be promoted. Don't know why anyone would ever believe a word Meghan Markle says. SJZ had the balls to call her out. #SJZisasexgoddess

· · ·

Scroll.

How have CSN not cancelled SJZ's ass already? Been 24hours already. #firethatbitch #SJZ&Meghan

Scroll.

Please CSN don't fire SJZ. I schedule a tug every Wednesday at 7pm just for her. #SJZisasexgoddess #SJZ&Meghan

She continued to scroll through the Tweets, noting that a poll the *New York Times* published some twenty minutes prior — in which over three hundred and sixty thousand Twitter users had already voted in — showed that forty-five percent of America wanted her fired, that forty-nine percent felt she was within her rights to question Meghan Markle's claims of depression, and that just six percent of those who voted, voted to simply select the "Do not care either way" option. She stared at the results, knowing that the percentage points could change any second as the poll continued to be fed to new social media users, but the digits hadn't shifted by the time the door of the conference room juddered, causing her to palm her phone back into her pocket.

"Shit!" Phil whispered as he raced out of his seat to turn the lock back on the door. When he pulled the door open, the three faces he had met with earlier stared at him, their brows knitting together in search of any signs that this whole drama might just be over. "We just wanted some privacy while we uh… discussed the matter," Phil said.

Jambon nodded, then strolled inside, followed by the network's two shit-hot, hot-shot, lawyers.

'Well?' Jambon said, as he sat, spreading his arms wide on the conference table.

Sarah-Jane looked at Phil as he walked back the length of the conference table to sit next to her, and when he was settled, she squinted back down at Jambon and folded her arms.

"I'm not apologizing," she said.

Jambon exhaled an audible, tired sigh.

"Sarah-Jane, I don't think you understand. You don't have an option. You either apologize or, I'm serious, you're done at CSN."

Sarah-Jane sat back in her chair; her arms still folded.

"You won't fire me, Jambon. I know you won't. I'm too price-less to CSN. Where would this network be without my fucking face, huh?"

Jambon slapped both hands to the conference table as he stood up.

"Goddamn it..." he snapped. Then he pointed his finger, "Sarah-Jane Zdanski, you're fired!"

NATE BENNETT

It was pretty cool how Costello slid my police badge across his big desk to me. As soon as I picked it up, I felt the power surge through me again. Then he tossed me a bunch of keys.

"Car number forty-three. Go get that footage!" he ordered us, and then we left, pacing all the way to the car numbered forty-three, parked up at the back of the precinct.

"Who's driving?" Zucha says after I beep off the alarm.

"Who d'you fucking think?"

I snatch open the driver's side door and hop inside. I've missed the smell of the warm leather in these cars. Though I think I'm still a little pissed that I'm stuck with a partner. I've never worked with a partner. I prefer to do my shit alone. I work the streets best when I'm alone. But I guess what Costello said made good sense. I have to do what I do the way I do it, but without getting myself into too much trouble. That's why she's here. To stop me from getting my ass suspended again.

"How long you been on the force?" I ask as soon as she gets her chunky ass into the passenger's seat. I roar the ignition before she has a chance to answer.

"Just three weeks."

"Three weeks? Jesus."

She shrugs her shoulders at me. She looks scared, as if she thinks I'm gonna bite her.

"So, you just graduated?"

"Yes, sir. I did, sir."

"You don't gotta call me no "sir" Zucha," I say. "It's Nate. E'rybody calls me Nate."

"Sure thing, Nate."

She's definitely nervous 'cause she's running her hands up and down her pants. She's already sweating. And we haven't even driven out of the precinct yet.

"Don't worry, Zucha," I say. "This is as easy an investigation as we're likely to get. We just gotta get our hands on that tape. Like candy from a baby."

She smiles at me. Not a real smile, but a kinda nervy grimace.

"But we've no warrant and—"

"You don't need a warrant when I'm around," I say. Then I click my signal on and we pull out of the precinct—heading for Woodville.

I flick the switch under the steering wheel as soon as we're outside and the sirens blare. Loud. Really loud. And I immediately love it. I've missed the sound of that wailing; the sound of power.

AIMEE STREET

I bend over the glass counter, flicking my eyes from the sativas on the left to the indicas on the right—pretending I understand what I'm studying.

"I'm uh… I'm celebrating today," I say, standing back upright and smiling my crooked teeth at the trendy dude behind the counter, "so I'm looking for something uplifting, I guess."

"Ah," he says, sliding back the glass, "have you ever tried Ghost Train?" He stretches his arm under the glass counter, reaching for the yellowy-looking bud in the corner. "This strain comes from Africa…. Supposed to cure back spasms and muscle injuries, that type of thing. But the high is amazing… really energetic."

"Perfect! I'll take an eighth," I say. Then I rustle inside my bag to grab some of the loose money I'd spilled in here from the bowl back at the hotel.

"Forty dollars," he says, zipping the top of the plastic bag he's just dropped the bud into. Then he punches the amount into the cash register and grins at me as I hand over two twenty bills some gullible idiots gifted to me.

"What you celebratin', girl?" he asks.

"Oh," I say, "Let's just say I've had a bit of a windfall today."

He pushes another laugh out of his nose.

"Well… I think your day is about to get a little better," he says.

He drops the bag of weed into my open palm, and I wink at him before spinning on my heels and skipping myself outside. I'm still buzzing from this morning. And that's before I even take my first hit of this Ghost Train shit.

I turn left out of the dispensary and as soon as I do, I hear a car begin to purr behind me… as if its engine decided to ignite as soon as I set foot back outside. I glance over my shoulder and then take a sharp inhale. The silver SUV. With blacked-out fucking windows.

"Hey!" I shout, racing toward it. "Hey, you!" It speeds up, zooming past me. "Hey…" I continue shouting as I chase after it. "Hey!" By the time its wheels are spinning around the corner at the end of the street, my efforts are all in vain. So, I don't bother anymore. I decide to stop, and I bend over, clutching both of my knees and breathing in and out as sharply as I can.

"Y'okay?" a stranger asks.

I look up at him through the scraggly strands of my curly hair, still doubled over, still panting short, sharp breaths.

"Yeah," I say. "Fine."

Then I spin around and begin to walk toward home, my brow feeling like it has an added weight to it. I'm definitely being followed. That's three times I've spotted that SUV today… and in two different towns, too. It was outside my bedsit this morning when I left at eight a.m., then outside the hotel when I finished my presentation… and now again—outside Hemp HQ, literally waiting for me to come back outside. I lick across my crooked teeth, trying to think it through. Maybe it's somebody I've scammed in the past catching up with me. I should lie low for a while. Though this is nothing new, I guess. I've always had a feeling that I'm being followed—as if this level of paranoia is part of who I truly am even before I first started smoking weed.

I let out a sigh, stop walking, and then remove the bag's strap from my shoulder before reaching into the front pocket for the weed. I feel for my personalized vaporizer in my jacket pocket and begin tearing at the leaves from the bud with my fingers, before flicking the flakes into the chamber. It cost only two extra dollars for me to have the name 'Aim' etched into this thing. It's my pride and joy. I don't go anywhere without it.

Then I close the chamber, pocket the packed vaporizer into my blazer and I begin skipping, excited by my record haul of eight hundred dollars this morning and, just as I reach the corner that the SUV skidded around a couple minutes ago, a body appears and we crash into each other.

"Shit, I'm sorry," I say.

"No, I'm sorr— "

I look up to see that old, familiar smile. He's always smiling. Even though he's about as depressed as any human could possibly be.

"Hey, Mykel," I say, wrapping my arms around him and hugging him as tightly as I possibly can. It's been so long since I've held him. We can do that, me and Mykel—not see each other for months on end, which is weird, seeing as we've been like a brother and sister pretty much our whole lives.

"Man, have I missed you?" he says.

He looks at me, gripping on to both of my shoulders while he beams another of his cheesy grins.

"You look good," I say.

"I feel good," he says, "now that I've bumped into you."

"Literally,' I say, snorting out a laugh, "Hey…" I reach into my pocket and pinch at my vaporizer. "Wanna go get stoned?"'

MAGGIE ZUCHA

I think this guy might be some sort of fudge nugget. As if he's living up to, like, the stereotype of some sort of TV street cop or something. As if he thinks he's in *The Wire*. He sure does look the part though, with his rough, stern face and that ugly deep, fresh cut on his cheek. As soon as he turned on the sirens, he sat more forward in the car, as if he was testing the limits of his seat belt, and we've been speeding ever since. I haven't looked at the speedometer. But I'd like to, if I wasn't pushed back into my seat by the force. Two separate cars have had to skid to a stop so as to not crash into us already. I actually let out a fart and a scream at the same time when one almost slammed into the side of me. Nate didn't hear my fart, I don't think. But only 'cause my scream was louder.

He pulls left onto Woodville and slows down, eyeballing the buildings on my side of the street before stretching his arm across my line of vision. Finally, my normal breathing returns and I actually begin to think I liked that; that I enjoyed the speed and the sirens.

"That's it," he says, braking the car to such a sudden stop that it causes me to fly forward before the seat belt yanks me back to the seat. "Let me do all the talkin'."

He gets out so quickly that I have to release my seat belt in a panic before I can run after him and up the path that leads to a long row of small commercial buildings.

This is the first time I'm actually gonna be a cop. Like for real. All I've done so far is sit in the precinct for eight hours a day adding to my rubber band ball before packing up my empty lunch box and going home when the time comes. I've learned some things, I guess. I've learned that I should just laugh when somebody makes fun of somebody else, even when I'm the butt of the joke. Just laugh. It's how to survive; how to get along. Oh, and I've learned it's expected that we were all supposed to have voted for Trump at the last election, and that Biden stole the election. That's what I've heard 'em all talking about in the precinct anyway. I don't think Biden stole the election, seems a bit farfetched to me. I just think Trump's a sore loser. Though, I dunno what to think anymore sometimes. Politics just seems a little too hard for me to understand. I sometimes wish we could just go back to the days when America was a normal country, like when I was a kid growing up and W. was our president. The world just seemed better back then. Friendlier. Safer. It's kinda got so weird on the TV and on the internet now that I like, uh, I dunno... I kinda just started to think Trump had gone a bit cray cray by the time his second election came around. That is why I didn't vote for him the second time. Though I sure as hell didn't tell the guys at the precinct I voted for Biden when I was asked. I just said, "Course I voted for Trump. We were robbed."

When Boris asked me on my third day at the precinct, when my rubber ball was only the size of a golf ball, where I had been on January sixth last year, I told him I was at home watching the attack on the Capitol unfold on TV.

"They're martyrs, right?" he said.

"You bet they are," I replied. Then I got back to adding to my ball of rubber bands, hoping he wouldn't ask me no more questions about Trump, or Biden. Or January sixth. Or, anything to do with anything on the news. 'Cause I don't understand half the stuff they talk about on the news. The stories move too quickly. It's impossible to keep up.

"Zucha," Nate says as he stops outside an office door, "follow my lead. Remember the task: we've to retrieve the footage. That's all! We never lose focus of the task in hand."

"Sir, yes, sir!"

He stops, puts his arm in front of me and gives me a weird stare as if he's just eaten something that tastes disgusting.

"What's with all this "sir" bullshit?" he asks.

I shrug my shoulders and then begin shaking my head.

"Dunno, it's like I can't... I dunno... I can't stop saying it."

"E'rybody calls me Nate."

I nod.

"Got it, Nate! I'll follow your lead... and I'll stay focused on the task in hand. Retrieve the footage. That's all we gotta do. Retrieve the footage."

He kinda like smirks at me, or something, then he pushes the office door open and we quickly move ourselves inside. It's quiet in here. A small white office with two large glass desks. Though there's only one man sitting at one. The other desk is empty.

"Oh," the man says, looking over his glasses at us. "What can I do you for officers?"

"Who runs this place?" Nate barks.

"I do... well, me and my partner, Roseanna. She's working from home today."

He walks out from behind his desk, rubbing his hands together.

"We need to know where you keep your recorded footage from the CCTV camera out back."

"Oh," the man says, "what is it you're looking for?"

"That's confidential police business," Nate says.

The man stares at me, then back at Nate.

"Well, uh... a recording of all CCTV downloads straight to my computer here. I can call it up for you... what date was the footage shot?"

"June fourteen. But we don't want to view it. We just need to delete it."

"Delete it?" The man says, rubbing his hands together, nervously. "Have you uh... have you guys got a warrant to delete it?"

"Nope," Nate says.

"No?" the man says, shaking his head. "Well, then I don't believe you have a right to delete any of my recordings, do you?"

"Oh… we do," Nate says.

"Well…" the man places his hands on his hips, "if you don't have a warrant, then what gives you the right?"

"This," Nate says. Then he slaps him across the cheek with the back of his hand.

BENJI WAYDE

We have an old TV with a video player in it that Grandpa used to watch sometimes in the bedroom and Grandma has allowed me to bring it downstairs while she's clearing out the attic so I can watch the VHS tapes on it. Only cuz I kept asking her over and over and over again if I could watch them. But she said I didn't have too long. That we have to bring some stuff over to our new apartment at ten o'clock. And, that I could watch them only if they helped me to write my eulogy.

I kinda feel that I should stay up in the attic. Not helping her clear out cuz I only get in the way when I'm helping Grandma clean. But prob'ly cuz I should stay in the same room as her. To be there for her. Next to her. So, she isn't so lonely. Her eyes have been yellowier today. Yellowier than they were yesterday. I think it's cuz it is our last day in house number forty-nine. But maybe it's cuz I was on the rooftop of the Northfarm Shopping Mall last night and she might think I was trying to do what I wasn't trying to do. I just wanted to feel the wind in my face. That's all.

I stick the TV plug into the socket then I press one of the VHS tapes into the slot that looks like a mouth under the screen. When it makes a small motorbike sound, I sit back down into the sofa that a man is coming to collect later today cuz this sofa that we've had since I can remember won't fit in our new apartment and Grandma will have to buy a new one.

The television screen comes on. It's all blue. Just blue with a black-and-white striped box in the top corner. I look next to me on the sofa at my notebook and my tablet. My tablet has a smashed screen. I didn't smash it. It was already smashed when Grandma bought it for twenty dollars at a garage sale on Luby Hill.

I decide to pick up my notebook while I wait on the VHS to play and not my tablet. I really need to write this eulogy today. Grandma said that if I see Grandpa on the tapes then that might help me write. So far all I have written is:

I love you Grandpa

I don't know what else to write. What more can I say than "I love you Grandpa"? That's all I really need to say about him. That's what I told him in the hospital the night before he died. He was lying there with his eyes closing every few minutes. Grandma was crying. So, I knew he was going to die. That's when I leaned into his face and kissed him on his cheek and I whispered, "I love you, Grandpa."

He opened his eyes and smiled up at me. Then he tried to touch my face with his hand. But his hand couldn't reach that far, and his eyes closed. And I never saw him awake ever again. And I never will. Not until I go to Heaven, too.

I look at the one sentence I have written in my notebook and then at the TV I have just left on the carpet next to me. The screen is still blue. Maybe there's nothing on the VHS tapes. I crawl closer to the TV to check, but as I'm looking for buttons I might have to press to start the tapes, I hear Grandma up in the attic blowing her nose into a tissue. And then I think I hear her cry. A small cry. Like a little sob. It makes me want to cry. But instead of crying, I walk into our tiny kitchen and begin to fill the kettle. I haven't heard her cry for the past three days. I hope she's not crying because I was standing on the rooftop of the Northfarm Shopping Mall. I hope she knows I just wanted to feel the wind in my face.

When the kettle clicks, I grab one of Grandma's Jamaican tea bags from out of the little tin she keeps them in. She loves Jamaican Tea. I tried it once. It just tasted like 'sgusting warm water. Grandma loves them, even though a box of Jamaican tea bags cost five dollars. She says they're her luxury. My luxury is Cola Bottle candies. I would eat them all day if I could. But Grandma says candies are not good for my belly. So, I only have them on Fridays.

I pour the hot water over her tea bag, like Grandma teached me to do, and then I stir it a little like she teached me to do, before I squeeze the spoon against the tea bag to watch the flavor all squirting out like Grandma teached me to do. Then I pour in some milk from the fridge and stir it with the spoon five times. Just like Grandma teached me to do.

I hope this will make her smile again... make her cheeks move her glasses up on her face.

I carry the mug up the stairs, then I see the ladder in front of me and I think "oh no." It's not easy to carry the hot mug up the ladder, so I climb it slowly, watching the water in the mug sway one way then the other. When I reach the top without spilling any of the hot water over my hand, I see she is still sitting with her back to the wall and her legs stretched out in front of her. Her eyes have gone even more yellowier. I can tell.

"Hey, Grandma," I say, crawling into the attic and pushing the mug ahead of me as I move.

She swipes the newspaper behind her. As if she's hiding it behind her back. I dunno why she's done that. She never hides the newspaper from me. She normally tells me I should read the newspaper. So, I know what's going on in Birmingham.

"Oh, you are a gem, Boy," she says, picking the mug up.

"I, uh... I thought I heard you crying again," I say. "Were you crying again, Grandma?"

She looks down at the wet tissues beside her and then back up over her round glasses at me.

"Just blowin' ma nose, is all," she says. Then she blows into her mug and takes her first sip. "Thank you, Boy." And her glasses move upward on her cheeks again. That was a great idea.

Making the tea. I knew it would make her smile. "See anything good on those VHS tapes?"

"I haven't gotten them to play yet," I say. "Uh, Grandma…"

"Yes, Boy?" she says.

"Last night…" She coughs. Then she takes another clean tissue from the box and wipes her top lip with it. "I, uh… I only wanted to feel the wind in my face. That's all."

"I know, Boy," she says. She reaches her hand out and touches my face. Just like Grandpa wanted to do but didn't have the energy to the night before he died. I press my cheek into her hand and then I turn to it and kiss it. "You were just trying to feel the wind in your face. I know." I think she believes me. I hope she believes me. "Why don't you go watch those VHS tapes… see if it helps you to write something nice for Grandpa tomorrow, huh?"

I kiss her hand again. And then she takes it away and looks downward at the paperwork on her lap. There's lots of it. Lots and lots of it. So, I crawl backward on my hands and knees, before my feet touch the ladder and I can climb down it.

I wonder about what other people will think if they heard I was standing on the edge of the roof of Northfarm Shopping Mall last night. They might think the same as that security guard. That I was gonna jump. And that I was doing a suicide. But I wasn't. I wasn't. I just wanted to feel the wind in my face.

When I get downstairs, I pick up my tablet and tap at the Facebook sign.

I don't think the security guard would have told anybody I know that I was standing on the roof. But just in case he did, I'll write something on Facebook. Something that will let everybody know I am good, and I am okay and that I would never do a suicide. I just want everybody to know everything is normal. I've got a Yoga class later today. I can tell everyone on Facebook that I'm going to Yoga. Then everyone will know I'm okay. And that everything is normal. If somebody says to them, "I heard Benji Wayde was found on the rooftop of Northfarm Shopping Mall," then they'll be able to say "Oh, no, he's okay. I saw him post on Facebook that he was going to Yoga today. So, everything must be normal."

It takes me a long time to type because I don't know where all the letters are on the keyboard cuz they're all in different places. After I've typed it all out... I stare at it. To make sure I wrote it correct and there are no mistakes.

Looking forward to midday yoga class at IAMYOGI studios today. #Namaste

Great. My typing is getting better. Not faster. But better. I don't make no mistakes no more. Not like I used to when I first got the tablet and didn't even know what the keyboard was for.

I hope my Facebook post gets some likes. Sometimes my posts don't get any likes. Sometimes they get four or even five. When I posted about Grandpa dying last week, I got twelve likes. And nine comments. That's the most I've ever gotten. I was happy with that. It made me feel happy, even though I was feeling the saddest I ever felt.

I stare and stare at my Facebook post, to see if somebody will like it. But nobody has. Not yet anyway. Sometimes it takes a long time for likes to show up. So, I put the tablet back down on the sofa that a man is coming to take from us later today and then I stare at the blue screen on the TV. I'm not sure what I'm supposed to do to make the tape play. And I don't want to call Grandma for help cuz she is trying to clean the attic out. So, I get off the sofa that a man is coming to take from us later today and I crawl on my hands and knees over to the blue screen. I press at the flap of the mouth where the tape went into and then I hit my hand against the side of the screen. It stays blue. With that black-and-white striped box in the top corner. I look around the side of the TV. And that's when I see six buttons. One has a P on it. And an arrow. Maybe that means "play." So, I press it. And then I hear the tape inside the mouth make a noise like a tiny motorbike and the screen blinks from blue to black. And when it blinks again a beautiful face is on it. A bit like my face. Only it's pretty.

I slap my hand to my mouth. And a tear falls down my cheek. I've only ever seen her in photographs before. But now I can see her move. I can see her smiling. I can hear her laugh.

"Ugh, Dad," she says. "Please... put that ruddy camera away."

She slaps at the screen, and it spins around to Grandpa. Grandpa when he was younger. Grandpa when he had hair. Smiling at the girl who just called him "Dad." Smiling at my Momma.

NATE BENNETT

Zucha gasps from behind me as soon as I've bitch-slapped this geeky fuck. She can learn the hard way. That's how I learned the streets. How we all learn.

I hop on top of him, my knee pressing into his chest, my two hands held lightly around his neck; ready to squeeze if I need to.

"Tell me, you geeky freak, how many copies are there of the footage shot by your CCTV camera out back on June fourteen?"

He coughs and spits and chokes, and his face starts to glow red. So, I lean off his neck a little... to give him a chance to answer.

"Jesus Christ," he says, gasping. "We have one digital copy that downloads straight to that computer. And my partner keeps USB thumb drive copies of the recordings at home."

I look back over my shoulder at Zucha, to see her standing still, her arms down by her side and her head kinda tilted to one side like a puppy dog.

"Whatcha think? You believe him?" I ask her.

"Why wouldn't you believe me?" he says, trying to sit up.

"Stay the fuck where you are," I shout, pressing my knee harder into his chest.

"Listen," he says, "what the hell do I have to hide? We don't even know what's on the footage you're looking for."

I ease off him, then stand back up before brushing down my shirt. I hate to see the uniform creased.

"Let me see you delete the digital copy from your computer!" I order.

He gets to his feet, rubbing at his neck, then takes two steps toward his work desk and begins swirling his mouse around. "What date do you want me to delete again?" he asks, his voice shaking.

"June fourteen, bitch," Zucha says before I can answer. I spin back around to stare at her. And I wink, impressed. This bitch sure is learning fast.

He clicks his mouse some more, then waves me over to stare at his screen.

"June fourteen. Here you go, I'm gonna hit delete…" He clicks his mouse again. "Now, it's gone."

I grab his mouse from him and open the trash can in the bottom corner of his desktop.

"It's still here, bitch," I say. So, I click the file, then I delete it from the trash. Now I know it's erased from this computer permanently. I'm used to deleting files permanently.

I turn to him, grin, then bitch slap him again.

"What the fuck?" he says, holding his face. I grab him by the collar and shove him against the back wall.

"Who's this partner you mentioned, who has a copy of this footage on a USB thumb drive?"

"Roseanna," he says, all panicky. "Roseanna Redford. She's my business partner we—"

"Where does she live?"

He coughs and splutters, and huffs and puffs, and his throat makes silly noises, as if he's trying not to cry.

"Kickham Avenue. 101."

"Well, we're gonna pay her a little visit. If you contact her before we get there, then we're gonna come back to deal with you, you understand?"

He nods his head. So, I release my grip on his collar to allow him to breathe.

"You better keep it shut, bitch!" Zucha yells at him.

She really is getting the hang of this.

As soon as I let him go, he slides down the wall, and almost cries like the little bitch Zucha told him he was. I stand over him, then grab his cell phone from his pocket, rip off the back cover, take out his SIM card and snap it in half. Then I walk to his work desk and yank at the cable of his landline, snapping it so hard from its socket that the plastic piece breaks into pieces.

"Let's get to that address," I say, turning to Zucha.

"Yeah… let's go," she says.

We pace toward the front door like the two bad ass mutha fuckers we are and just as we're about to leave I notice a copy of the *Daily Connecticut* lying on the floor among the rest of the mail. So, I snatch it up and turn over the pages until I can see my name. Costello said news of me returning to the force made it into this rag of a newspaper. I find my old head shot from about ten years ago that I used to wear on my police badge in black-and-white down at the bottom of page five and I huff out a laugh to myself.

"Disgraced officer back on the streets," I whisper-read the headline.

"Whatcha say?" Zucha asks.

"No… nothing. Nothing," I say, before rolling the newspaper into a ball and throwing it across the office. Then I push the door open, and we walk out into the strong wind. As good as that felt, this job ain't done yet. I can see why Costello wanted me back for this job, though. It might seem an easy enough investigation to retrieve some CCTV footage. But we have no warrant to demand that the footage is deleted… so, any average cop just wouldn't do. It had to be me. It had to be a cop who knew how to work the streets.

"That was awesome!" Zucha says, almost bending over with excitement when we reach the car.

"That's the power rush you're feeling right now," I say.

Then I walk over to the driver's side and open the door before being stopped in my tracks just as I'm about to climb inside. There's a cell phone on the seat. What the fuck is this? I bend down pick it up, stab at the screen and see a text message with my name on it.

Nate, ring this number asap. If you don't, I'm gonna reveal all of your secrets to the world.

"What the fuck?" I whisper.

"Whatcha say?" Zucha asks, staring up at me as she slides into the passenger seat.

"Uh… nothing. Gimme a sec."

I slam the driver's door shut and walk to the back of the car as I dial the number on the phone, the cut on my face beginning to sting again.

"Nathan Bennett," a distorted voice says. And as soon as I hear it, I already know I'm in trouble.

"Who the fuck is this?"

"Ohh, *who* this is is the least of your concerns, Nate. The only concern you should have right now is what I have to say. I see you're back on the streets again. It's crazy they'd let a guy like you back in uniform. Only in America, huh? I bet you're chuffed to be back on the streets, but don't be. 'Cause I'm about to fuck your day up…." I squint up and down the street, to try to find who this mutha fucker is. "Nate, I've hacked into your home computer—"

"Holy fuckin' shit."

"Holy fuckin' shit is right. You sure do like them kiddies, huh? Now, you listen here… I will out you as the sick paedo fuck you are unless you do as I say, understood?"

"I… I…."

I almost collapse on the spot, forced to drop to one knee while I hold on to the back bumper of the car with one hand.

"Shuddup stuttering, you pervert. You don't have the time to stutter. You've orders to follow. And if you don't follow 'em, then I am only one click of a button away from making your browser history public knowledge."

"What do you want from me?" I say, my fist clenching, even though there's nobody to punch.

"I told you already… I need you to follow my orders."

The cut on my cheek burns, and my fist balls up even tighter, digging my nails into my palms.

"Listen you mutha fucker, whoever you are, I will hunt you down. I will fuckin' kill you!"

He laughs into the phone, which makes my cut burn even more, and my fist begins to shake.

"Stop acting tough you little pussy and listen up. You will carry out my orders otherwise everyone will know that you jerk off to kiddie porn every night. And by the looks of this browser history, it *is* every night."

"Tell me!" I shout, slamming my fist onto the bumper of my car. "What the fuck is it you want me to do?"

Then the mutha fucker hangs up.

3

SARAH-JANE, HER HAND FLAT AGAINST HER FOREHEAD, WAS PACING back and forth across the cowhide rug that spread over the center of her polished panel wood dressing-room floor.

"Shit! Shit! Shit!" she grunted.

Phil had already given up asking her to, "sit down, and calm down."

While he sat in her makeup chair, swiveling slowly from side to side with his knees spread wide and his crotch on display, Howie — her show's lead producer for twenty-five years, and Simon and Erica — her two junior producers — were squeezed into the cream leather sofa on the opposite side of the room, their knees pressed tightly together.

Howie couldn't keep his eyes off Sarah-Jane as she continued to pace back and forth, his mind whirring in rhythm with her feet. He was fretting; feeling incredibly antsy and anxious that the thirty-odd years he had spent in the TV business had come to a sudden halt the moment Sarah-Jane dared to question Meghan Markle's mental health in front of ten million watching Americans. He was under the impression that they had all been canceled. Not just Sarah-Jane. Howie Laine had been Sarah-Jane's lead producer since the day she first strolled into the CSN studios back in 1997. They had come a long way since then despite the tabloid magazines frequently reporting of a friction-filled relationship. But Sarah-Jane appreciated the friction. She felt Howie pushed her and was just as responsible for her long run at the top as she, herself, had been. Despite being a great team player, Howie's main concern as Sarah-Jane continued to pace her cowhide rug was himself. He wasn't ready to call it quits. Certainly not when he felt he was on top of his game as a lead news producer. He was nearing his sixties though, and the threat of retirement had been long filling him with dread. He hated the notion that his dream life producing live TV would ever have to end; let alone be forced to end through no fault of his own.

Simon and Erica were certainly redundant in Howie's thinking. Simon may have only been with the show for just over five years but while he proved to be somewhat innovative in terms of creating feature ideas, he was young and talented enough to secure employment at another network if he were to go looking. Erica was new to the business, however, having just joined *The Zdanski Show* some six weeks prior to the Meghan Markle debacle. Like Simon, she had proven to be innovative and full of fresh ideas, but she had limited experience in television production and her chances of landing something new with such a limited résumé might prove somewhat difficult.

"Shit, shit, shit," Sarah-Jane repeated again, still pacing.

"You could walk into the studio of any TV network in the country, Sarah-Jane," Howie offered. "Let's just set up *The Zdanski Show* somewhere else."

Sarah-Jane stopped walking, slowly soaked in what Howie was saying, licked across her perfect-white teeth, and then sighed, exhaustedly.

"Shut the fuck up, Howie," she spat. She held a finger up. "Just for one minute. Just for one minute. I need to… I need to think…."

"Fox has already been in touch," Phil said just as Sarah-Jane began to pace again.

"Fuck Fox," she spat. "T'fuck, Phil? You think I'm gonna go with my tail between my legs to become a puppet at Fox News?"

Phil cleared his throat, then closed his knees so he could sit upright in Sarah-Jane's makeup chair.

"'Course not," he said, "I'm just letting Howie know that another network has already been in touch with an offer. We know we could go to another network. Look, Sarah-Jane, Howie's as worried as you are. We all are. We've all lost jobs here today, not just you...."

Sarah-Jane exhaled another audible sigh; so heavy it sounded like a sob. Then she pushed out an uncomfortable laugh, stopped walking and held her hands to her hips.

"Now's the first time you decide to say more than two fuckin' words, Phil? You've been pretty silent for the past twenty-five years... now I can't shut you up, huh?"

The three others on the sofa offered tired laughs, mostly because they were brimming with the nervous tension Sarah-Jane had exacerbated throughout the dressing room with her anxious pacing.

"I'm just sayin'," Phil said, sitting back in the makeup chair again and spreading his knees wide, "we're all just as concerned as you are about what's gonna happen next."

Sarah-Jane swiveled around to face the trio on the sofa.

"Listen... this is all I can say at the moment—because I know as much about the future as you do. We're waiting to hear back from ABC News. That's the only network I've ever said I'd leave CSN for. It's the only other balanced news network in America. We haven't heard back from them yet... but whatever happens — *whatever* happens — the five of us are a team. We will be sticking together. Wherever I go next, we all go."

Howie nodded, and as he did, his shoulders relaxed, allowing him to sit back into the sofa just as Erica decided to lean forward, holding up her iPhone.

"Ya know, according to the polls, you have the backing of the country. On average, more people think you were right to question Meghan than oppose it."

"Those polls aren't gonna help her," Simon said, opting to talk for the very first time since Sarah-Jane had locked them all inside her dressing room, moments after she had been informed of her show's cancellation by the network owner Michael Jambon and his two most senior lawyers. "CSN won't take her back just because of the results of some random Twitter polls."

"No… no, that's not what I'm saying, Simon," Erica said, pushing back her thick-rimmed black glasses onto the bridge of her narrow nose. "The point I'm specifically making is that most of America supports Sarah-Jane."

"Most of Twitter," Howie said, shrugging a shoulder. "There's a distinct difference between 'most of Twitter' and 'most of America.'"

"Well, let's call it 'most of the online population of America'."

"Okay… and how's that gonna get us our show back?" Simon said. "Or a good offer from another network?"

"Fuck the networks," Erica said.

"Huh?" said Howie, sitting back up, and joining his two colleagues on the edge of the cream leather sofa.

"We don't need another network," Erica said. "What's the average viewership of, say *Live with Kelly and Ryan* these days? What… five million on a good day? *The View*? Four million on a good day. And they're the number one shows behind ours. What do we get now? Six million when we have an A-lister?"

"We got ten million for Meghan," Sarah-Jane said.

"Meghan is an exception, and you know it. Ten million never happens. Not anymore. We spike at seven million when we have a shit-hot guest on. But we mostly even out at just under six million…. Yet we're *the* most watched show in America. I bet when *The Zdanski Show* first started out you were hitting three times that number, right?"

"More," Phil said. "For our debut show, we hit thirty mill."

"Well…" Erica said, pushing back her thick black-rimmed glasses on the bridge of her narrow nose again. "That was before I was even born… and it only proves exactly what I'm trying to say…."

"Which is?" Howie asked, swiftly standing up from the sofa, striding three steps forward and then spinning around like a fashion model at the end of a catwalk, just so he could look Erica in the eye while she answered him.

"The numbers are going down."

"Yeah, because everybody has more choice. There are more networks now."

"There are also more people. There are more people in America now than there's ever been."

"Spit out what you're trying to say, Erica," Howie said, waving his hand dismissively.

"A podcast."

"Are you kidding me? She is the most watched face in America," Howie said, pointing both of his hands toward Sarah-Jane as if she was the grand prize in a game show. She was standing in the center of the bear-skin rug, a curled finger pressed tightly against her lips, listening to her most experienced producer grow frustrated with her most inexperienced producer.

"A visual podcast," Erica says, "that will go out live on YouTube and that will also be distributed to every podcast channel around the globe."

"She's America's biggest TV star," Howie said, looking incredulous. "Why would we walk away from TV? Asking Sarah-Jane Zdanski to switch from TV to online is like asking LeBron to switch to the NFL."

"No, it isn't," Erica said, exasperated, "that's a ridiculous argument to make. Sometimes I genuinely wonder, Howie, if you are still tuned into what is happening in the real world—"

"Okay, enough, you two," Phil shouted, still swiveling gently from side to side on Sarah-Jane's makeup chair. "We've had offers about podcasts over the years, of course we have, but…" he sticks out his bottom lip and shakes his head.

"It's not for me," Sarah-Jane said, finishing Phil's point. "We've studied the data. The turnover from TV to digital would be major surgery for us. We'd literally lose our audience. Those who watch live TV don't listen to podcasts… our loyal viewers don't engage in news that way."

"We need to lose your current audience then," Erica said. Sarah-Jane laughed, causing Erica to curl up the corner of her top lip, unsure if her boss had produced the laugh in a dismissive manner or not. "Well, we're losing your current audience anyway. Look, we might think we're number one around here. And we are on TV. But TV is not number one anymore. And that's the cold hard truth of it."

"It would be career suicide," Sarah-Jane said.

And then she put her hand to her forehead and nodded, knowing full well what everyone was thinking in that moment. It was rich, given what had happened over the previous twenty-four hours that Sarah-Jane would be accusatory about "career suicide."

"Wanna know how many tune in to the Joe Rogan podcast these days?' Erica said. 'Fifteen million. Every goddamn episode. A good episode. A bad episode. It doesn't matter. Joe will get up to five million views on YouTube and another ten million will listen to the podcast…. Fifteen million. Logan Paul… that guy has thirty million subscribers to his YouTube channel. *Thirty million*! These are humongous numbers that simply don't exist in TV… not anymore."

"What the fuck has Logan Paul got to do with us?" Howie said. "We're journalists here, not YouTube clowns. We're in the news business."

"I'm talking about the numbers… the numbers. This is where the numbers are. This is where America is. Everybody's online. They're listening to podcasts. They're watching YouTube. Not watching *Kelly Clarkson* or *The Talk*. The consumption of news… it's changed, Howie. TV is no longer king. You all know that. You *have* to know that."

Howie sniffed and scoffed and shook his head.

"Please," Sarah-Jane said, taking her curled finger away from her lips and holding it up. "I appreciate your enthusiasm for all things digital, Erica. I do. We all do. That's why we hired you. To look after our social media and to make sure we made the most of our online presence… but listen, we're not gonna jump from TV to a podcast just because Logan Paul gets in big numbers for making an ass of himself. It doesn't compute. Howie's right. We're in the news business."

"You're missing my point. News is going to be—"

"Enough!" Sarah-Jane shouted at her newest recruit, causing Erica to stare down at the laces of her black Doc Martin boots. It was a bit harsh that Sarah-Jane had raised her voice. Erica had done nothing wrong but try to steer her boss in a new direction. That was more than anyone else in the dressing-room had offered thus far. Erica's cheeks blushed red while she was pretending to fidget with the laces of her boots. And as the dressing-room silence lingered, Sarah-Jane decided to force out another audible sigh, mostly because she felt bad for being so blunt with her youngest team member. Although Erica Murphy was twenty-six years old, she had the fresh face of a teenager hidden behind her oversized, black-rimmed glasses. That fresh face was framed by a blood-red blunt-cut bob with grungy, blunt-cut bangs. Howie had likened her appearance to the Scooby Doo character Velma when she first joined the production team. But the joke didn't go over well. Not with Phil, who insisted the newest recruit be judged as they all were—on work performance alone and not on her cartoonish appearance. Yet, Howie was equally annoyed by her work performance as he was her grungy, hipster look. Erica's insistence that Sarah-Jane's numbers on Twitter held more importance than the viewership numbers *The Zdanski Show* got on CSN every Wednesday evening was a nonsensical irritant to him.

"Power," Erica said, looking up from her Doc Martin boot-laces. "Power. Absolute power. That's what you should be aiming for, Sarah-Jane. You... you're the big name around CSN. Yet you have to answer to us, you have to answer to a director, to a network president, to a network owner, to network lawyers. You're Sarah-Jane fucking Zdanski. Why should you answer to anybody? If you run a visual podcast, you own everything. Every. Damn. Thing. You will be the host. The producer. The director. The president. The owner. All of the control... all of the power shifts right onto your lap."

"It's not gonna happen," Phil said. "We'll try cut a deal with ABC News and we'll make sure all five of us are part of the ticket."

"What if ABC doesn't pick up the show?" Howie asked.

"She's Sarah-Jane Zdanski for crying out loud," Phil said. "Of course they'll pick up the show. She's the most sought-after anchor in America."

"*Was* the most sought-after anchor in America… until she accused Meghan Markle of faking her depression," Howie said. "Now ABC probably won't touch us… just like CSN don't want us anymore. Sorry, Sarah-Jane. I love you. I do. But you pushed the envelope too far… I'm just—"

"We understand your fears, Howie," Sarah-Jane replied, interrupting her lead producer. "We do. We all do. Let's just see what ABC News has to say when they get back to us and we'll…."

Sarah-Jane trailed off, not only because her phone buzzed in her pocket, but because all of the other phones in her dressing room buzzed too, almost in unison.

"The news is out," Simon said, turning the screen of his phone to face the room.

"Motherfuckers!" Sarah-Jane spat. "They told me they wouldn't release a statement about canceling the show until they spoke to me first."

"Fuck 'em," Phil said. "CSN is in the past."

"No. No. Nope," Sarah-Jane said. "I gotta go up and speak to these motherfuckers. Jambon's trying to get ahead of the story… make it out that we're the deserved victims. Come on Howie… me and you, let's take the elevator. You guys…" she spun around, to take in Simon, Erica and Phil staring blankly back at her, "you just… you just get to, uh… I dunno. Try to figure something out. Try to figure out what our next move is."

"You want me to look more into the podcast idea?" Erica said.

Sarah-Jane stared at her newest production assistant, deep in thought. Then she shook her head. Slowly.

"No. Forget about podcasts, Erica," she said. "Phil, I want you to ring ABC… let's hear what they have to offer."

NATE BENNETT

The phone rings as I'm driving, and I almost fumble it to the pedals before gripping it tighter. Then I tap at the green button and press it tightly to my ear.

"What?"

Zucha turns and stares at me.

"Get your ass to your bank," the distorted voice says, "Take out all of your savings and await my next call. And, Nate, you need to take out every damn cent you own. Clean your account out. If you don't, my finger is hovering over a button that will out you as the sick paedophile you are."

Then the mutha fucker hangs up. Again. And my cut immediately stings, so I pull a U-turn, causing Zucha to lean into me.

"What the hell, Nate?" she says, grabbing for something to hold on to.

"We've gotta go somewhere else first."

"But, what about the guy in the office? Don't we need to get to his partner's house before he does?"

I jam on the brakes, causing her head to fly forward before her seat belt snaps her back to her seat. Then I slap both of my hands to my face and try to breathe as slowly as I can into them; just like the therapist I was forced to go to taught me to. When I take my hands away, I open the car door and step out onto the street.

"Ma'am," I shout at a car, holding my badge aloft. The car

skids to a stop and the driver rolls down her window, her eyes wide. "We need your vehicle for emergency police business."

I curl my finger at Zucha, calling her out of our car.

"Officer, I need to work I can't—"

I hold a hand up to the driver as she gets out of her car, shutting her up.

"Ma'am, we'll get your car back to you within an hour, but right now we need it for official police business."

I notice her keys are still in the ignition, so I hold her driver's door open and motion for Zucha to get in.

"Go to the address, make sure you get the USB thumb drive. And don't let it outta your sight. I'll catch up with you."

Then I slam the door shut and turn to the driver. She's hot. Kinda. I mean, I definitely would. So, I go easy on her, even though my cut is stinging on my cheek and my mind is lost on what this mutha fucker on the phone is asking me to do. But I put my hand on the shoulder of her pretty blouse and give it a little squeeze.

"I promise I'll get your car back in one piece. Please get a cab to wherever you need to be, and all will be compensated by the Birmingham Police Department. You have my word on that, Ma'am."

"But I... I...."

I ignore her, by patting her shoulder before racing back to my car. When I'm inside, about to flick on my sirens, I notice Zucha still hasn't moved. She's staring at me through the windshield of the car I've hailed down for her, as if it's the first time she's ever sat behind a wheel.

I roll my window down.

"You know how to drive, don't you?" I shout.

She nods. And so I immediately wave her on and watch as she drives away slowly.

"Fuck me," I say to myself. Then I step on the gas, screeching my way across the wrong side of the road before flicking the switch to blare my sirens. I normally love the sound of the sirens wailing around me... but right now my head is so messed up I don't know how to feel.

I fly through a red light, forcing two cars to skid to a stop while my head continues to race. My knuckles are white wrapped around the steering wheel. I wish they were wrapped around the mutha fucker's neck who's blackmailing me. I swear when I get my hands on him, I'm gonna strangle him to death. And I'll fucking laugh in his face as he's choking.

I skid into the parking lot at the back of the bank, switch off the siren and then run for the door before I'm stopped in my tracks. I've gotta wait for the person in front of me to move forward before I can be buzzed inside. I huff and puff and kick the ground, before slapping my hands to my face again so I can try to breathe more slowly—just like the therapist told me I should do any time I feel like I wanna smash somebody's head in. When I'm finally buzzed into the bank, a bald man in a three-piece navy suit walks toward me with his hands behind his back, trying to look all important.

"Officer, we'd much prefer if our customers were wearing masks, I know—"

"I'm exempt," I say, holding my badge up. "Breathing difficulties."

"Oh, so sorry," he says. "Uh, how can we help you here at Citigroup today?"

"I need to make a withdrawal."

"Oh," he says, as if he's surprised somebody might wanna withdraw cash from his fuckin' bank. "Let me lead you over to Clive at our front desk here... Clive!" he calls out.

I cringe. Because Clive is a kak. And I hate dealing with fucking kaks.

"Hello, officer," he says, smiling, showing me his bright pink gums.

"Clive," the guy in the navy suit says, "this officer here would like to make a withdrawal."

"Sure thing," Clive says, still showing me his gums. "How much would you like to withdraw, officer?"

I suck in a deep breath, 'cause I can't actually believe I'm doing this.

"All of it," I say. "Every damn cent."

AIMEE STREET

He tries to spoon the tea bag from his mug, but it falls, splats, and squelches onto the table. And I immediately fall to my side, onto the bench I'm sitting on, snorting and chuckling. In between sucks of breath, I stare up at him, to see his face glowing bright pink from trying to hold back his laughter, veins popping out of his temples, his hand slapped over his nose and his mouth, his eyes squeezed shut and streams of wet webbing away from them.

"Fuckin' hell," I say, gasping for air. When I rise back up on the bench, I have to wipe a tear away from my own eye. A tear of laughter. The two of us are quite literally laugh crying because a tea bag had the audacity to fall from a fucking spoon.

"Hey," he says, sniffling his nose and recomposing himself, the pink draining from his cheeks. "Did I tell you about the time a friend of mine asked me to put a tea bag in my mouth because he wanted to pour boiling water into it?

I shake my head.

"No… what the fuck?"

"Yeah," he says, "he was trying to make a mug out of me."

I fall to my side so hard that I miss the bench this time and, instead, I crash to the floor, holding my sides. My shoulder hurts. But, not as much as my sides are hurting from the laughing. I hear his chair screech backward and I know he's standing; standing because he can't contain the laughter while he's sitting. I look up through the legs of the table to see him almost hyperventilating; his hand covering his face again, his shoulders shaking and shuddering like a vibrator. He eventually bends over and holds on to his knees while I get to my feet to brush myself off, the tears now streaming from my eyes and dropping to the tiled floor beneath me.

When I eventually sit, leaning my head on to my folded arms on top of the table, I try to steady my breathing until he finally takes his seat opposite me and I look up to see the pink draining from his cheeks again.

"Fuckin' hell," he says, "are we funnier because we're stoned, or do we just find everything funnier because we're stoned?"

"Ha," I say, "If I had a quarter for every time I've asked myself that question... Know what my conclusion is? You're laughing either way... so who's laughing now?"

"The stoners," he says, holding his mug of coffee up and clinking it off the top of my Margherita glass. Mykel's been sober for almost a year now. He doesn't trust himself when he drinks. He's right not to trust himself. He's an asshole when he drinks. Yet he's the soundest guy in the world when doesn't. I've missed him. I always miss him. He's been family to me.

"Oh jeez," I say, tapping my finger at my phone. "It's eleven. I'm supposed to be at a class right now."

"A journalism thing?"

"Yep. Libel Law."

"Not your bag?"

"Hasn't been my bag for ages. I've been in and out of college for the past few months. I just... I don't know... I've given up. All they're doing is teaching us traditional old-school media. But the media's evolved way quicker than the education system... so I'm left studying the same shit other journalism students were studying in 1997."

"I've no idea what the fuck you're talking about," he says, and then he begins to cackle again.

"Ah, something will turn up," I say, reassuring myself.

"It always does with you," he says. "Lucky Aim."

He's always called me that. As far back as when we were

about seven or eight. He says I get all the luck in the world, whereas he never gets any at all. That's why he calls me Aim. He thinks I always hit the bulls-eye. I guess he has a point. I can't escape it. I *am* lucky. Always have been. Opportunity just always seems to present itself to me.

"So, what you gonna do if you don't give journalism a try?" he asks. "How you bringing in money now?"

His eyes look really heavy. Stoned heavy; stoned like I haven't been for a long time because I vape these days and it dilutes the weight of the high as opposed to smoking. Mykel chose to smoke a small joint of my Ghost Train instead of using my vaporizer. It sure has made his eyes look glassy and weighty.

"Ya know me," I say, smiling my crooked teeth at him. "Something will come up."

And then I look up at the television in the corner of the room, showing Sarah-Jane fucking Zdanski and Meghan Markle. Again. "Are they ever gonna shut the fuck up about this interview?" I ask.

He turns to look over his shoulder at Zdanski beaming one of her faux smiles into the camera, then he swivels back to face me.

"Aim," he says, getting out of his seat and then shuffling his way in beside me on the bench. He's sat really close. Too close. So close our hips are touching. Not this shit again. I thought he only ever did this when he was drunk. "I, uh… can't seem to get a job, either. I will. I'm trying. I'll get something… y'know."

"'Course you will," I say, leaning on my folded arms and staring up at him. "The likes of me and you… we gotta take it one day at a time. I say that to you all the time, Mykel. It was how we were brought up." He smiles at me, rounding his chin. "Oh hey," I say. I grab my bag under the table and reach for some of the cash gullible idiots poured into my plastic bowl back at the hotel earlier before scooping a handful onto the table. "Take it. I had a good morning. It's yours."

"What the hell, Aim?" he says. "I can't take this."

"Take it," I say, sitting back upright.

He leans towards my face. His lips slightly ajar.

"Jesus, no, Mykel," I say. He quickly turns away, his heart

cracking again. His pride wounded. Again. "I thought you only ever did that when you were drunk."

"I just… Aim," he pauses, and looks around. "I just don't know what to do when I'm not with you. I don't know where to go… who to go to…."

"Listen," I say, placing my hand on his shoulder like the way family are supposed to show affection to each other. They're certainly not supposed to make out with each other. "Me and you… never. I don't mean that in a bad way, Mykel, but come on… we're like brother and sister. We're not…." He shakes his head, a blush of pink racing up his cheeks again. Only this time he's not trying to contain his laughter. But his heartbreak. Again. Every time I see him these days, I end up breaking his heart. "I— I gotta go, Mykel," I say. He swivels around on the bench, blocking me from getting out.

"No. Please don't go, Aim. Don't."

"I got to, Mykel. I've somewhere I gotta be. But we'll do this again sometime… hang out. Get stoned. Have a laugh."

"Aim, don't. Please!"

I climb up on to the bench table to step past him before jumping down and walking on. When I reach the front door of the bar, I look back over my shoulder at him slumped at the table, his face buried into his folded arms. But I don't offer him a "good-bye." Instead, I push the door open and step out into the wind.

BENJI WAYDE

Momma smiles like I smile when I am smiling in the mirror. And she *is* pretty. Even though I don't think you're s'posed to think your own Momma is pretty. But she is. She is as pretty as Grandpa always tells me she was. Grandpa hadn't spoke about Momma in a long time before he died. But when I was a boy and not a man he used to say, "Yo Momma was the prettiest... just the prettiest." I overheard him say to Grandma one day when I was about ten years old that "Vanessa was the prettiest... just the prettiest. Until she started messing with that poison."

That's when I spent a year thinking Momma had died because of poison. But it wasn't poison. It was heroin. It's a drug. A really bad drug. Momma took a really bad drug. And she died. Grandma says I never had a daddy. But I have to have a daddy. Everybody has to have a daddy. You can't be born without a daddy. When I learned that at school and came home and told Grandma that everybody has to have a daddy, she just told me that whoever my daddy was ran away when I was in Momma's tummy and because he was gone before I was born then that means I don't have a daddy. That makes me sad. If I had a daddy, I think everything would be better and happier.

"Ah, here she is," Grandpa says. The screen goes all shaky. And wobbly. And then I hear her voice before I can see her. Grandma. When the screen stops shaking and shows her walking into the room carrying a brown bag of groceries, she looks really different. Her hair is brown. And her lips are bright red. And her eyelids are painted light blue.

"Ugh, Sidney, will you put that camera away," Grandma says.

It's the exact same thing Momma said when Grandpa pointed the camera at her earlier.

"And now… you are looking at the most attractive super-model in all of Connecticut. No scrap that," Grandpa's voice says, "all of America. Ladies and Gentlemen, the beautiful, Missus Darlene Wayde."

"Shuddup you," Grandma says into the camera. And then she smiles. A really, really wide smile. If she was wearing glasses back then like she does now her glasses prob'ly would have lifted off her face cuz her smile was so big. It makes me feel happy. Cuz I can see how much Grandpa made Grandma feel happy. So, I pick up my notepad and pencil and I stick out my tongue and grip it between my lips cuz that's what I always do when I am writing. I tried to write one time without sticking my tongue out between my lips cuz my old teacher Mr. Shanley said I shouldn't be doing that. But I couldn't write without sticking my tongue out. I kept forgetting what the next letter was. But when I do stick my tongue out, I can write long sentences. Really long sentences. That's why Miss Moriarty told me one day that I was a good writer.

I press the pencil into the paper to make a period. And then I read what I've just writed.

I love how much Grandpa made Grandma feel happy.

That will be a nice thing to say at the church tomorrow. Really nice. Maybe I could talk about some of the times Grandpa made Grandma happy. I could talk about what I've watched on this video. How Grandpa said, "Missus Darlene Wayde looked like a supermodel" and it made her smile really big. And that one time Grandpa brought Grandma for a meal in New York City for her sixtieth birthday. I was only a young boy then. But I remember it. I remember how excited Grandma was when she dressed up all nice to go to New York City. And I could talk about the time

Grandpa put a record on the record player and when Grandma walked in the kitchen to tell him to turn down the noise, he grabbed her hands and started dancing with her. She tried not to laugh. But she did. She laughed. And it made me laugh too. Maybe I should do that. Dance with Grandma. It might make her laugh again.

The screen of my tablet blinks and when I pick it up it says I have one notification on Facebook and I get a little bit excited cuz I bet somebody liked the post I writed out earlier. So, I press my finger on the screen.

IAMYOGI liked your post.

One like. Already. From the yoga studio I do my yoga at. I like the people at Yoga cuz they talk to me like I am a friend. Sometimes when people talk to me and when I talk back, they look at me all funny and then they smile and then they walk away without saying anything else. But Victoria and Nina and Claire at yoga never do that. They talk to me, and I talk to them and then they talk to me and then I talk to them and sometimes we talk and talk for a long time like adults are supposed to do. Maybe we will talk for a long time after my yoga class at noon today. Sometimes we do. Sometimes we don't. But I always love going to yoga cuz it makes me feel like a adult. Grandma even lets me walk to yoga on my own even though I have to go through Gray Bridge to get there. And around Gray Bridge is very empty and it could be dangerous. Grandma didn't let me go down there when I was younger. But because I am a adult now, she lets me walk that way all on my own so I can go to Yoga.

"Oh," Grandma says. I look up and she is standing under the doorway. I didn't hear her coming down the stairs. She looks at the TV with the video player in it, then back at me. "Bringing ghosts back to life are you, Boy?"

MAGGIE ZUCHA

I'm supposed to be in a hurry. But I ain't never driven one of these Nissans before, and I'm not sure if the pedals suit my wide feet. And the wing mirrors are not right either, but I'm not sure how to fix 'em. That makes it scary when I have to turn. I'm driving around like my ol' grandmother used to drive before we had to tell her she shouldn't be driving no more. And driving like my grandmother is the opposite of what I'm supposed to be doing, which is getting to this address as soon as I can. 'Cause I'm supposed to be a cop. In the middle of an investigation. The adrenaline was rushing through me after we got that guy at the office to delete the footage from his computer. But now I'm kinda all alone. In a strange car. Heading to a stranger's house. And I'm not really sure how I'm supposed to be feeling. Or even what I'm supposed to do.

Though I guess this sure does beat the hell out of adding more rubber bands to my rubber ball back at the precinct. It's just I'd rather be doing this if I was a passenger in Nate's car and speeding to this address with the sirens blaring and not me chugging along like my ol' grandmother.

Nate sure is something. He kinda scares me. But he's kinda cool in some ways, too. I have never felt a rush like the one I felt back there when we were getting the job done. As if I held some sort of power for the first time. 'Cause I think I've always felt weak. And stupid. A little bit weak. And a little bit stupid. Lots of people have told me I'm stupid. I think that's why I filled in the application form when I saw the advertisement looking for new police recruits. I was just working my boring-ass job in the insurance office when I saw that ad in the newspaper, and I just remember thinking "to hell with it. I'll be a cop… then everyone will see I ain't stupid." It took me an afternoon to fill out the application form and then I kinda forgot all about it until I got an email two months later, inviting me to some sort of recruitment day. Now here I am. A fully graduated officer of the twenty-second precinct of Connecticut. Driving a strange car to go visit a stranger's house. All on my own. On my first day on the streets.

"Whoop, whoop," I shout, fist-pumping the air to try to cheer myself up; to get my adrenaline rushing again. But then I have to place my hand back on the steering wheel 'cause the car overtaking me seems to have come from nowhere. It's alright. I don't have much farther to go. Next turn is Kickham Avenue. And then I'll… well, I dunno what I'll do. I'll just ask her to show me the USB thumb drive and then I'll take it. I'll just take it. That's what Nate told me to do. He told me to retrieve the USB. That's all I have to do.

I spot her address as soon as I turn on to the street. It's big. And pretty. Very pretty. Like romantic comedy pretty.

When I stop the car outside, I hold a hand up to my eyes to see if I'm shaking. Maybe a little bit. Then I climb out of the car, walk up the long pathway and, when I finally reach the bright red door, I whisper to myself.

"You got this, Maggie."

And that's when I hold my finger against the doorbell.

BENJI WAYDE

Grandma sits in beside me on the sofa a man is coming to take later today, and it makes me think that this might be the last time me and Grandma ever sit on this sofa. All I remember is us sitting on this sofa. Watching TV. But instead of watching the bigger TV in the corner right now, we are both looking down at the small TV with the video player in it on the carpet.

"Oh my," Grandma says. "Your Grandpa was obsessed with his ruddy video camera. Not for long. Just for about a year. Then he got sick of it. He was an awful cameraman. You'll see more wallpaper on these VHS tapes than you will see of any of us, Boy."

I laugh. Cuz I've already seen the wallpapers more than I've seen any person.

"Don't suppose your wee Momma was on any of these tapes?"

"She was, Grandma," I say. "For a little bit. Two times. She smiled and then she put her hand out to the screen and pushed it away. Both the two times she did the same thing. Push the screen away."

The glasses rise on Grandma's cheeks. And I know she is smiling.

"That was your silly Grandpa," she says, "he used to just stick that camera in our faces." And then a tear rolls down her cheek. And it makes me sad. "Oh, Boy, I can't believe he's gone." Her hand covers her nose. And her shoulders are shaking. And she is crying hard. Really hard. So, I rub her head and then I get down on my hands and knees on the carpet and I crawl over to the TV with the video player in it and look to the side of it where the buttons are. There's a button with two arrows. So, I press that one. But it just makes the screen go all fuzzy and funny and it makes a funny noise like a small motorbike again. So, I press the button with the square on it. And the tape stops sounding like a small motorbike and the screen goes blue, with a black-and-white striped box in the top corner. When I look back at Grandma, she has her glasses off and is wiping her eyes with her sleeves. So, I crawl back to her and wrap my arms around the back of her knees and then I lean my head on her lap. I know I'm not supposed to lie on Grandma's lap like this no more. Cuz I am a adult now. But I think it might make Grandma feel better. It might make her stop crying. So, I stay like this with my head on her lap and my arms circled around the back of her knees really, really tight. And I say nothing. And she says nothing. For a long time. A very long time… Until my tablet screen lights up and I know that somebody must have liked the post I put on Facebook. So, I stop gripping Grandma's knees really tight, and I take my head from her lap so I can pick up my tablet and take a look.

A comment. I don't really get comments. Not many.

I click into Facebook and then drag my finger down until I see the comment. It's from Olive Burdett. One of Grandma's old friends who we haven't seen in a long, long time cuz she moved out of St. Michael's House about three years ago—just before Coronavirus.

Hope you are well, Benji. Thoughts and prayers are with you.

And she put a love heart at the end of it. A love heart. Maybe she is just being really nice cuz Grandpa died. And not because she found out I was standing on the roof of Northfarm Shopping Mall yesterday. But I don't think she knows about that. She can't know about it. Grandma won't have told her. She hasn't spoken to Olive since she moved out of St. Michael's House.

When I put the tablet back down on the sofa and look up at Grandma, she still has her glasses off. But she is not crying. Not anymore. Her eyes just look yellowy but there are no more tears. So, I sit right next to her, really close so that we are touching. And we both stare straight ahead at the blue screen on the small TV with the video player in it. In silence. For a long, long time. Until Grandma blows her nose into her hands and then rubs them together. When she turns to look at me her eyes are really yellow. Really, really yellow.

"So, Boy," she says, "written any of your eulogy yet?"

"A little bit," I say. I pick up my notebook from the carpet and open it to the page I was writing in. "I wrote this," I say, "I wrote, "I love how much Grandpa made Grandma happy" and I'm gonna talk about the times he made you happy like when he brought you to New York for a special dinner when you were sixty and you got all dressed up nice. And the time when Grandpa used to put on the music really loud in the kitchen and then he would grab your arms and make you dance with him. Actually, I was thinking, Grandma," I say, looking up at her. I close my notebook and put it down on the sofa a man is coming to take later today. "Would you like to dance with me? I know how happy you were when you used to dance with Grandpa and maybe if you dance with me, you might feel happy again."

Her yellowy eyes blink, and when they do a tear falls out of both of them. And I feel bad. And sad. Cuz instead of making Grandma happy I made her feel sad again.

"I would love to dance with you, Boy," she says.

And I get excited. Cuz I haven't danced in a long, long time. Sometimes I used to play music in my bedroom and dance in the mirror. But I ain't never danced in front of somebody cuz I don't know if they will think I am really bad at dancing. And they might laugh at me.

Grandma pushes herself off our sofa and then she is over in the corner of the room, where the radio is. She presses some buttons. And my hands get sweaty cuz I'm not sure if Grandma will think I can't dance. When she turns around to face me, there is a slow song playing and I think it might be a song she used to listen to with Grandpa from way, way back before I was even born. She walks over to me, puts one hand around my back and grabs my hand with her other hand. And then we are just turning around in a circle really slowly. I step closer to her, and she puts her head on my shoulder. And I hope she is not crying while her head is on my shoulder. I hope she is happy cuz we're dancing. Cuz that's why I asked her to dance. To make her not sad anymore. She grips my hand tighter, and we continue turning in a really slow circle and I start to think that I might be good at this type of dancing. At slow dancing. Maybe that's because I am slow. And that makes me good at slow things. The song is nice. Really, really nice. It's about the first time the singer had ever seen somebody's face. And I wonder if Grandma is thinking about the first time she ever saw Grandpa's face. And then I start to think of the first time I saw Grandpa's face and I remember that the first time I saw Grandpa's face I would have been a baby, so I wouldn't be able to remember it.

I squeeze Grandma even harder so that our bellies are squished against each other, and we continue to turn in a circle really slowly... Until the doorbell rings and Grandma lifts her head from my shoulder. Then she rubs her eyes with her sleeves, walks over to the radio to turn it off and then disappears to go answer the front door. And I feel sad that we've stopped. Cuz I think we were both enjoying the dancing.

"Hello, are you Missus Wayde?" I hear a man's voice say. "We're here to take the sofa."

AIMEE STREET

I stop in the large doorway of what once was a sandwich deli, but is now just one of the many dilapidated, boarded-up stores around here, just so I can refill the chamber of my vaporizer away from the wind. I gotta reignite my high. I can't believe I was literally on the floor laughing my ass off just ten minutes ago, and now I feel like a paranoid wreck, checking over my shoulder every ten steps I take to make sure Mykel isn't following me. I love him. I do. I'll always love him. But it's best I love the memory of him, and not have to put up with him trying to make out with me. He doesn't get it. He's not listening to me. He's never listened to me. We're family. Not boyfriend and girlfriend. We never have been. Never will be.

I tear off some of the bud and flick it into the chamber before pressing down the standby button on my vaporizer until it buzzes in my hand. Then I stand back and watch the folks of Birmingham, Connecticut going about their days while I bring the nozzle to my lips and begin to inhale.

I gotta get myself some happy. It's not as if I haven't had the biggest take I've ever had for a scam this morning. I can't believe there's almost eight hundred dollars in that bank account. I'll withdraw it tomorrow. Then close the account down.

As I'm blowing out a large cloud of vaporized weed, I bounce up and down on the spot—trying to convince myself that I should be excited. Fuck the fact that Mykel tried it with me again… forget about it. Forget about him. Well… forget about the man he turned into. Not the six-year-old boy I swore would be my best friend forever. As I'm inhaling again, trying but failing to forget about Mykel's innocent six-year-old face, a silver SUV with blacked-out windows drives by—almost in slow motion. I immediately step out from the doorway of the old sandwich deli to stare at it through the cloud I've just exhaled, trying to catch the license number as it begins to pick up speed. 380 K-something. It speeds up before I catch the last two letters, screeching its wheels to turn onto O'Leary Street and out of sight.

"Fuck it," I say to myself, pocketing my vaporizer before tightening my bag strap against my shoulder. I run as fast as I can, jumping over a parked red Vespa before skidding on to O'Leary Street. "Hey," I scream after the SUV. "Stop! Stop right there!"

It speeds up, moving further away and screeching its brakes as it skids around another corner. I'm not letting up. I strap the bag tighter against my shoulder as I sprint, grateful that when I turn after him, I'll be running downhill—down the hill that leads to the old Home Depot. Two heads turn as I race by them on the sidewalk, screaming from the back of my throat at the SUV, as if my screams are gonna help propel me forward. By the time I turn, he's already down the bottom of the hill, making another right. But I still continue at full throttle; determined to not let him get away. Not this time. I need to find out who the fuck this is….

So, I sprint. As fast as I can—so fast that I have to skid to a stop when I get to the corner at the bottom of the hill. And when I look up the next street, I see that he's already taking another right. This fucker is literally going around in circles. He's gonna come back around again… isn't he? Because he still wants to follow me, as much as I'm now following him. I take a deep inhale with my hands on my hips, then I decide to jog back up the hill… certain he's gonna come back around the same way. I can meet this guy head-on.

I put my hand in my pocket as I jog, to make sure my vaporizer is still tucked away safely. I'd be lost without that. I'd have to go back to smoking weed, and it's just not the same. While I'm zipping up my pocket, I hear an engine around the corner at the top of the hill... and I'm sure it's him. I'm certain it's him. So, I stand against the wall... and wait... and wait....

The nose of the car creeps out. A silver nose. And then it turns onto the street I'm on, its blacked-out windows catching the glare of the sun. I try to squint through the blacked-out windows, to make out the driver. I can't see shit through them, though. But I do have this fucker's full license plate now.

"Hey," I say, running toward the SUV. "Hey, you!"

The wheels spin. Backward. Then the entire SUV spins, like something you only see in the movies, before it speeds away from me again. I race after it, then change my mind. I spin on my heels instead, back down the end of this street, back down the hill where the ground blurs in front of me as I run... maybe because I'm running too fast; maybe because of this Ghost Train weed. I've never run this fast in my life. And I've been running my whole life. From everything. And everyone.

I skid around the next corner; certain I'll bump into him at the end of this block because I know he's driving around in circles. I huff and puff as I pass the same couple I barged through on the other side of the block. They probably think I'm crazy. They're probably right. I race for the corner, certain that when I reach it by foot, he'll be getting there at the same time with his wheels. So, I sprint. Huffing and puffing even louder. Huffing and puffing so loudly that I run straight out on to the road when I reach the corner, missing my turn and instead ending up in the middle of the road.

My shoulder thumps against metal. My back scrapes along the ground. My temple smacks into the concrete. And everything's blurry; the sky above me; my hand as I wave it in front of my face; the scruffy New Balance trainers that step out of the silver SUV. And then everything seems to go dull... and dark... and dizzy... and—

4

ALL FIVE OF THEM WERE SEATED AT THE SAME END OF THE OVERLY large chocolate-brown marble island in the middle of Sarah-Jane's plush kitchen, just so they could face the floor-to-ceiling windows that framed the picture-perfect postcard view of the Manhattan skyline. The blue from the sky above New York was providing a triangular shard of light into what was, otherwise, a purposefully dark paletted penthouse—layered with rich chocolate-colored patterns and bespoke chocolate-colored furnishings.

"Simon, you've been way too quiet," Sarah-Jane offered up. "You've barely said two words since we lost the show."

Simon lifted his nose from his phone.

"I've just been reading this," he said. "Trying to decipher what America thinks of it all."

"And what does America think of it all today?" Sarah-Jane asked.

"On average it's fifty-five to forty-five in your favor," Erica cut in to answer ahead of Simon. "Each and every poll on Twitter pretty much says the same thing. Just over half the population think you shouldn't have been fired simply for having an opinion."

"And the other half?"

"Well, every poll is split somewhat these days, isn't it? America is always split. America has been conditioned to be split.

We're split over everything. On Trump? America's split. Abortion? America's split. Guns? Split. America's even split on Kyle fucking Rittenhouse. Heck, America is now split on whether or not we can say the word 'gay' for fuck sake. So… what you did, calling out Meghan Markle, of course it was gonna divide the polls. America is bipolar. There is no such thing as middle ground in this country anymore. The fifty-five percent who think you did the right thing; they feel you're a martyr against the liberal left. The forty-five percent who think you were wrong to question Meghan, well… they *are* the liberal left."

"That's why we should take the Fox offer," Howie said. "Before it's too late. They could rescind the offer, y'know? If they find out ABC has turned us down, too… and the heat is turning up online—"

"I'm not fucking working for Fox, Howie," Sarah-Jane spat, just as she tossed a pen to the chocolate-colored marble top of her kitchen island.

"Think of it this way," Howie replied. "What if we approach Fox and we say to them, "we'll be your balance". That we'll come to Fox, produce a truly balanced political show and it will prove to the nation that Fox are giving serious balanced debate a platform. It will give the network kudos. Everyone will tune in 'cause it will make such a wave that Fox is going straight and… y'know, it could be a win-win all around."

"Are you…?" Sarah-Jane squinted across her kitchen island. "Are you for fucking real? You seriously want us to move to Fox News?"

"It's the only offer on the table, Sarah-Jane," Howie said, furiously scribbling a mess of twirls on his notepad.

"Listen, fuck it," Simon said, pocketing his phone and speaking without being spoken to for the very first time since the Meghan Markle debacle. "We're just going around in circles here and I've something to say… I, uh… I've been offered a job. CSN wants to retain me… for *Top Of The Morning*. They're looking for a producer to work alongside Troy Keiper. They're giving him more airtime and they're telling me I'm the ideal producer to get the best out of him."

"They've made a great choice," Sarah-Jane said, without hesitation. "Great choice."

"Oh, please tell us you're not leaving, Simon," Erica said. "Seriously?"

"Well… I mean. I'd rather stay here… with you guys. I love you guys. And the thing is, *Top Of The Morning* is not even offering me more money for all the hassle it will be, getting up at three a.m. and all. I know it's a first-world problem, dismissing a hundred grand a year. But ya know how impossible it is to live in this city on just a hundred grand a year?"

"Dude, you don't live in this city," Erica said.

"Exactly," Simon said.

Erica creased her lips into a smile, then she pushed her black, thick-rimmed glasses back on the bridge of her narrow nose.

"Gimme one sec," Sarah-Jane said. She began to scroll through her phone while everybody else sat at one end of the kitchen island sheepishly readjusting their positions on the high stools they had been sitting upright in for almost an hour now. This had been their fourth meeting since *The Zdanski Show* had been canceled the previous Wednesday night. And they hadn't made one inch of progress since then. Which was worrying. Very worrying.

Phil hadn't said much. Not at this meeting Sarah-Jane had opted to host at her penthouse after their offices at CSN studios had been cleared out the previous day and their access passes revoked. But he was still evidently riled that ABC had opted not to take on *The Zdanski Show*. He had received a phone call the night before this meeting, informing him that while ABC were huge fans of Sarah-Jane Zdanski, they feared the backlash hiring her off of her Meghan Markle faux pas would bring to their brand.

Sarah-Jane placed her phone back onto the cold marble of the kitchen island and everybody remained silent, until that phone buzzed, and Sarah-Jane scooped it back up.

"Yes!" she said, grabbing a fistful of air. "I got it for you, Simon. I got *Top Of The Morning* to double their offer. Two hundred K a year to be Troy Keiper's producer."

"What?" Simon said, his eyes popping wide open. "You serious?"

"I texted them that you'd be worth every penny of that salary and then some."

Simon climbed down from his stool, and walked, grinning, to the opposite side of the island so he could hug his boss—or former boss, as she was now going to be.

Sarah-Jane massively respected Simon Franklin. His ideas were always innovative. But with no show to produce, she knew she had to let him go when *Top Of The Morning* came calling.

"You're a doll, SJ," Simon said, leaning onto the shoulder of Sarah-Jane's black hoodie for a hug.

"You deserve every cent of it," Sarah-Jane whispered back to him, rubbing his back.

And then her phone vibrated against the marble again and she stabbed a thumb at the screen before squinting over the top of Simon's hair so she could stare at it.

"Oh, they want you over there ASAP!" she said, just as Simon stepped back from his embrace. "They want you meeting with Troy Keiper today to discuss some ideas."

"What? Now?"

"Yep. Looks like you gotta get your ass back to CSN Tower."

"Holy shit. Two hundred K a year, I can't believe it. I owe you, SJ. I owe all of you. Thank you."

"Get your ass outta my kitchen," Sarah-Jane said through a toothy grin.

Simon picked up his satchel, hugged Howie and Erica before shaking the hand of Phil — a man he always felt a need to tip-toe around but one he tremendously respected nonetheless given the ogre's distinct nose for a news story — then he walked himself down the chocolate-colored carpet of Sarah-Jane's penthouse hallway, holding a palm up at his ex-colleagues and waving a goodbye.

"Hey, before you go," Sarah-Jane called out. Simon stopped and spun around in the shadows of the luxurious dark brown hallway; his silhouette only partially lit by the crack of light glowing from under Sarah-Jane's hall door behind him. "You never said 'cause you had your face in your phone the whole time. But... what exactly do you think we should do next?"

"Oh, that's obvious," Simon's voice called back. "You all know the answer to that. Some of you just afraid to admit it to yourselves."

"What the hell does that mean?" Howie said.

"It means Erica's right. Online is where the numbers are.... Remember Dax Sheppard? Blond, goofy-looking guy who used to annoy the celebrities on *Punk'd*? His interview podcast hits twenty million people per episode. *Twenty* million." Simon's silhouette shrugged. "That's the *Punk'd* guy. Imagine what numbers you could get, SJ."

Then he turned around, opened the front door of Sarah-Jane's thirty-million-dollar penthouse, and left.

As soon as the door closed, Sarah-Jane folded both of her arms onto the marble worktop of her kitchen island, then collapsed her forehead on top of them.

"Fuck," she said. "Now the team's falling apart."

"You let him go," Howie said. "You let him go 'cause you know we're all screwed, don't you?"

"Calm down, Howie," Phil said.

And then Sarah-Jane's head slowly rose from her folded arms, her green eyes not shining as bright as they usually did. They looked tired. Heavy.

"I've made a decision," she said. "Erica, you're right. We gotta forget about TV. We need a podcast. Ring Fox News, Phil. Tell 'em to go fuck 'emselves."

"This is too big a risk," Howie said, shaking his head.

"Well, it's a risk we're gonna have to take," Sarah-Jane said. Then she opened up the notepad lying in front of her and began to scribble some notes.

"It's not a risk," Erica said, pushing the glasses back on the bridge of her narrow nose.

Her three colleagues all glared across the kitchen island at her.

"Of course it is," Howie said, squinting. "We are literally dissing the millions of devoted fans we already have. Just so we can start from scratch."

"It's not scratch. We've got Sarah-Jane. We've got the Zdanski name. The Zdanski brand. If we launch, with a great story, we could be huge. Within weeks we could be breaking the numbers we've been doing on TV. Hell, if we launch with the right story, we could blow those numbers out of the water from the get-go."

"Uuuugh," Howie said, slapping his palm onto the brown marble kitchen top. "It's a fucking podcast for Christ sake. Anyone can create a podcast. Anyone can set up a YouTube channel. My fucking niece has a YouTube channel. And she's nine!"

Sarah-Jane folded her arms under her chest and sat more upright on her stool, taking in her most experienced producer verbally sparring against her most inexperienced producer yet again. Phil was resting the jowls of his chins onto the palm of his hand, staying as mute as he usually did.

"No offense, Howie," Erica said. "But your niece isn't Sarah-Jane Zdanski. Trust me. I've been studying the figures on the YouTube clips CSN cut up and put out there of our show. Jesus, we get more eyes on a YouTube clip than we do live on TV. This is just the reality of it. The Jake Gyllenhaal interview we did two weeks ago? We peaked at five point two million viewers when we went out live. But one clip of that interview, where you asked him about Taylor Swift, that's been watched up to eighteen million times on YouTube. The Meghan Markle interview, we peaked at nine point nine million when it went out live. But that clip of you telling her you didn't believe her… that's been viewed a hundred and sixty million times online. That clip is being shared on social media a million times every three hours."

Howie huffed.

"Fuck social media," he barely said, mouthing it to himself.

"Actually, Howie," Sarah-Jane said, unfolding her arms, "we've never really gotten to the bottom of this, but what is your problem with social media exactly?"

"It's toxic, isn't it?" he said, flopping his forearms onto the kitchen island like a toddler. "Social media has single-handedly ruined news. It's fucked this nation up. Social media," he said, sitting more upright in his stool and wagging a finger, "has turned news from a harmless form of education into a weapon of mass destruction that's aimed straight at the nation's mental health."

"Huh?" Erica said.

"More and more people are suffering mentally, right?" Howie said. "We know that. It's social media. We're all comparing ourselves to other people... filling our minds up with lies and bullshit and more lies and more bullshit till we're all fucking feeling manically depressed with bullshit. Social media isn't regulated. That's why everyone is served lies as facts. It's why the whole of America is stressing out."

"Well, that's actually another plus point," Erica said, swiveling on her stool to face Sarah-Jane. "Something I've been meaning to bring up. If we go down this path, of producing a visual podcast, none of what we do will be officially regulated. We can get away with whatever the hell we want...."

"Please!" Howie scoffed, "You think Sarah-Jane Zdanski is suddenly gonna start lying to the nation after a quarter decade of being America's most trusted news anchor?"

"I'm not saying she should lie... of course not," Erica said. "What I'm saying is, she gets to control the narrative. She gets all of the control. All of the power. She becomes anchor. Producer. Editor. Director. President. Network owner. She won't have to answer to anyone. We get to control every second that goes out on the air."

Phil gently eased his chins up from his cupped hand, then glanced at Sarah-Jane before producing a huff—his usual tic to let everybody know that he was finally ready to offer his two cents.

"If we go online, we're still gonna have a show to produce," Phil said gruffly while staring at Howie. "I know it's not gonna be on a TV network. But it'll be online, and available everywhere anybody goes... if you're out for a walk, you can listen, if you're out in your car, you can listen. You will be able to listen and watch Zdanski on the go... on the move. It's gonna be a show. A show that needs to be produced. And there is no better man at producing a show than you.... Whatcha got now, Howie? Eight Emmys?"

Howie nodded with his mouth all screwed up.

"It's true," Erica says. "It's still gonna be a show. Nothing much changes. We won't have an epic studio and four different cameras, and we won't have floor managers and a team of sixteen researchers, but we'll have a show. A show that needs producing every week. We need you, Howie."

Howie covered his face with his hands, then rubbed the ball of his palms in a circular motion into his eye sockets before showing his face to the kitchen island again.

"Okay, I'm in," he said. "But we gotta make it a killer launch. It won't work if we don't have a killer launch."

"Exactly," Erica said. "If we launch big. We'll stay big. What we've gotta do to make this transition work is to find a story. A huge story. A story that will send shockwaves right through the heart of America."

NATE BENNETT

"And another fifty makes that a total of two thousand, three hundred and fifty dollars, Officer Bennett."

I don't thank him. Because he's a kak. I just slide the notes toward myself and scoop 'em up. Then I turn and begin speed walking toward the doors. I gotta get back to the car. That mutha fucker can't leak my browser history. I'd lose everything. I'd lose my job... for good this time. I'd lose Abigail... for good this time. There's no way she'd get back with me if she found out I jerk off to kiddie porn.

"*Uuuuuugh,*" I roar as I punch the side-door of the car when I finally reach it. Then I lean my arm on the top of the car and put my face onto my arm. I can't believe this is happening to me. Who is this mutha fucker on the phone? I'ma fuckin' kill him when I get my hands on him.

My phone rings. Not the one that was left in the car for me. But my own phone. My real phone.

I sigh before pressing the green button, then I throw my eyes toward the gray sky.

"Hey, Costello," I say, trying to sound composed; as if my whole life isn't actually falling apart.

"Fill me in, Nate," he says.

"Uh...." I look around the near-empty parking lot and feel the wind picking up in what's left of my hair. "We uh... we managed to delete the footage from a computer at the address you sent us to—it's been deleted permanently. I had to get heavy with the guy in there and it's lucky I did… because he told us there was also another copy of each day's recordings on a USB thumb drive back at his partner's house."

"Fuck!" Costello says. "You on your way there now?"

"I am, yeah."

"How's Zucha doing?"

"She ah… she…" I stare through the wind. "She's doing great."

"Well, you'll both only have done great if you get that USB to me as soon as you can."

"Don't worry, Costello," I say. "We won't let you down."

"You'll be letting America down if that footage leaks… trust me! Get it secured as soon as you can. This is why I brought you back!"

"You got it, Chief."

And then he hangs up, leaving me to stare at my reflection in the side window of the car. The cut looks rough, as if I took a chunk out of my cheek with a carving knife and not nicked it with a cheap-ass razor. Then I stare at the heavy bags under my eyes. They've been there ever since I was suspended a few months ago. Not being able to work has aged me. I look like I'm turning sixty next month, not fifty. But fuck it. I don't have the time to worry about how I look, so I snatch open the car door and hop in.

As I'm screeching the car out of the parking lot, the tires puffing out clouds, the siren blaring again, it hits me.

It's Costello. It has to be. That'd make total sense. He knew I was coming back to work today. In fact, he bloody organized the whole thing. Plus, he's the one who gave me the keys to this car… the car I found the burner phone in.

"Holy shit," I roar, slapping my hand repeatedly against the steering wheel. "It's Costello. *Has* to be!"

MAGGIE ZUCHA

My heart begins to thump again, like it did back at the office when Nate was smacking that guy around. A part of me felt a little sorry for that guy, but I was, like, I dunno, all caught up in the moment or something and it kinda felt good. Like a rush. A rush that made me feel different. As if I was someone. I sure as hell had never screamed in somebody's face before like I screamed in that guy's face. I even surprised myself. But it worked. We got him to delete the footage from his computer—and now we know where the only other copy of the footage is: behind this bright red door.

"Oh," she says, holding her hand to her chest as she pulls the bright red door open, "everything okay, officer?"

"Are you Roseanna Redford?"

She nods, and pulls the door open wider, inviting me inside. My heart thumps more with every step I take down her echoey hallway. I'm being a proper cop now. An actual street cop like the ones you see in the movies. And on the TV. Visiting a house. Questioning a suspect. Searching for evidence.

"What can I do for you, officer?" she says while I'm staring through the first door I see along her hallway.

"Your business partner, at the office on Woodville... he uh, he told us you keep copies of the footage from the CCTV cameras out the back of your office on a USB thumb drive, is that correct?"

"Uh-huh," she says.

"Well, I need to take the USB thumb drive you have from June fourteenth."

She clutches her chest again with her hand. I bet the tits she's clutching are fake. They look fake. So do her lips. So does her hair. Her ponytail looks like the tail of a racehorse.

"What's on it?" she asks. "Are you sure everything's okay?"

"Roseanna, everything's fine... we just need to watch the footage to, uh... it's uh...."

Shit. I'm tripping up over my words. Stuttering. Stumbling. Like I did every time I had to do a Show and Tell thing at school.

"You ah... have an ID? Where's your police ID?" she asks me.

I grin at her, then I reach into my back pocket to take out my cop badge for the first time in public. The only other time I've flashed this was back at my own home, in my own bedroom, in front of the mirror for over an hour the first day they handed the badge to me.

"Here y'go," I say.

She moves closer, stares at it, then nods, her hand still pressed against her fake tits.

"So, you were saying," she says, "you need the footage to...?"

"To uh... we just need to view it. It is, uh... oh, yes... it's confidential police business," I say, remembering what Nate had said back at the office, and feeling a little smug that I managed to remember it.

Roseanna flicks her head toward the doorway and begins walking past me. So, I follow her into a gorgeous high-ceilinged lounge room that smells like a department store.

"Wow. You do well for yourself, huh?" I say.

She doesn't answer. She just continues to walk across the large room, all the way to the other side, all the way to the tall shelving unit on the back wall.

"June fourteenth, you say?"

"Yep."

She slides a wicker box from the shelf, and I hear it rattling with lose USB thumb drives. I watch her pick one out, squint at it, and then set it aside. Then another one... then another... I look around her living room while she continues. It's crazy how the other half lives. I guess I'll never live this way. Certainly not on a cop's salary. I thought a cop's salary would be pretty good when I applied for the job. But it's not. I make forty-eight thousand dollars a year. Less than I was getting at Fullams Insurance, and less than the average wage. I guess I'm not doing this for the money, really. I'm doing it 'cause I want to feel as if I'm doing something. As if I am someone.

"June fourteen. Got it," she says.

I turn back around, walk toward her and hold my hand out.

"Thank you."

"I, uh…" she hesitates and closes her fingers around the USB thumb drive. "You got a warrant? You need a warrant to take somebody else's possessions, right? Maybe I should just ring my partner… see what he says about letting you take this recording…."

"I, uh… I, uh… no, Roseanna. You don't need to do that. I just need to uh…" She shuffles her hand into her pocket and takes out her cell phone. "You don't need to… Roseanna. I am a police officer. Just hand over the USB thumb drive," I say. I feel panicky as I'm saying it.

She lifts the cell to her ear and we both stare at each other while a weird ringtone vibrates from her phone. Then she shoves it back into her pocket and kinda, like, grins at me or something. It looked like a grin. I think. Or maybe it was a smile.

"I just need to go to the bathroom," she says.

"But Roseanna, I, uh… I need the USB thumb drive, and then I can get out of your way."

"Won't be long," she calls out as she's running away from me, and up her stairs.

I sigh, before deciding to look around her living room some more. It really is something. The TV must be sixty inches. That's three times bigger than mine. Maybe if I become a detective or a station chief or something I might earn enough money to afford a screen like that. I dunno… I guess I just gotta enjoy the ride of being a street cop for a few years anyway. See where it leads me…. It sure has started out weird. I mean, I was bored outta my head for, like, the first few weeks after I graduated and was given a placement in precinct twenty-two. But now that I'm out on the street, I think I'm really gonna enjoy this ride.

I pick up a framed photograph of Roseanna on the side table next to her giant TV. She was pretty when she was younger. Very pretty. But she musta kinda, like, messed with her face or something. She just has one of those faces that looks as if it's had lots of work done. It's too tight. And too shiny. And that pony-tail isn't kidding anyone. Then I hear a thud. From upstairs.

"Roseanna!" I shout, placing the framed photo back down. I speed-walk toward the stairs. "That you?" I pause at the bottom step, to listen for a reply, but it's silent. The whole house is silent. As if I'm the only one here. Talking to myself. So, I place my foot on the first step and grip the thick railing to begin climbing. "Roseanna… Roseanna! You here?"

BENJI WAYDE

It's not nice lying down here. It's hard. And itchy. And it kinda smells. A bit like leftover dinner when you take the tin foil off the next day. But there's nowhere else to sit now that the sofa is gone. So, I'm just lying across the smelly, itchy carpet, with my head resting on my arm so I can stare at the TV with the video player in it. All's I'm staring at are the old cupboards that we used to have in our kitchen when I was a little boy. Grandpa and Momma are sitting at the table, talking about school. Sometimes Momma's hair comes on to the screen, but most of the time I can just see the cupboards. If Momma was in school when these videos were made, then I am not alive. Momma was twenty when I was born. Grandpa told me that before. He told me that he told her that if she went to college like he had told her to she wouldn't be dead now. And then I asked him if he thinks I should go to college, and he said that going to college "wasn't for everyone." So, I was confused about Momma having to go to college. But I'm always confused about Momma. I don't ask too much questions about her cuz Grandpa and Grandma get sad when I talk about Momma. They miss her more than I miss her cuz I don't remember her. What I remember when I think of Momma is the photograph Grandpa and Grandma used to have on the shelf in the corner of the living room. Until it was moved to the wall by the stairs. It's still there now. I wonder where Grandma will hang that picture in apartment number seven. Momma is smiling in the photograph. And she looks pretty just like Grandpa always says she was pretty. In other photographs that Grandpa and Grandma showed me before she wasn't as pretty as she is in the framed photograph. But I bet she was pretty most of the time cuz Grandpa always told me she was "just the prettiest."

"I don't see the point," Momma says.

"Well," Grandpa says, "the point is that you will prove to yourself that you can see it through. You've been going to school for thirteen years. What's one more year?"

But I can't hear what Momma says next cuz the bottom step is creaking, and I know Grandma's gonna pop her head inside the door cuz we gotta go now. She shouted down the stairs to me a few minutes ago, "Boy, we're gonna go in five minutes."

But I couldn't get up off the carpet. Even though it's a bit smelly down here. Cuz I really wanted to see more of Momma. Even if it only was a little bit of her hair that I could see. But I could hear her. I could hear her voice. I could hear Grandpa being really kind to her. Trying to tell her how important school is.

"C'mon, Boy, we gotta go," Grandma says.

I lean up off my arm and I pick up my notebook and the pencil. And because I saw that Grandpa was being really kind to Momma on the TV, I open the notebook and begin to scribble while I stick my tongue between my teeth.

I love that Grandpa was really kind.

And then I get up off the smelly carpet and put my coat on cuz I've been hearing the wind outside and that's how I know it is cold. It's always cold when there's wind. Grandma is already out the door with her big heavy winter coat on. So, I go after her and we walk across the grass, and I think of the times Grandpa used to bring home cola bottle candies from the store on Emmett Road for me when he had extra coins on Fridays. And I think of the time he spent all that money on Grandma to bring her to New York City for her sixtieth birthday. And I think of the times he used to help some of the neighbors in St. Michael's House with their plumbing cuz when Grandpa was younger, he was a plumber for three years. He never took money from the neighbors when he fixed their plumbing. I can talk about those things for my eulogy when I am saying that I loved Grandpa because he was kind. Cuz he was kind. Really, really kind.

The wind is strong and is blowing back my coat and it reminds me of last night when I was standing on the roof of Northfarm Shopping Mall.

I put my arm inside Grandma's while we walk through the wind and over the grass, cuz the wind is so strong that it might blow her over. Then she lets me go, takes out a key and turns it in a lock on a red door. There are three numbers on the red door. Seven, eight and nine. But we're just apartment number seven. There are three apartments in here. I think two old ladies live in the other two. I tried to find out who lived in number eight and nine after I was told we were moving in to number seven and I think they're just two old ladies. A bit like Grandma. Maybe their husbands are dead as well.

It kinda smells in the hallway. A bit like our carpet. Grandma turns to the door with the crooked number seven on it and when she pushes it open and I look inside, the room is tiny. Really, really tiny. Much tinier than the living room back at house number forty-nine. I bend down and pick up the copy of *The Daily Connecticut* that's been dropped in the mail box. And Grandma immediately tears it out of my hands.

"Nope," she says. "You don't have time to be reading the newspaper today, Boy. Lots of work to do."

Then she makes the newspaper into a ball in her hands and walks back outside and into the wind again. I stare at her through the curtains as she lifts up the big lid of one of the bins and drops the newspaper inside. Then she slaps her hands together and walks back inside to me.

"Oh, Boy," she says, holding her hands on her hips. "This is so small." She opens the other door and then holds her hand to her face. So, I walk after her to see what she can see and I see that it's the kitchen. A small kitchen. Like a little square with a door on the other side. No room for our table. She walks across the small kitchen to the door and opens it. A toilet. With just a sink. No shower. Then she walks back past me, into the tiny living room and opens the other door on the far wall. A bedroom. With two small beds that have no sheets or pillows on them.

"Do we sleep in there together, Grandma?" I ask.

"We do, Boy," she says. "We gotta share a room from now on."

"Good," I say. "Then you don't have to sleep on your own."

She looks up over her round glasses at me. Her eyes are still really yellowy. Then she pats me on the shoulder.

"You're a real angel, Boy," she says.

She always says that.

I sure did feel a bit like an angel when I was standing on the roof of the Northfarm Shopping Mall last night with the wind blowing in my face.

Grandma pushes her glasses up and covers her face with her hand and I think she is going to start crying again. But she doesn't. She takes her hand away and puts it into the pocket of her cardigan.

"Here, Boy," she says, "take hold of this." She pulls out a long bright yellow measuring tape and I pinch the end of it like I used to do when I helped Grandpa in the house doing some things sometimes and then she walks backward away from me and puts the small black box she is holding on the ground. "Now, Boy, take your end all the way to the end of that wall." So, I walk backward, until I hit the back wall and then I place the tape down on the ground at the corner.

"Darn it!" she says.

"What's wrong, Grandma?" I ask.

"Nothing, Boy," she says. "Nothing...."

She pushes her glasses up and puts her hand across her face again. And her shoulders start shaking. So, I let the tape go and it makes a horrible scary noise as it whips back into the black box Grandma is holding. And then everything goes silent. Until Grandma starts squeaking. Trying to not cry. So, I step toward her and grab her tight. Really, really tight.

AIMEE STREET

There's something nibbling at my hair.

No.

Pulling at it.

Not ripping it. Just pulling at it.

Gently.

A huff…

Wait…

What is that?

A dog's nose sniffing at my head?

No.

A cat?

Wait…

Fingers. Thick, fat fingers. Like sausages.

I need to open my eyes. I gotta open my eyes. But I can't. My eyelids. They're too… they're too darn heavy.

"Aim," a voice whispers.

The sound of my name helps me open my eyes. Briefly. Like a blink. Like a reversed blink. I saw light. A sharp ray of light. But that was it. Darkness again. The backs of my eyelids. I groan. And moan. My head swaying subtly from side to side. My throat creaking.

"Aim."

The same voice. Whispering. Whispering while rubbing two fat fingers through my hair.

I manage to open my eyes again. Another reversed blink. The ray of light was sharper this time. Longer. Lingering. And almost blinding me before my eyelids snapped shut again. *Ouch*! My shoulder. My right shoulder. The one I hurt when I fell off the bench in the bar laughing at Mykel. Same one I hurt when... oh shit... I got knocked down. Holy shit. I got knocked down! I open my eyes again and try to stare through the sharp ray of light. A hand. Is that a hand? I dunno... my eyelids are too heavy. And I see darkness. Again.

"Aim... you're okay."

I open my eyes. Blinking them rapidly so the sharp light goes away, and I can see more clearly. It *is* a hand. So, I try to sit up.

"Hey," the voice says. "Stay where you are. You've been in an accident."

"Who the fuck are you?" I ask, blinking my eyes again until the light dims and I can make out the face of the man attached to the hand. Or at least part of his face. All I can really see are his massive nostrils as he stares down at me.

"I'm nobody," he says, pressing his hand to my forehead.

My eyelids close again. And I remain still... my brain jumping from thought to thought again. From question to question. From one thud of my shoulder against the floor of the bar to the other thud, when my shoulder smacked against the front corner of an SUV. A silver SUV. With blacked-out windows.

"Ouch," I say, reaching for the side of my head.

"Where's it hurt?" the voice asks.

I tap just above my ear, and when I bring my fingers down and blink my eyes open to stare at them, there's wet blood on two of my fingertips.

He swivels around toward the front seat, grabs a tissue, and then spins back to dab the tissue against the side of my head.

"Thank you," I say, breathless. "Did you... did you save me?"

He doesn't answer. He just continues to pat at my head, making me wince so much that I have to suck cold air in through the gaps of my crooked teeth.

"Shhh, shhh," he says. "Take it easy."

I blink my eyes back open so I can squint up at him. All I can see are his long nostril hairs. They're grossly long.

I sit more upright, pushing myself away from him until my head knocks against a cold window and I can't go back any further. So, I look around for the first time. I'm in the back of a car. What. The. Fuck?

I reach above my ear again. Then take my fingers down to look at them. Not as much blood this time.

"Who are you?" I ask, blinking my eyes rapidly until the blur recedes and I can take all of him in. And not just his nostrils.

He's old. Well old. About sixty. Sweaty. And dirty. Which is weird. 'Cause his car is spotless. Almost gleaming—as if he's just driven it straight from the dealership.

"I told you... I'm nobody," he says. He balls the tissue he had been patting against my cut between his two hands then tosses it into the front passenger seat. "It's only a small cut... just above your ear."

Jesus. He breathes really loudly through his nose every time he says something, making those damn nose hairs dance.

"Did you see what happened to me? I got knocked down, right?"

He coughs. Without covering his mouth. He's as disgusting as he looks.

"You did."

"And what happ—"

"You dropped this," he says.

He twists around again and grabs at something from his driver's seat.

"Oh shit," I say, snatching my vaporizer from him. I sit more upright in the back of his car. Frightened. Curious. Weirded-the-fuck-out. He places his hand on my knee and gives it a little squeeze which kinda makes me feel... I dunno... I don't know how to feel... "Thanks," I mumble. He's been trying to help me; having me lie down in the back of his new car; patting his tissue against my cut; squeezing my knee.

"I, uh… I think… I think I may need to go to the hospital," I say.

He squints his baggy, bloodshot eyes at me.

"You've just got a small cut above your ear. Maybe a bruise or two. But you'll be okay. No need for a hospital visit. What you need is a hot coffee."

I look around myself, at nothing much… the cream interior of a spanking new car. It doesn't suit him. He looks like he roughs it up on the streets of Connecticut, probably around Anner Street. So, having a brand-new car doesn't compute. It doesn't add up. Something's going on here. This doesn't feel right. *I* don't feel right. My temple. My shoulder. This new Ghost Train weed…

My head starts to spin quicker. So, I slap my two hands to my cheeks and while I'm doing that, he squeezes my knee again.

"Please," I say. "Don't touch me. I need to… I need to…"

"You need a hot coffee," he says.

I take my hands away from my face and stare at him again, as he breathes in and out through the long bristles hanging from his fucking nostrils.

"Thank you for helping me, but I, uh… I gotta go," I say.

I snatch open the door and as soon as I do I see the light gleaming against the bright silver panels of his SUV.

"Nope," he says, dragging me back into the car. "What you need is a hot coffee."

BENJI WAYDE

Grandma has stopped crying. But she is still feeling really sad. I can tell. Cuz she's not talking. And Grandpa used to say she could talk anybody to death. And it's true. She could. Grandma can talk and talk and talk all day. But that's why I love her and why we always spend lots and lots and lots of time together. Cuz she's a good talker. And I'm a good listener. But she doesn't want to talk today. Except for when I ask her questions. And I keep asking questions cuz I don't like it when Grandma is all quiet.

"Where we gonna put your radio, Grandma?" I shout into the tiny living room from the skinny bed with no sheets on.

"Mother divine," Grandma says. And I know she is a bit angry cuz she only ever says "Mother divine" when she is a bit angry. "Are you going to think of every item back in our house and ask me where I'm going to put it in here?" she says. "Just, please, Boy, enough with the questions."

I feel bad. Cuz I made Grandma a bit angry. But I just didn't want it to be too silent. I don't like it when it's too silent.

I kneel on the skinny bed and look out the small window. Again. It looks onto the front of the apartments that we look onto the backs of when we are in house number forty-nine. We're only moving a little bit away. But it feels really different. Really, really different. I guess it should be different cuz Grandpa ain't here anymore. But I try not to think about him cuz it makes me sad. But when I do stop thinking about him all I can hear is the silence.

"Where you gonna hang the picture of Momma?" I ask.

And before I am finished asking, I know I already forgot that I was supposed to stop asking questions. But Grandma doesn't say anything. She doesn't even say, "Mother divine" like she does when she's a bit angry. She just stays in the living room, pulling at the measuring tape. She told me earlier that she didn't need my help with the measuring tape. Maybe it was cuz I was asking too many questions and she wanted me to go away. But there's not really any place to go away to in this apartment. If we were at home, in house number forty-nine, I could go upstairs to my bedroom and shut the door and play a game.

"Hey, Boy," Grandma says. I get off the bed and walk into the living room to see her. She is on her knees, writing another number from the measuring tape into her notebook. "Why don't you go back home, play one of your games in your bedroom, huh? It'll be your last chance. We gotta move our stuff over later."

I look around the tiny living room again and I wonder where we are going to put the little tables that are in the corner of our living room that we eat dinner from. But I don't ask Grandma where the little tables are going to go in here, cuz I remember that I'm not supposed to ask where all the things are going.

"Grandma," I say.

She stops writing and looks up over her round glasses at me.

"Yes, Boy?"

"If I go back home, can I not play a game in my bedroom, and maybe watch some more of Grandpa's VHS video tapes instead?"

She presses her hand against the wall and gets to her feet. Really slowly.

"What's so special about those tapes, Boy?" she asks.

"Momma," I say.

And then Grandma walks over to me and puts her hand on my shoulder.

"You seen much of your Momma on those tapes?"

I shake my head.

"Not much. Two times she pushed the screen away when

Grandpa put it on her, and then the other time it was just her and Grandpa talking but sometimes I could see her hair and some of her ear. But most of the time I could just see the cupboards in the kitchen. 'Member the old brown cupboards we used to have in the kitchen when I was a small boy?"

Grandma's glasses move up on her face. And that makes me smile.

"What were they talking about... your Momma and Grandpa?"

"Momma's school," I say.

"Well, that's no surprise," she says.

"Why is that no surprise?" I say.

"Never mind," she says. "Your Momma and school. That was an often-spoken topic."

I am not sure what she means but because she said "never mind" I don't ask any more questions. So, I think I should change the subject and talk about something else.

"Where we gonna put Grandpa's old TV with the video player in it?" I ask.

"Mother divine," Grandma says, putting both of her hands against her cheeks. Then she puts them on her hips and looks at me over the top of her round glasses and I feel bad cuz I made her say "Mother divine." Again. That's two times. In one day. "Okay, Boy," she says, turning me around. "Go back to the house while I'm measuring up here... go, go, go. Go watch your Grandpa's VHS tapes."

NATE BENNETT

As I skid around another corner, my knuckles white from gripping the steering wheel so tight, I am trying to convince myself that it can't be Costello who's trying to blackmail me. It's too small-time to be him. A couple grand from my savings? What would he want with that? But I dunno what to think any more... My head is that fucked up. Maybe he and Governor Haversham are in on it together. They probably planned all this. Get me back on the force and then they can get me to go rogue and do... do whatever the fuck it is they want me to do for them. But why the hell have I got all my life savings in my pocket... what's that all about?

"Mutha fuckers!" I yell, punching at the steering wheel.

Bastards musta hacked my computer... found my kiddie porn, then decided to bring me back to the force. To do... to do what? Empty my fucking bank account? None of it makes sense.

I reach into my trouser pocket, take out the burner phone and stare at it. The number still hasn't rung back since it ordered me to the bank to take out all of my money. What the hell am I supposed to do with this cash? Whoever it is can have it all... I don't care. Anything to make sure they go away; that they don't leak my browser history.

"No. Can't be Costello," I say to myself as I pull a hard right, causing a truck to jam on its brakes and skid to a stop. Me and Costello go way back. More than twenty years. It was 2001 when we first met. We both graduated two months after the Twin Towers came down. He's the same as me. We both hate kaks. We talk about it all the time. We're old buddies. He wouldn't do this to me. He wouldn't...

I press harder on the gas pedal and watch as the speedometer rises over one hundred. I gotta get to Zucha. Poor bitch probably doesn't know what's going on. She's not the only one. This has been one hell of a morning. Though at least it's not boring. At least I'm driving around in a cop car again with the sirens blaring over my head. And not just watching Fox News while slumped on my sofa in my stinking towel robe.

I skid to a stop outside the address and stare at the house. It sure is big. I bet the bitch who lives behind that door doesn't know what's on that USB thumb drive. I bet she's as innocent as they come. Hell... I don't even know what's on it. Maybe if I found out, I might be able to put two and two together... and maybe this whole morning would start to make sense.

I push out a laugh. Because I begin to wonder if I'm going through an initiation test... just like I did when I first started as a cop. Some of the guys made me arrest a homeless guy on my first day, telling me he had robbed a sex shop. Turns out it was all just a big laugh for the rest of the street cops at my expense. Maybe they're pranking me again... because this is my first day back in months. Though this sure is a helluva lot more elaborate than arresting an innocent homeless kid and patting him down in search of vibrators.

I feel for the cash in my trousers pocket. Then I begin to shake my head again because I don't even trust my own thoughts anymore.

Then, out of the corner of my eye, I see a woman jumping down from an upstairs window at the side of the house before she begins to run as fast as she can across the lawn. This morning sure is getting a whole lot weirder.

I snatch open the car door and squint at her as she races away.

Then the front door of the house opens and Zucha appears, puffing and panting for breath.

"Get after her, Nate. She's got the USB!"

5

SARAH-JANE WAS ENJOYING THE SUSHI, IF NOT THE CONVERSATION. She was bored. Bored from listening to the same celebrity names being mentioned and the same weak news ideas being pitched. Each of them had been through their Rolodexes of politicians and showbiz personalities before slapping those Rolodexes shut... until whichever room they happened to be meeting in at the time finally fell so intolerably silent that the same Rolodexes would be reopened, and the same names would be mentioned, and the same weak news ideas pitched.

Since *The Zdanski Show* had been canceled two-and-a-half weeks earlier, and access to their offices at CSN Studios revoked, Søsa Restaurant — which they were now sitting in the dimly-lit back corner of — had been their third meeting venue. They had held two meetings in the plush kitchen of Sarah-Jane's penthouse before she decided against hosting colleagues in the same place she literally paid thirty million dollars for to seek respite from work. She then decided to rent an office space in Tribeca where the four remaining members of the Zdanski team — Sarah-Jane herself, Phil, Howie and Erica — met a total of four times in the space of one week before the boss admitted in a sulk just two days ago that the office space she was spending ten thousand dollars a month to rent wasn't inspiring enough for creating innovative ideas. Which is why, during their last meeting there, she snapped in frustration, "Fuck this, let's just meet in restaurants from now on." So, she chose this specific restaurant for their next meeting. Her favorite restaurant. Søsa Restaurant. Where she was always led, by a fawning middle-aged restaurant manager, to the shadows in the far corner of the dining area dimly lit by blood-orange bulbs that glowed under red-velvet lampshades. A restaurant she didn't have to repeat over and over again in that she had a nut allergy because they already knew. She felt comfortable here. She basked in the relaxed setting of Søsa Restaurant.

"I still think the best thing for you to do is get Trump on," Simon said. Again.

Simon had been invited to this meeting primarily because it was sold to him under the guise of a leaving dinner thrown in his honor. He had already settled into a faster-paced life at *Top Of The Morning*, mesmerized by the buzz of the overly competitive morning TV ratings war. But rather than discuss how his first week at *Top Of The Morning* had gone, talk at this table had only consisted, thus far, of how Sarah-Jane could relaunch herself on her new visual podcast. Before the dinner order had even been taken by their waitress, Simon had already become aware that he was at yet another Zdanski work meeting, and not necessarily a personal farewell dinner. He looked at his watch after offering up Trump's name once more, conscious he had to be up for work at three a.m.— a little over five hours from now.

Sarah-Jane shook her head while sucking in a mouthful of nigiri sushi from the pinch of her chopsticks, then, when she finally swallowed, she placed her chopsticks to the side of her bowl and audibly sighed.

"Stop. Please. Let's stop going round and round in circles with the same names. Trump's not gonna work. He's not a big draw anymore. That guy can't even get a post to go viral on his own bloody social media site these days. And Biden's not good enough. So don't mention that name again either. We gotta think beyond... I dunno... beyond presidents."

"Think beyond presidents? You mean, get an interview with God?" Erica said.

Sarah-Jane giggled. It was the first time she'd naturally giggled in her colleagues' company since CSN had canceled her show. The ease in which her giggle returned in that moment, however, could be attributed to the comfortable setting she was enveloped in rather than Erica's 'God' quip. Sarah-Jane adored the ambience of the roped-off back corner of Søsa Restaurant mainly because it reminded her of who she was. Sarah-Jane fucking Zdanski. Only, she was well aware she was now Sarah-Jane fucking Zdanski minus *The Zdanski Show*. And that was an entirely different Sarah-Jane fucking Zdanski altogether. If she didn't retain her relevancy as the queen broadcaster in America, there'd be no VIP treatments in the dimly-lit back corners of her favorite restaurants anymore. She'd have to eat at the regular tables. With the regular schmucks. And she despised even the very notion of such an existence.

"I know I keep repeating myself," she said, picking her chopsticks back up, "but we just *have* to get this right. We need to make a huge splash with our debut show. If we don't, we're just gonna be one of the millions of podcasts out there, lost somewhere in the ether among all the noise."

She glanced at Phil while snatching a bite from the pinch of her chopsticks to see him doing exactly what he had been doing ever since the waitress had arrived at their velvet cloth draped round table—stuffing his mouth with a forkful of noodles.

"Ya know what I think could be a good interview?" Erica said, trying to not stare at Phil as he vacuumed noodles down his throat. "Chris Rock. If we could get his first interview after the Oscars slap... that would be pretty mega."

Sarah-Jane swished her tongue around the inside of her cheek.

"Yeah, we have a request in with his reps at the moment. But that's more of a show number two kinda interview... not a launch strategy. Whaddya think, Phil?"

Phil leaned back in his chair and subtly shook his head while he gulped down another mouthful of noodles. Then he leaned forward to shovel his fork back into his bowl again, without saying anything.

"Olivia Rodrigo?" Erica suggested in the resulting silence. "She's won three Grammys this year. Is the hottest young pop star on the planet... she's a big name. About to get a whole lot bigger."

"No, not a popstar. Come on. We've said this already. We've mentioned Britney, Kanye… Beyonce. A pop star isn't gonna cut it. We gotta go beyond pop stars."

"So, you're going beyond popstars… and beyond presidents?" Simon said.

Sarah-Jane scoffed a laugh from the back of her throat before unfolding her velvet-red napkin and dabbing it at the corners of her lips.

"What about Dr. Fauci?" Simon said. "He's been America's grandfather these past couple of years."

Sarah-Jane shook her head again.

"No. He's already been mentioned."

"But you could come at it from the angle of 'this is the end of COVID.' We would market it as us interviewing the King of COVID to officially mark the end of the pandemic."

"It's still not strong enough… nowhere near it," Sarah-Jane said. "We need to a have a 'pow' moment. We need to make a huge splash. Get all of America talking."

"Why don't you get Meghan Markle back on?" Simon suggested. "Maybe talk it out…."

Phil blew a raspberry through his lips, while still managing to suck a mouth full of noodles down his throat.

"No chance," Sarah-Jane said. "She and her team were reluctant to do our show in the first place. They're not coming back… certainly not to help me relaunch myself."

Then she sighed. A deep sigh. Before picking up her chopsticks again while those around the dimly-lit red-velvet table stared at her. In the silence, Sarah-Jane tapped a finger at the screen of her phone, creating a glow in the back corner of the restaurant.

"Where the hell is Howie?" she said. "It's ten p.m. He's almost an hour late already."

She tapped at her screen, until the shrill of a ring tone cracked through the silence.

When he answered, Howie immediately sounded as if he was panting for breath.

"Howie, where are you? We're already halfway through dinner."

"Sarah-Jane…" he paused to pant some more, "I'm just walking up the steps from the subway. Two blocks from the restaurant. Order me the usual… Temaki rolls. I won't be long. But… boss, I got something for you… something incredible."

"What? What d'you mean you got something for me?"

"I'll be with you in a few minutes…. This… this," he said, panting some more, "you gotta see this for yourself."

Then he hung up. And the glow from Sarah-Jane's phone disappeared, dimming the back corner of the restaurant into near darkness again.

"What's he mean he's got something for me?" Sarah-Jane said, raising one of her perfectly sculpted eyebrows before pinching more sushi between her chopsticks.

Simon shrugged across the table. So did Erica. But Phil didn't react at all, other than to continue sucking noodles from his fork.

"Think he's lined up a guest for the show?" Erica finally asked.

"Maybe," Sarah-Jane said. "He sounded weird though. Was he running?"

"Think he's found a story?" Simon asked.

"Maybe. A story is probably where we should be looking. The next big story. Rather than a big-name interview. We sometimes rated higher when we had a big shit-hot news story as opposed to an A-lister on."

"Y'know, I was wondering," Erica said, stabbing a knife at her fancy food as if she was getting more enjoyment out of playing with it than eating it. "When you first launched *The Zdanski Show*, you said you had thirty million tune in to your debut, is that right?"

"Uh-huh," Sarah-Jane replied, her mouth full.

"What did you launch with?" Erica asked.

Sarah-Jane took the time to swallow before answering.

"A school shooting," she said. Then she licked her lips while reaching for her glass of Chateau Margaux. "The Median High School Shooting, straight outta Kansas. It's where Phil and I are from. We got to the story first…. Reported live from the scene for our local public access channel and then CSN offered us our own show that very day. We launched two months later with the exclusive insight into the school shooting... interviewing all of the loved ones of those who were killed."

Erica blew through her lips.

"Well, that shit wouldn't work today."

"Hell no," Sarah-Jane said. "There's a mass shooting every day in America. That's not news anymore. It isn't 1997."

"So, in the nineties mass shootings were big news?"

"Explosive," Sarah-Jane said. "Certainly ones as raw and emotional as a school shooting."

"What, wait? And then mass shootings suddenly became more common? So popular they happen every day now. Why is that? How the hell did mass shootings become popular?"

Phil tossed his fork into his bowl, causing a clank to echo around the dimly-lit back corner of the restaurant.

"'Cause we made them popular," he said.

They were the first words he had spoken since the waitress had placed his bowl of noodles in front of him.

Erica pushed her plate away, deciding she was finished playing with her sushi, then she picked up her phone and began tapping at her screen. Simon, in the silence that followed Phil's first words, was itching to change the subject; desperate to talk about the thrill of his new job. But when he looked across the circular table at his former boss, he knew her mind was whirring with a selfishness he couldn't relate to, and that she wouldn't take kindly to him boasting about booking Tom Hanks for an exclusive interview the following week. It looked, to Simon, as if Sarah-Jane's star was literally fading right in front of his eyes. The sheen of invincibility that shone effortlessly from her as soon as he had first been introduced to her a little over five years ago was definitely dimming; just like the back corner of the restaurant they were all seated in. He knew she could handle the vitriol that was firing on social media channels; a vitriol that was being counterbalanced by support in her favor. Because this had always been the way. Controversy had followed Sarah-Jane like a welcome companion. That's why hers was the most watched face on TV.

The vitriol raging among half of the American population over her handling of the Meghan Markle interview wasn't what was bothering her. Simon knew that. He knew she was harboring no guilt whatsoever in that regard. Her mood was completely selfish. Her dimming glow was all about her own personal status in America—a status that was now in danger of toppling from the very top. Simon observed, somberly, as Sarah-Jane ever-so slowly lifted another pinch of sushi between her chopsticks and placed it on her tongue. It was when she was placing her chopsticks back down to the side of her bowl that she heard a ruckus behind her. As she was chewing, she swung her head over her shoulder to squint out of the shadows and into the bright lights of the main restaurant.

"That's okay," she shouted. "He's with me. He's with me."

The waiter clasped his hands together and bowed at her, then he stepped aside to allow Howie to walk past him and into the dimly-lit back corner of the restaurant.

"Holy fuckin' shit!" Howie said as he approached his colleagues. Phil grunted while Sarah-Jane stood to hug the executive producer who was still panting.

"What is it, Howie?" she said, sitting back down.

Howie continued to pant. Heavily. As if he had just run a marathon and his finishing line was the dimly-lit back corner of Søsa Restaurant.

"I've got it," he said, almost out of breath. "I've got your launch show. Just wait until you see this."

Then he tossed a USB thumb drive onto the red-velvet covered table, where it spun to a stop right next to Sarah-Jane's chopsticks.

BENJI WAYDE

The wind is strong. Really, really strong. And I wonder will Grandma be okay walking back on her own without blowing over on the grass even though it is only a really short walk. I should prob'ly go back to flat number seven and wait for her to finish measuring. But I was asking too many questions that she didn't want me to ask no more. And I want to watch Grandpa's VHS tapes anyway.

I turn the key in the door of house number forty-nine and walk straight into the living room and then I feel sad cuz when I walk in the sofa isn't here anymore and I had forgotten it had been taken away by a man earlier. The small TV with the video player in it and my tablet and my notebook are on the carpet where I left them. So, I get down on my belly and touch my smashed tablet screen to see if anybody has liked my Facebook post about going to Yoga at midday.

Eight more likes and three more comments. That makes me happy. Really, really happy. Eight likes is a lot. One of the comments is from Melanie Samson who used to live on the row of houses behind ours in house number fifty-five. She wrote: "*thinking of you x.*" And there's another one from Sean McAuley who used to be in my class back at school before he was suspended for lighting fireworks in the gymnasium, and I never saw him again until he popped up on my Facebook and I sent him a friend request and he accepted it right away. Sometimes he likes what I post. Sometimes he doesn't. This is the first time he has ever commented.

Hope you are doing okay, brother. Peace and love, brother.

That's a odd thing for him to type. But he's prob'ly only being nice to me cuz he knows Grandpa died.

I notice a red circle in the top corner of my screen. A private message. I never get private messages. When I click into the private message, I see the name of who private messaged me. Steven Meyers. He is not nice. He bullied me at school and used to call me Bender. And then every student started calling me Bender Wayde instead of Benji Wayde.

I press my finger on his name and the message pops up.

Hey, man. Wanted to reach out to say I hope you're feeling well this morning. You were always a good guy. Not a bad bone in your whole body. Sorry I was a bit of a dick at school.

And I can't believe he is private messaging me. I should message him back and say he wasn't a dick at school and that he is nice and a good guy too even though that is a lie. I don't like to lie. But I don't like not being nice to every person. I don't know what to write to him, though. And that makes me think of Grandpa's eulogy that I have to write, and I put my tablet down and pick up my notebook instead and open the page where I have written only two sentences. One that says how much Grandpa loved Grandma. And the other about how kind Grandpa always was. I look at the Facebook message from Steven again. And then I look at the blue screen of the small TV with the video player in it. And I don't know what to do next. And my face just falls down onto the smelly carpet and I start crying. Not because Steven Meyers private messaged me because I think it's really nice that Steven Meyers private messaged me. I think his message makes me feel happy. But I am crying cuz I feel sad that the sofa isn't here no more. And Grandpa isn't here no more. And me and Grandma won't be here no more soon. And we'll be in that silly, stupid small flat number seven and I'll have to share a bedroom with Grandma which isn't a bad thing cuz she won't be alone at night-time when she is falling asleep but is a bad thing cuz I won't be able to play my games in my bedroom anymore. And now my tears won't stop dropping on to the stupid, smelly carpet.

I try to sit up to stop the tears from falling on to the carpet and I wipe my face with the sleeve of my sweater. Then I reach to the side of the TV with the video player in it and I press the arrow button. Right away the blue screen turns into our old kitchen cupboards again and when I hear Momma say, "Uhh, Dad, why do you even care?" I stop crying and I sit up and stare at the old kitchen cupboards again. "Because you're my daughter," Grandpa says. "And you'll always be my daughter."

And then there is a horrible noise like a screech and Momma is standing up and I can see half of her face. And then she walks to the cupboard and takes out a glass and turns around and I can see all of her. Her jeans. Her T-shirt. Her arms. Her neck. Her face. Her sneakers. All of my Momma. I don't think I've ever seen all of my Momma before.

"Dad," she says, "why do you always make me do things I don't wanna do." And then there is another horrible screech sound and I see Grandpa walk over to my Momma and put his arms around her and give her a big, tight squeezie hug. Then he whispers something in her ear. But I can't hear what it is.

NATE BENNETT

I jump over the bush, then hook my arm around the lamppost so it can swing me forward. It works. I'm on top of her in seconds, almost within reach of her bobbing ponytail.

I huff and puff as I reach my hand out to grab for it, and then I yank her to the ground. I stand still for a second, staring at the ponytail in my hand while she's flat out in front of me.

"Connecticut Police Department," I say standing over her, tossing her fake ponytail to the lawn.

"What the hell is it you guys want?" she says, twisting around and leaning up on her forearms. She's kinda hot. I definitely would.

"You know what we want, Roseanna," Zucha says, finally catching up with us. "We want that USB thumb drive!"

"I... I..." Roseanna stutters, "what did you do with my husband? I can't reach him by phone."

I stare at Zucha, then nod my head toward Roseanna on the ground before stepping away.

"Show me how much you're worth," I whisper out the side of my mouth.

Zucha pauses to eyeball me, and then licks her lips before jumping on top of Roseanna, grabbing at her face.

"Where's the fucking USB thumb drive, bitch?"

Roseanna begins shaking. Groaning. Crying.

I stare at the tears squeezing out of her eyes with a grin stretching across my face because I've missed the streets so much. Then the fucking burner phone vibrates in my pocket... slapping away my high.

"What?" I snap, answering.

"Get your ass to Anner Street," the distorted voice says. "I'm gonna ring you back in ten minutes. You better be there."

Then the mutha fucker hangs up.

AIMEE STREET

My head is still spinning. Maybe not as fast as it was. But it won't stop flashing from one thought to another: from one question to another—without any semblance of sense shining its way through.

I feel for the cut at the side of my head with my fingers again and then stare at them. No fresh blood. He's probably right. I'm fine. All's I need is a drink. I guess he did a good job lying me down in the back of his car and then closing the cut above my ear. Maybe that's why my mind won't stop flashing from one thought to another. Because I genuinely don't know whether this guy is helping me. Or out to scam me.

He looks back over his shoulder as he slows into a parking space, then he turns off the ignition, gets out and opens my back door—as if I'm some sort of diva. He holds an arm out for me to balance on to as I jump from the back of his big-ass SUV, and as soon as my feet land on the concrete, he stoops down to meet my eye.

"S'what way you take your coffee?"

"Why've you been following me?" I snap.

He flicks his head toward the Starbucks then walks off, heading for the front door.

I glance around the mostly empty parking lot, then down the street behind me that stretches along rows of old wooden houses until they're out of my line of vision. I could sprint down that street no problem. By the time he gets back into his SUV to chase me, I'd be behind of one of those houses... hidden among a maze of backyards.

I look back and see him just as he's pulling the entrance door of Starbucks toward himself, then I glance back down the long street of houses while tightening the strap of my bag against my shoulder. My good shoulder. Not the one that feels bruised as fuck. The wind whips my hair all over my face and strands of it start blowing into my eyes. So, I brush them away as I turn around to face him and see that he's holding the door open, waiting for me.

"Whatcha gonna do, Aim?" I whisper into the wind.

I march forward, gripping my bag tighter around my shoulder and running my tongue across the front of my crooked teeth. I nod at him as I pass him and then I feel the familiar smell and stillness of a Starbucks and my mind almost calms with it.

"S'what way *do* you take your coffee?" he asks again as the door closes behind us.

"I can't stand coffee," I say. "Do they make Margaritas here?" He pushes a laugh out of his nostrils, making his gross nose hairs dance again. The sight of them makes me wanna vomit. "Just get me a bottle of still water."

I huff as I walk away from him to the far corner of the store next to the toilets where I drop my bag from my shoulder and swing it onto the bench. I sit down beside my bag, my elbows on the table, my hands cupping both sides of my chin and I stare at the bald patch on the back of his head as he talks to the young woman behind the counter. I wonder if he's someone I've scammed in the past; a face I've blocked from my memory. But I'm not running away. 'Cause he's intrigued me; intrigued me enough to sit and have a drink with him. One drink. Then I'm outta here.

He turns all of a sudden, gripping a large paper cup full of coffee and a plastic bottle of water, striding toward me.

"Who the fuck *are* you?" I whisper, just as he places the bottle in front of me.

He chuckles through his hairy nostrils again, and slumps into the bench opposite me, causing it to creak under his weight.

"That's the thanks I get for helping you?" he says.

"You fucking knocked me down!"

He takes a sip of his coffee, then places it down on the table, gurning his ugly-ass face at me as if it's my fault it's too hot.

"You ran out in front of me," he says, swiping his fingers across his lips.

I close my eyes... and try to think. I was running. Definitely. I was... chasing...

"I was chasing you!" I snap. He blows into his cup, places it back down on the table, then holds my stare, saying nothing. I glance away from him, over my shoulder at the doorway. Maybe I should just go. Make a run for it. "Have I, uh... have I scammed money from you?" I whisper as I turn back to face him.

He sniggers. Again.

"No," he says. He takes a sip of coffee. "You haven't taken a cent from me, Aim."

"How the fuck do you know my name?"

He puffs out his cheeks, resting his elbows on to the table, before leaning toward me.

"It says it on your little vaporizer thingy there."

I scoff before licking my tongue across the front of my crooked teeth again. I do that when I'm nervous. Then I snatch the bottle of water from the table and try to open it. But it's tight. Too tight. Embarrassingly tight. It's actually burning the skin on the inside of my fingers. He holds his huge hand out and after a pause, I relent with a sigh, handing him the bottle. As soon as he twists the cap it releases with a gasp and I swear he's grinning at me as he slides the open bottle back across the table. I don't bother to thank him. I just look over my shoulder again. Toward the door.

"Cut the bullshit and get to it," I whisper, as I turn back to face him, "why the fuck are you following me and what do you want?"

He sits back on his bench and crosses his arms.

"Aim," he says, "I'm not following you. I haven't been following you."

"You fucking have," I spit back.

Then I take a large gulp of my water. Because I need it. My throat needs it. My temples need it.

"So, what is it you do?" he asks.

"Whatcha mean *do*?"

"What do you work at? Do you work? Are you still at school?"

I shrug. Then I take another gulp of water.

"You know what it is I do... that's why you're here, isn't it? That's why you've been following me. I've seen your car three times this morning. That one out there." I point my hand toward the door. "Registration 380 KJD. Three fucking times. Outside my home. Outside the Harriett Hotel. Outside the bar I had a drink with my friend in earlier. You've been everywhere I've been this morning. *Everywhere.*"

"Maybe you're too young to work." He shakes his head, causing his fat cheeks to wobble. "Are you a student? What are you studying?"

I grip my bottle, squeezing it so hard that water splashes over my wrist and onto the table.

"Stop playing fucking games with me. Who are you? Why are you following me?"

He places both elbows onto the table and leans closer again.

"You think, perhaps, the strain of weed you're putting in that thing might be a little too strong for you, Aim?"

I stare down at the pocket my vaporizer is in, then back up at his stupidly long fucking nose hairs.

"I'm outta here," I say.

I flick my fingers at my bottle of water, sending it toppling, and then I toss my bag over my shoulder before striding toward the door.

"Don't you wanna know how I can help you?" he shouts toward me.

MAGGIE ZUCHA

I sit on her fake tits and grip at her face, pushing her fat, fake lips toward me.

"Where's the fucking USB thumb drive, bitch?" I say, like a real boss.

She starts panicking. And crying. Like the little scared bitch she is. So, I grab her face harder.

As the tears pour out of her eyes, I begin patting at her pockets with my other hand, then Nate's phone rings again and I'm not sure if I'm supposed to stop now while he goes to answer it. But I don't stop. 'Cause I'm enjoying this.

"Where the fuck is it, bitch?" I snarl into her face. She huffs and puffs and then I let go of her mouth so she can talk.

"I don't have it on me," she cries, spitting out snot and tears.

"Where the fuck is it?"

"What did you do with my husband... where is he?"

"Zucha," Nate says from behind me. I look over my shoulder, still sitting on Roseanna's fake tits. "We gotta go."

"But I don't got the USB thumb drive yet... she don't have it on her."

"We haven't got the time," he says, spinning around and jogging toward his car. "Bring her with us!"

I stare at Nate's back as he runs away and then I begin to pick her up by the collar. But I'm not as strong as my adrenaline rush made me think I am, and I fall back on top of her, and we tumble back down to the grass.

"Get up, bitch," I say, as I start getting back to my feet. "You're coming with us."

She rants and raves about where her husband is as I'm putting her in cuffs, but I just ignore her, still kinda mortified from falling and tumbling on top of her. When the cuffs are tight, I lead her to our car where I notice Nate looking worried in the driver's seat. He's running his fingers through his hair fast, yanking at it.

"Hey," I say when I open the back door, before pushing Roseanna inside. "Everything okay, Nate?"

"Fine," he says. "We just gotta get going. C'mon."

"What about the car I drove here in… the Nissan?" I say as I'm climbing into the back of the car after Roseanna.

I stretch to pull her seatbelt across her and as I'm trying to click it in, Nate lets out a groan.

"Ahhh, fuck the Nissan," he says. "I'll explain that later to the chief."

Then he starts the engine, flicks the siren on and speeds off so fast that my head tumbles on to Roseanna's lap. Again.

BENJI WAYDE

Momma leans her chin on Grandpa's shoulder and they both stand at the kitchen cupboards hugging really, really tight. Saying nothing. Not for a long time. A very long time. It makes me feel happy that Grandpa is hugging Momma like the way he hugs me, and I wonder if I have rested my chin in the exact same place Momma is resting her chin on Grandpa's shoulder as I watch them on the small TV with the video player in it.

I pick up my pencil and open my notebook, and I write another sentence under the two sentences I have already written about Grandpa for his eulogy.

Grandpa gave the best hugs.

When I am doing the eulogy on the altar tomorrow, I can talk about the time he hugged me really tight cuz I said "Hello" to a woman on the street after Grandpa had teached me not to be shy on the street no more. And I can talk about the time Grandpa hugged Grandma when she told him that her cancer had all gone away. And I can talk about this video. About Grandpa hugging Momma in the kitchen really tight and Momma resting her chin on his shoulder like the way I used to.

"I'm happy you've decided to go back to school," I hear Grandpa say. And it makes me look back up at the small TV with the video player in it. Momma pushes him away from her and slaps her hands down by her jeans.

"That's not what I said, Dad. Jesus! Don't you ever fuckin' listen to me?"

And then she walks away, and Grandpa looks at the screen and then he walks over to it and it kinda goes all shaky and then the screen blinks to blue. I hear a noise, like a small motorbike in the video player and the VHS tape pops back out. The tape must be finished. So, I take it out and then I pick the other one up from the carpet and put that in the video player before I press the button with the arrow on it at the side of the TV.

The video player makes another motorbike noise and then the screen shows Grandma looking real young with her brown hair and her eyelids all painted light blue again. It's like she is staring straight at me.

"Are you nervous for her?" she whispers to the screen.

"Who?" I say to the TV.

Then Grandpa's voice says, "I'm always nervous for her."

And I look behind me as if Grandpa is here. But he's not. He's only behind the camera. Not behind me.

Grandma sits on the sofa that was taken by a man earlier and she starts fiddling with her fingers. She looks nervous cuz she is nervous. She told Grandpa she was nervous.

"Oh, here she is now," Grandpa says.

The screen goes all shaky and then I see our stairs with the old green carpet on it and suddenly Momma appears at the top of the stairs in a beautiful dress. A red dress with red gloves on, too. Red gloves that go all the way up her arms. Nearly to the top of her arms. And her hair is all straight and long over one shoulder. I ain't never seen Momma with straight hair before. When she walks down the stairs, really slowly, and comes closer to the screen I see she has red lipstick on to match her red dress and her long red gloves. She smiles. And I can really see now why Grandpa used to say my momma was "just the prettiest." Her smile makes me smile. I can feel my whole face smiling, even though I should be sad cuz Grandpa just died and me and

Grandma have to move over to the silly, stupid, small flat number seven.

"You look a picture," Grandma says. And the two of them hug at the bottom of the stairs.

"Careful, Momma," my pretty Momma says, "you'll smudge ma makeup."

They walk into the living room, and I can see that Grandma is close to crying. But she doesn't cry. She just keeps fidgeting with her fingers.

"I'm so proud of you," Grandma says.

And then Momma gives Grandma another hug. And I feel like I want to give the TV with the video player in it a hug. So, I do. I move closer to the TV and reach my arms around it.

"Now, Vanessa," Grandpa says. "You're three years off drinking age—so no alcohol tonight."

"Jeez, Dad," I hear my Momma say, even though I am still hugging the TV, "can you stop giving me orders for just one night, huh?"

And then I hear a doorbell and I look behind me out to our hallway and then I think that is not the sound our doorbell makes anymore so I get back in front of the TV and I stare at the screen. It goes all shaky and then I see our front door.

"Now you, Sidney," Momma whispers to the screen, "if you've got nothing nice to say, don't say anything at all."

Grandpa doesn't say anything back to her. And then Momma comes on the screen with her beautiful red dress and long red gloves on and she opens the door.

"Hey, Pauly," she says. She kisses a man on the cheek and when he walks into the hallway, he is wearing a big white suit with a white waistcoat and a black bow tie, and he puts his hand out for Grandpa behind the screen to shake.

"You look handsome, Pauly," Grandma says.

And then he gives Grandma a hug and a kiss on the cheek, and I think he must be a nice man to shake Grandpa's hand and to give Grandma a hug.

And then I hear a cough. But it's not Grandpa. Or Grandma.

Or Momma. Or the Pauly man. The cough isn't on the screen. It's behind me.

I twist myself around on the carpet and I get a real scary fright and I have to jump backward until I'm up against the wall and I can't move backward no more.

There's a man in our house. Tall. With a beard. And a stripey suit with a blue tie. And he has lots of rings on his fingers. On all of his fingers. Even his thumbs.

"Who-who-who are you?" I say.

NATE BENNETT

My body's rushing with I-dunno-what... maybe adrenaline. Maybe rage. I'm not sure I know the difference between those feelings at the best of times, anyway.

When I stare at my reflection in the visor mirror, I actually imagine pressing the barrel of my gun to my temple. I'd have the balls to do it... I know I would. I wouldn't be able to face the world if everybody knew what I jerk off to. So, I just gotta keep my head down, and do what this mutha fucker tells me to do. That way, I can get out of this alive.

"You cops have no right to—"

"Shut the fuck up, Roseanna," Zucha shouts from the back seat.

I eyeball her in the rearview mirror, her arm across Roseanna even though she's handcuffed and won't be going nowhere. Zucha will definitely turn into a fine cop, even if she is a chick. I'm not normally a fan of us having chicks on the force. But I'd rather have chicks than have kaks. They're lettin' way too many kaks become cops these days. The papers said a few years ago that they have to let a certain number of kaks in. What a heap of bullshit that is. We gotta put up with more kaks on the force just to tick off some politically correct boxes. I can't stand it. It makes me hate those mutha fuckers even more.

I screech the wheels onto Anner Street, wondering what the

hell this mutha fucker wants me down here for. I hate this hood…
it's full of kaks… full of the worst of the worst kinds of people.

When I flick the sirens off, I slow to a stop next to the rundown
stores all boarded up and painted over.

"Why're you bringing me here?" Roseanna says.

"I told you, shut your mouth," Zucha says, answering for me.

"You have no right to—"

"Shut the hell up, bitch!" Zucha screams.

"You can't tell me to shut up, I'm a citizen of—"

"Shut the fuck up!" I roar, turning around to face both of them.
Roseanna looks petrified. As if she thinks we're gonna kill her.
"Listen, all you gotta do is find that USB thumb drive for us…
then you're free to go."

"Well, then what the hell am I doing here? Why did you bring
me down to where all the homeless people hang out…? I don't
get it. I'm frightened. I don't know what you're gonna do
with me."

"Relax," I say. "We've another job to do… when we're done
here, we'll drive you back home and you can help us find the
USB."

I get out of the car, and immediately hear Zucha opening the
back door.

"No. You stay where you are," I say to her. "I gotta do this
alone."

"What is it you're doing?"

I shrug my shoulders. 'Cause I literally have no fuckin' idea
what I'm doing.

"Hey, officer," a kak with stained yellow teeth says to me.
"Can ya spare some change?"

I shake my head at him. Not to say I don't have change. Just to
let him know how disgusting he looks. Most of 'em around here
look like him, like somebody who hasn't showered in months. It's
the lowest of the low who live 'round here; the losers who've
never been able to sort their shit out.

I decide to walk up and down the street, eyeballing the ones
who have bothered to get out of their tents today. It's such a
pathetic life they live. I'd rather be dead than a lost cause.

"Officer, could you please spare me some dollars?" a loser with a stupid red wool hat asks.

"I'll spare you some advice," I say. "Take a fuckin' shower."

His eyebrows lower, then he just spins and walks away from me. So, I continue strolling, ignoring all the pity-me looks these losers are throwing my way... until the phone finally buzzes against my leg.

"What?"

"You on Anner?"

"Yeah, I'm here, what's going on? Is this an investigation? Are you a cop?"

He laughs, which makes me grip the phone tighter.

"I'm no cop," he says. "I'm just your worst nightmare, Nate. All I gotta do is press one button and your browser history enters the public domain."

"What the fuck d'you want me to do?"

"You got the money?"

"Wait... you want me to give my money to one of these losers?"

I take the phone away from my ear and stare up and down the street. Holy shit. This isn't a cop. This isn't a bigger investigation. Or an initiation test. This shit's real. This mutha fucker is seriously blackmailing me.

I press the phone back to my ear.

"I want you to give it to one of the Black guys," he says.

"A fucking kak? I ain't givin' my life savings to no kak!"

"Okay, I'll just press this button then... and let the world know Nathan Bennett jerks off to kids."

"You mutha fucker," I yell, causing lots of losers' heads to pop outta their tents.

"Hand over your money to a Black person on that street, or I'm gonna press this button."

"Here," I say, shoving my hand into my pocket when I see a young kak kid staring at me. "Here, take all this... it's yours."

He stares at the bills I pushed into his hands, then up at me with his stupid bloodshot kak eyes.

"You fo' real, officer?" he says.

"Fuck off, kid," I hiss, before lifting the phone back to my ear. "There, I've done it.... Over two grand to some little kak kid, now… is that it… can you fuck off and leave me alone?"

"Hell no…" the distorted voice says.

Then the mutha fucker hangs up.

AIMEE STREET

I take my hand off the door, allowing it to shut just before the glass almost slaps against my nose. And when I close my eyes, I sigh, fogging up the window of the door. After a long pause, I turn.

"I'm gonna give you two more minutes," I say, marching back toward him. "If you don't explain who the fuck you are and why you've been following me within those two minutes... I'm gone."

He points his whole hand to the bench I had been sitting on moments ago and, after standing and staring at him with my hands on my hips for what seems like way too long while water continues to gurgle and spill on to the table from the bottle I flipped over, I finally oblige and slide back down opposite him.

"You think you're a good scam artist, don't you?" he whispers across the table. "You think you're getting better at it."

I lick across my crooked teeth and then decide to match him with the same level of cockiness he's throwing across the table at me. Confidence is the one skill I know I possess. Sometimes I think it's the only skill I possess. It's why it made sense I became a confidence woman.

"I *am* damn good at it," I back at him.

"You'll be caught. You'll end up in prison." I shrug, but he just continues. "The thing about scamming," he says, leaning closer to me, "is that every job is a new job. And every new job is a fresh opportunity to get caught. And you will get caught, Aim. The more dangerous you play the game, the easier it is to get caught. You're trying to level up, aren't you? You're not playing with random strangers on the streets no more, taking their watches, taking their wallets. You're messing with the big boys now. Inviting executives to your pitches... employees of the Governor, for Christ sake."

I squint at him, then I rub my hands together, reminding myself that I am more than capable of matching this fucker for confidence.

"Do you work for the Governor?" I ask. He laughs. A real laugh this time, not a snide huff through his grotesque hairy fucking nostrils. "Who do you work for then?"

"I work for myself."

I feel my confidence wane. Because, I'm not sure what to ask next. So, I lean into the table and slap both palms to it.

"What the fuck do you want from me... tell me?"

"I'm just tryna help," he says. He leans back, stretching both arms across the back of the bench, trying to look calm and cool, while I remain leaning forward, holding his stare, my teeth clenched. I finally exhale a deep sigh, and I lean back on my bench too, before reaching inside my jacket pocket to grab for my vaporizer. In the silence, while we're still both staring at each other, my vaporizer buzzes and I glance down at it.

"Want a hit?" I ask.

He holds a hand up to wave a no. So, I bring the nozzle to my mouth and fill my lungs while continuing to hold his stare. When I exhale a cloud across the table, he ducks away from it.

"What do you wanna do?" he asks. "Instead of scamming innocent people... what do you really wanna do?"

"Smoke shit," I say. I lift the nozzle to my lips again and take another hit. It's when I'm blowing my exhaled cloud back in his direction that I realize I'm acting like a kid. I thought I could match this guy for confidence, but I've already stuck a pin in mine by saying I wanna smoke shit all day and by blowing weed clouds into his face. So, I relent... I give in. "I always thought I'd be a journalist," I say, shrugging. "I used to write for the school newspaper and used to produce a show for our God-awful community radio station...."

He pinches his bulbous nose before yanking his fingers away from it, likely taking a couple dozen hairs with him.

"And you somehow went from "I wanna be a journalist" to "I'm gonna scam people out of their money" instead?"

"Well..." I sit more upright, pressing the standby button of my vaporizer and turning it off. "It's an impenetrable industry, journalism, isn't it?"

He shrugs.

"I'd've thought it was a career path filled with opportunity... now more than ever."

"Uh-uh," I say, shaking my head. "I've written to all the newspaper editors in Connecticut. Not one of those fuckers replied to me."

"Ohh," he says, waving his hand back and forth as if my weed cloud is still smothering him, "newspapers. It's not 1997, Aim."

I push out a laugh and then realize I'm getting too comfortable in his company. Probably the way he wants it. I bet this guy's a scam artist too. He must be. Ugly looking. Scruffy looking. But with a big-ass brand new car. He worked his way up. He's where I want to get to. Maybe this guy can help me.

"Anyway..." I say, "I wanna know why you've been following me."

"Listen," he says, leaning forward on the table. "These days, if you have one of these," he wiggles his phone, "you're a fucking journalist. We're all journalists now. Every little shit who posts on Facebook, who rants on Twitter, who dances on Tik-Tok, they're journalists, right? I mean, maybe no one is reading or watching... but there's no doubt that it's easier to get into journalism now than ever before. Media is brand new. The whole industry has pretty much started all over again. And people like you need to take advantage of that."

I squint at him. Intrigued. He's talked more sense in the last twenty seconds than any of my lecturers have over the past two years.

"Easier to get into, maybe. But harder to make a living from."

"There are people earning more money from new media today than any journalist ever earned in old media," he says.

I run my tongue across my crooked teeth. Again. Not because I'm frightened. But because I'm so fucking intrigued.

"You should lecture on media," I say.

"I don't have a clue about media," he says, "I'm just well aware how much the world has changed. That's all." We sit in silence, him staring at the profile of my crooked-ass nose, me looking at the Starbucks employee as she wipes down the tables adjacent to ours. "How the fuck did you think you could be a con woman, but not a journalist?" he asks.

I shrug my shoulders before turning back to face him.

"'Cause when you're a con woman, everything is on you. I just had to decide to be a confidence woman. I didn't have to apply for the job."

He squints at me over the rim of his coffee cup as he takes a sip. Then he places it back on the wet table before burping silently inside his mouth. He might be intriguing. But he's also so fucking gross.

"Same in journalism, surely," he says.

"Huh?"

"Same in journalism. You go do the work, right? The work doesn't come to you. You find the stories. The stories don't find you."

I stare down at my lap, soaking in his words.

"Man, are you sure you don't wanna be a media lecturer?" I decide to say.

He laughs through his hairy nostrils again. And for the first time I watch them dancing without feeling an urge to throw up.

"Think about it. If you've been a con woman, then you already pass the qualifications required for being a journalist. You need confidence. You need to be proactive. You need to be adept at bullshit." I laugh. And then immediately stop, because I shouldn't be feeling this comfortable in this creep's company. "Go find a story," he says. "And then make it an even bigger story. That's what journalists do. Journalists don't apply for jobs, like con women don't apply for jobs. You gotta go out there and find your story."

"Okay. How about you?" I say. "How 'bout I make *you* my story. Let's start with who the fuck you are...."

"I'm nobody."

"Why the hell are you, a sixty-year-old man, lecturing a girl?"

His brow kinda points downward, as if he's saddened by what I've just said.

"I'm not sixty.... Secondly, I'm here because I knocked you down with my car... and I wanna make sure you're okay."

"You've been following me."

"Oh please," he says. Then he takes another sip from his coffee before putting his cup down. "Anyway, it seems you are okay, so I think I'll be...."

He moves, to slide his fat ass out of the bench.

"Stay sitting," I say. "You're... I dunno... interesting. Tell me... tell me more. How do you think I can become a journalist?"

He leans back on the bench again, then pinches his fat nose.

"I dunno... I just know you find the story; the story don't find you."

"And how do you expect somebody like me to just stumble onto stories?"

He squints his brow, and looks around the Starbucks at the employee moving chairs closer to tables for no reason other than the fact that she's bored, then at the table across from ours before eventually getting to his feet. I watch as he shuffles toward the counter, but I can't see what he's doing over there, not until he turns back around and marches toward me, holding a copy of the local newspaper. He says nothing when he sits back down as he turns the pages and quickly scans his eyes over them... until he eventually spins the paper around to face me.

"That looks like a great story," he says, stabbing his fat finger to the headline at the bottom of the page.

6

BY THE TIME HOWIE HAD FIRED UP HIS LAPTOP ATOP THE RED-VELVET-clothed circular table in the dimly-lit back corner of Søsa Restaurant, then sat himself between Erica and Simon before pressing play, his hands were sweating with excitement and he was sporting an uneasy grin—an odd facial expression for somebody who had just stumbled upon the most shocking footage they had ever witnessed in all of their decades of working in television. Because he had already watched it countless times before pocketing the USB thumb drive to carry it, late, to Søsa Restaurant, he instead observed the faces of those around the table after he had pressed play. Each of the faces, lit subtly by the blood-orange bulbs glowing from behind the red-velvet lampshades, squinted, then almost in unison, inched their noses closer to the screen before their eyes widened, and their bottom lips popped open...

Howie distinctly remembers Sarah-Jane placing a folded elbow on the table before pushing back the velvet-red chair she was sitting on and gagging from the back of her throat, as if she was going to throw up on the red carpet beneath her feet. She didn't vomit. But she did gag. Audibly. Phil couldn't keep his baggy eyes from the screen, opting to watch the footage over and over again as it played on loop while Sarah-Jane's head was ducked beneath the table. Simon slapped a hand to his mouth and kept it there for what seemed like an age before he felt a need to wipe away the lone tear streaming down his cheek. Erica's response was less emotional, but certainly more vocal.

"Holy fucking shit, holy fucking shit, holy fucking shit," she repeated, over and over again while Sarah-Jane continued to gag.

So, it had already become apparent to Howie, by the time he was sat around the glass conference table with his colleagues in a brightly lit office two days later, that everybody he looked at while they watched this footage for the very first time met it with a different reaction. Cody Williamson, who Howie was glaring at as the footage played out from a laptop in front of him, barely reacted at all. He just leaned his two arms on to the glass conference table, glared at the video, and puffed out his cheeks before leaning back in his chair and sighing audibly. Cody, who was impeccably dressed in a designer dark navy suit, complemented by a perfectly crisp, white shirt and a super-thin silver tie that glistened when he moved, stared at Sarah-Jane.

"This authentic?" he asked.

Sarah-Jane nodded.

"Yep. We had Phil check it out. Nobody knows video like Phil."

"A hundred percent authentic," Phil followed up with; his first words since setting foot inside the plush offices of his and Sarah-Jane's lawyer.

Cody puffed out his cheeks again. Then he rubbed at his cleanly shaven chin.

"This is huge. Absolutely huge," he said. "I assume you wanna run it as a story?"

"S'why we're here," Sarah-Jane replied.

"Ya gotta find who recorded this footage."

Sarah-Jane pushed her bottom lip out and shook her head.

"It was left anonymously, we've no idea who or even how it got into our old mailbox slot at CSN."

"Yep," Howie said. He was sitting opposite the impeccably dressed lawyer. "I got access to our old newsroom just to pick up all of our remaining things and in the mailroom slot, with a shit-load of other mail, was a brown envelope with this USB thumb drive inside it. This was weeks after the show had been canceled.

So, it could have been left there on any day. Of any week. In a mailbox slot that can be accessed by any member of the public."

"We need to get this to the police," Cody said.

"Not yet," Sarah-Jane shot back.

"We need to check the envelope and the USB thumb drive for any prints, any evidence...."

"We've checked into that," Howie said. "Nothing. Everything was wiped clean. Not a smudge on anything."

Cody knitted his two eyebrows together, then puffed out his cheeks again as though, for the first time in his life, he was stuck for words. He may not have reacted by gagging onto the carpet below him, like Sarah-Jane had, but he was shaken. Oddly shaken for a man who thought he had seen it all.

"We still gotta go to the police," he said. "We can't possess video evidence like this and not immediately turn it in."

"We're waiting to build our show. Should be about ten days," Sarah-Jane said. "We wanna report this footage for our launch show. It'll be the biggest news story of the year. Of a generation. That's why we're here, Cody. We need to know *when* we should go to the cops."

"Well, now!" Cody said, retightening the knot of his metallic silver tie. "As soon as you first watched this video, that's when you should have gone to the cops."

"Cody," Sarah-Jane said, leaning forward and fingering the top of her lawyer's hand. He glanced down at her touch, then back up at the most watched face in America. "Listen to what I'm asking you. I wanna break this footage as a news story in ten days' time when I launch my new channel. When do we need to go to the police?"

Cody took in Sarah-Jane's light-green eyes while she continued to stroke the top of his hand. Then he shook himself back to reality, before moving his hand away. Sarah-Jane had tested him before. Quite a number of times. She had often been eager to push the legal boundaries as far as she could in terms of breaking news stories. But this footage was beyond anything she had brought to him before. Way beyond it.

"Listen, you gotta go to the police as soon as you've seen this," he said. "So, what I'm saying is, if you wanna hold off till your show airs, then you gotta pretend you haven't seen this footage till just before your show airs. And if that's the case, then you aren't here. And you aren't talking to me about this right now."

"Of course," Phil said, leaning his arms onto the glass table, causing it to creak. "The meeting we're all having right now is about the Meghan Markle interview. Nothing else. We haven't spoken about anything other than Meghan Markle here today, understood?"

"Understood," Cody said, nodding. "But that's the bottom-line. If you don't want this footage to get out until you air your new show, then you haven't seen this footage. Not yet. Understood?"

Cody aimed his question at Phil and continued to eyeball the scruffy-looking producer until it was clear he wasn't going to get an answer. Cody had never quite taken to Phil. Not many had. But they couldn't help but want to be attached to Sarah-Jane Zdanski regardless of her insistence on having Phil in every room with her. Cody scooted his chair back so he could stand, then he began to walk around his overly bright office, his fingers inter-locked behind his back.

"Jesus Christ," he said. "This footage... soon as it gets out, there's gonna be riots on the streets. There'll be a movement. A fucking rebellion. This will really push America over the edge."

He walked all the way to the window, to glance down at the 9/11 memorial below him, a habit he'd never neglected in all the years he had worked here.

"We're well aware," Sarah-Jane said to the back of his head.

Then the conference room fell silent, while Cody replayed the footage he had just watched inside his mind. As he was staring down the height of fifty-five stories, Sarah-Jane was stuffing a notepad back into her designer handbag.

"Aren't we uh..." Cody finally said, spinning away from the window. "Aren't we gonna discuss the Meghan interview?"

"I told you, Cody," Sarah-Jane said. "There's nothing to discuss. Aside from that one thing I asked you to look into.... Yes?"

Howie's head pivoted from Sarah-Jane to Cody, then to Phil. Phil was looking down at the glass table at the blur of dusky pink carpet beneath his feet.

"What about releasing a public statement about the Meghan interview, get you back on side with the audience?" Cody posed, pushing his hands into his pants' pockets. "We can put something really clever together."

"We're happy with the audience reaction," Sarah-Jane said before standing and tossing the strap of her handbag over her shoulder.

"But… half of America hates you right now," Cody said.

"Half of America loves me," she replied, offering a sterile grin, "but, more importantly — and you always seem to neglect this, Cody — *all* of America is talking about me. And that's all that ever matters."

Then she strode toward the frosted glass door of the office, pulled it open and stepped out onto the plush baby-pink carpet of the fifty-fifth floor of the Freedom Tower—the home of Cody's equally reviled as it was revered lawyer's firm. Both Phil and Howie joined her in a corridor lined with photographs of Cody posing with clients; some of whom were celebrities; most of whom were unknown. But all of whom were rich. Super rich. Tens of millions of dollars in the bank rich.

"Okay," Sarah-Jane whispered as she turned to Howie, "you go and return the USB thumb drive inside this brown envelope to the mailbox at CSN you found it in. We haven't seen it yet. Take it out a day before we go live as if we've come across it for the very first time, then we'll bring it back here for Cody to pass on to the cops. We'll break the story the following night."

Howie nodded his head. Then he grabbed the brown envelope and tucked it inside his jacket. He was used to his boss's tricky ways. In fact, he had helped evolve her tricky ways over the years, so naïve and inexperienced was she when they first met ahead of her debut show back in 1997.

"Oh, actually," Sarah-Jane said, "I'll meet you two down in the lobby. Take the elevator ahead of me… I just need to," she tilted her head back toward the office they had just left.

"Okay," Phil said. Then he threw his arm across the shoulders of Howie and led him to the giant copper double doors at the back wall of the lawyer's offices.

Sarah-Jane rapped one of her knuckles on the frosted glass of the door she had just exited, then pushed it slowly open.

"Hey, Cody," she said.

Cody was standing at the window, staring down at the top of the 9/11 Memorial.

"Fuckin' hell, Sarah-Jane," he said, spinning around. "I've got some shady clients, but you — America's sweetheart — you're something else."

"Please," she said in a sultry whisper, "don't tell anybody about this."

"'Course I won't," he said, placing his hands back into the pockets of his suit trousers, "you pay me for two things: my legal expertise and my confidentiality. You always have my confidentiality. You know you have. I won't say a word. Just bring me that footage the day before you plan to launch your show, and I'll see it gets into the hands of the cops."

"You're a gem," she said. Cody offered her a smile that was familiar to Sarah-Jane, mainly because most men smiled at her that way. "And one more thing. Did you uh… you get a figure from CSN for me?"

"I did. They're willing to offer the entire six million dollars," Cody said. "Exactly what you asked for."

Sarah-Jane grinned, then she turned around, opened the frosted door again and made her way down the furry, baby-pink carpet of the brightly lit office toward the copper-colored double doors that were just about to closed on Phil and Howie.

NATE BENNETT

"You always this much a bully?" she asks, just as I'm pulling into her driveway.

I glare at her through the rearview mirror.

"Let's just say I'm not having a great day."

Then I catch a glimpse of myself, the wedges of crooked lines deep in my forehead, and the stupid cut on my cheek. I look like a loser. Maybe I am a loser. A fuckin' kiddie porn-watching loser. I don't even like watching that stuff. I just stumbled onto it 'cause I was bored. I used to just watch normal porn. Me and Abigail used to watch it together. But when she left me... I just got bored and ended up down rabbit hole after rabbit hole online and... I dunno... I guess it felt dirty. It felt wrong. And that's probably why I can't stop looking at it. Maybe Abigail is right. Maybe there is evil inside my bones.

"Okay, I'm gonna take the cuffs off you," Zucha says to her, "And you're gonna lead us straight to that USB thumb drive, okay?"

Roseanna twists to her side so Zucha can get to her cuffs while I get out of the car. I look across at the bushes that I leaped over earlier when I was chasing after her, and when she gets out of the back door, I grab her by the back of her neck and push her toward them. Cos that's where she said she dropped the USB. In the bushes while we were chasing after her.

"Jesus," she says. "You fuckin' guys. I swear I'm gonna report you both."

"Just ask for Chief Chris Costello," I say. "He's my super... you can make any complaints directly to him."

"I mean if this is how you treat regular people who do nothing wrong, I hate to think how you treat criminals."

"If you don't find me this USB thumb drive, I'll show you," I say.

Then I shove her into the bushes.

"Find that fucking USB, bitch," Zucha shouts.

I take the time Roseanna is down on her hands and knees, rooting through the bushes, to check the phone that was left in my car this morning. I haven't heard a word from this mutha fucker since I was on Anner Street.

"Got it!" Roseanna says. Then she pokes her hand out of the bush to show us a silver USB thumb drive with a blue lid.

"Good girl," I say, snatching it from her before I turn around and pace back to the car, Zucha skipping after me.

"Hey, fuckin' pigs," Roseanna shouts. "You're not gonna help a woman up? Hey.... Hey!" she shouts. "Abusers. I'm gonna report you."

We hop into the car, ignoring her roars.

"Okay," Zucha says, "let's get this USB to Chief Costello and Governor Haversham."

"Nope," I say squinting at the thumb drive as I twirl it around in my fingers. "I wanna see what's on this fuckin' thing first."

AIMEE STREET

I read the article, nodding my head as my eyes dance across the words. And when I'm done, I lean back on the bench and fold my arms.

"I agree," I say, "that is a story. But it's already been written."

"The story here," he says, leaning forward to stab his fat finger at the headline again, "isn't that he's back on the job. It's *why* he's back on the job." He tries to take a sip from his coffee before realizing his paper cup is empty. "It says here that this guy was suspended for six different physical attacks on members of the public. Five of them were for attacks on Black people. How was he not fired? What's he back on the streets for exactly? This guy..." he stabs his fat finger against the newspaper headline again, "this fucking scumbag of a police officer... he is a walking, breathing story for any wannabe journalist like you. I bet he was put back in uniform for a reason. Whatever that reason is... that's the story. That's *your* story."

What he's saying makes sense. Perfect sense. Much more sense than any of my lecturers ever made about engineering a career in journalism. So, I nod. Then I find myself shaking my head.

"I, uh, don't have my notebook or pen, or anything to go around following him today."

He picks up his phone and wiggles it at me.

"It's not 1997, Aim," he reminds me.

"But this police district he's at, that's almost an hour away, I don't... I can't get there."

"You find the story," he says, "the story doesn't find you. If you want the story, you gotta go get it."

I lick my tongue across my crooked teeth. Again.

"Well... by the time I get there his shift will be over, and the story might be gone."

He stands, nudging the table nearer to me, just so he can get his fat belly out.

"Follow me," he says.

As he walks away, I look around the empty Starbucks at the employee leaning against one of the tables she's just wiped clean, scrolling through her cell phone. Then as I make my way to follow him, the door swings closed in my face, and I glare out the window at him before focusing on my own reflection.

"Fuck it," I whisper to myself.

Then I push the door open and join him.

"You sure you're okay?" he asks.

"Fine... why?"

"'Cause about half an hour ago I just hit you with my car."

"I'm fine... just a little stiff," I say, clutching my shoulder.

"I'm sorry," he says, "you just ran out in front of me and I... I didn't see you."

"I'm fine," I say.

"Good," he says. "Then come with me."

We walk across the empty parking lot, then across the busy street until we get to a row of stores that line up in front of the old warehouse that used to make potato chip packaging when I was younger but has been closed down for I-dunno-how-long now. My mind is whirring with so many questions that I can't really find the time to ask one. Not until he stops walking and I almost bump into the back of him.

"What are you doing?" I ask, staring through the window he's stopped outside of and into a rundown little office where I can make out one guy standing behind a desk, shuffling through some paperwork.

"I'm gifting you my apology," he says.

MAGGIE ZUCHA

It's *really* dark in his house. And, like, kinda stinky. A warm kinda stinky. As if he hasn't opened a window in months. Heck, I don't think he's even opened the blinds in months.

He switches on a lightbulb above us, even though opening the blinds would've been enough, then he bunches up some of the clothes hanging over the back of his couch and throws them onto the armchair opposite it—as if he thinks that's made any difference.

"Through here," he says, walking toward a door at the back of his living room. He pushes it open, and I can immediately see a huge computer screen taking up most of his back wall; probably the biggest computer screen I've ever seen in my life. This room, a tiny kinda, like, office or something, is even messier than the living room. I count, in my head... eight... nine... ten empty snack packets lying around. Different flavors of Cheetos, but mostly the Flaming Hot ones. That's why it smells so warm in here, I bet. Cheetos. Though it's probably as much to do with the bin underneath the desk overflowing with wet tissue papers... ugh... it's gross. So gross I have to hold a finger to my nose.

"Don't mind the mess," he says. "I don't got no time to clean up."

"It's fine... fine," I say. "I can be a bit of a messy bitch some-times, too."

I surprise myself saying that. Don't think I've ever called myself a bitch before. I guess I gotta get more used to cussing though, 'cause that sure seems to be the way with us cops. Everybody back at the precinct cusses. Nate seems to use a cuss in every second sentence.

His ass juts out toward me as he bends over his desk to place a plug into the socket. Then he leans back a little and holds down the standby button on the huge computer screen.

"Takes a while to warm up," he says.

I look around the pokey office again, finding four more empty packs of Flaming Hot Cheetos in the far corner next to the broken shelf.

Then a picture flashes up on the massive computer screen… of Nate—looking much more fresh-faced than he is in real life, pressing his cheek against a beautiful, beaming bride.

"Oh, wow… your wife sure is pretty," I say.

"She ain't that pretty no more," he says. Then he sits down into his office chair and clicks his mouse, while I stand behind him still holding a finger to my nose.

"Uh… can you turn away for a second?" he asks. "I just wanna shut down some files that might be sensitive…."

"Sure," I say. I turn around to face his wall, noticing the framed picture of him graduating on to the force.

"How old were you when you became a cop?" I ask.

"Twenty-six," he answers.

"Oh, wow… so what was that? Like five years ago?"

I laugh. He doesn't. In fact, he doesn't even answer. He just continues to click his mouse. Clicking and clicking while in the reflection of the framed photograph I notice his massive screen blinking from one file to another.

"I was over and back from Afghan from age eighteen to twenty-four," he says. "When I came home, I just wanted to go back out there. And somebody said, 'y'know what you need to do, Nate, you need to become a cop. You'd be a great cop.' And I just thought, how the fuck did I not think of that before? Soon as that guy said I needed to be a cop, it all made sense to me…. Okay," he says, "here we go."

I spin around, and see him slotting the USB thumb drive into the socket at the side of his screen. Then he double clicks his mouse and suddenly a file pops up; a freeze-frame of black-and-white CCTV footage of what looks like the back alleyway behind the office we were in this morning.

Nate taps at his mouse once more, pressing play, and I take a step closer to him so I can watch over his shoulder, still holding a finger to my nose.

BENJI WAYDE

The man in the stripey suit with the rings on all his fingers walks closer to me and I can feel that I am really scared and frightened even though I can't hear my heart beating quicker which is what used to happen when I was frightened when I was a young boy. But my hands are sweaty, and I am blinking a lot. That's how I know I'm scared.

"Never mind who I am," the man in the stripey suit says, "who the hell are you?"

"M-m-m-me?" I ask.

"Yes, you stuttering fuck. Who the hell are you?"

"M-m-my name is Benji. Benji Wayde."

"Benji? Get the fuck outta here," he says. And then he stretches his arm down to me and I put my hand inside his and he shakes it. Really hard. I can feel all of the rings on all of his fingers squishing against my fingers. "Well, aren't you all grown up, Benji? You look about forty-five with that moustache. How old are you now, kid?"

"Twenty-one," I say without stuttering. "I was twenty-one in January."

He puts his hands inside his stripey trousers pockets and smiles at me.

"Twenty-one huh? That makes you a man. Are you the man of the house now that your Grandfather has popped his clogs?"

I stare at him, cuz I don't know what clogs is.

"W-w-why are you in my house?" I ask.

He laughs.

"Your house? Get the hell outta here, kid. This isn't your house. It's mine."

I try to push back more, but I can't. Cuz I'm already against the wall. But I stand up. And I am taller than him. I'm prob'ly faster than him too if I have to run.

"Are y-y-you the-the-the man who is moving in here?" I ask.

He laughs again.

"Me? In here? Get the hell outta here," he says. Again. Then he pinches the collar of his stripey suit and leans nearer to me, "See these threads... these cost more than this fuckin' house is worth."

And now I'm confused. Really, really confused. So, I just stare at him. And he stares at me. And my hands get even sweatier. So, I rub them against my butt. And when I'm rubbing them, he looks away from me and down at the TV with the video player in it on the carpet, and then at the VHS tape lying beside it.

"What's this?" he says, "Nineteen eighty-fucking-two?"

When he looks back up at me, I shake my head. Even though I don't know what he is asking about nineteen eighty-two.

"It's-it's-it's a VHS tape," I say.

And he laughs. Again.

"Tommy!" he shouts.

I look over the man in the stripey suit's shoulder and see a big man, tall and angry looking with a bald head and a little spikey beard walking into the living room.

"Wh-wh-what... who-who?"

"Shut the hell up stuttering, kid. You sound like an owl. Hey, Tommy," the man in the stripey suit says, turning to the big, bald, angry man. "Did I ever tell you about Vanessa Wayde?" The big, bald, angry man shakes his head. "Nah, I guess it was probably before your time with me, Tommy. Fit she was. Fit as fuck. Tight little ass on her. Hey, kid... how long is it since your Momma died, huh?"

I rub my hands against my butt again cuz they're still really wet.

"S-s-seventeen years," I say.

"Seventeen years?" he says. "Fuck me. Don't the years fly? Anyway, Tommy," he says, "About eighteen-nineteen years ago, this retard's Momma was worth visiting this place for. Then she went and fucked herself up, didn't she, kid?"

"I d-dun-dunno," I say.

"Course you know," he says. "Well, she ain't here no more is she?" Then he laughs. And when he looks at the big, bald, angry man next to him, the big, bald, angry man laughs too. Really loud. And it makes me feel scared. Really, really scared. "Well, we know your hot momma ain't here no more, but where's that little darling grandmother of yours, kid?"

"Sh-she's over in our new apartment. Apartment number seven. W-w-we're moving today."

"Not today," he says. "This morning. You're supposed to be outta here already. Not lying down on the carpet looking at... VHS tapes."

I rub my wet hands against my butt again.

"You heard him," Tommy says. His voice is all gruffly like a cartoon dog. "You're supposed to be out of here by now. Get on your bike."

"I-I-I don't have a bike," I say. "It got stolen."

And then they laugh again. Louder this time. And I know they're laughing at me cuz they already know I have the mental age of somebody half my age. When they stop laughing, the big, bald, angry man walks toward me and grips my sweater. Then he lifts me up so high that even my tiptoes can't touch the carpet no more.

"You don't live here," he says, pressing his nose against mine. Then he turns around to the man in the stripey suit and says, "Hey, this kids' face... I think I know it. Wasn't he in today's newspaper?"

"Hey, you put him down right this minute!" Grandma says.

The big, bald, angry man lets go of my sweater and I fall back against the wall and my butt crashes down on to the carpet.

When I look back up, Grandma is standing in the doorway with her hands on her hips.

AIMEE STREET

I'm beginning to think my spinning head is all down to this Ghost Train weed. 'Cause it sure is the weirdest fuckin' day I've had in I-dunno-how-long.

I continue to pace outside the office, bored from studying the prices of the different car models listed on the poster stuck to the window. I finally stop and decide to take another hit of my vaporizer. But only because I thought about my weed. If I hadn't been thinking about weed, it wouldn't have entered my mind to take any more. In fact, I was actually thinking how much this Ghost Train seems to have me feeling more paranoid than ever when I was actually reaching into my pocket to retrieve my vaporizer. That's addiction, I guess.

I'm sucking from the nozzle when the door finally swings open and he walks out, a key ring hanging from his thumb, his finger trying to stuff a bank card into his fat wallet. I try to catch the name on the bank card. Begins with a J. Ja... probably James. Probably Jared. I guess he looks more like a James.

"It's all yours... for twenty-four hours," he says, holding the keys out for me to grab.

"What the fuck?" I say, blowing out a weed cloud. I take the keyring from him, then click the button on it while I raise onto my tiptoes to look around the lot, to see which car he has rented for me. "Oh," I say, falling back onto my heels, realizing it's the most basic car in the lot—the cheapest car on the poster I memorized while I was waiting.

"A Nissan Altima," he says, "the most driven car on the roads of Connecticut. In silver... the most driven color on the roads of Connecticut." I smile a polite thank you before it transitions into a full laugh. He's clever. Very clever. I'll be driving around in a car that will practically go unnoticed. "Go get your story," he says.

I step off the path, toward the Altima with more questions whirling in my mind, and just when I reach the driver's door, I decide I have to ask one of them before I set off.

"Why you doing this for me?" I say, looking over the top of the car.

He shrugs.

"You keep forgetting," he says, "I knocked you down. I'm tryna help... that's all."

I kinda believe him. But I also kinda don't... not really. He's definitely the creep who was following me around all morning. He has to be. But he's also been the kindest anyone's been to me in I-dunno-how-long. Probably ever. On top of that, this fucking weed is hella strong. And I really don't know what the fuck is going on anymore. Except for the fact that I'm driving to Birmingham, on the lookout for a story—doing what I've always wanted to do. Being a journalist. A real freaking journalist.

I snatch open the car door, nod another thank you toward him and then climb in, starting the engine before I've even shut my door or put my seatbelt on. The car growls and splutters and then growls again. I haven't driven in so long. Not since I was learning to drive at school.

I slam my door shut, and click the gear stick into reverse before skidding the tires backward.

"Hey," he says, knocking his pointed knuckle against the passenger side window. I fumble around the buttons on my car door, until I finally find the one that takes down the window on his side. "You uh... you know where you're going?"

"Oh," I say, squinting. "Birmingham, yeah?"

"Yep," he says, "but where in Birmingham?"

"To... uh... I dunno."

He shakes his head with a grin, then winks at me before shoveling his hand in through the open window.

"I rented you a satnav as well," he says. "Where you need to go is programmed in."

"Okay, thank you," I say, finding the buttons on my door again and then holding down the one that takes the passenger window back up. He continues to stand there, staring through the glass at me while I try to stick the satnav to the windshield. When it finally sticks, I press the green "play" button.

"Destination," the satnav barks at me, *"Birmingham Police Station. Estimated travel time, forty-one minutes."*

NATE BENNETT

I yawn. Because I'm bored; bored of looking at a black-and-white still of a concrete alleyway. We've pretty much been staring at two oversized black bins for forty minutes... waiting to see the footage Costello told us would shake America.

"It'll happen," I say to Zucha, before darting my eyes to the bottom corner of my computer monitor to catch the time. 11:05. Then I lean forward and scroll with the mouse so I can fast-forward the video in double-time.

"You not think we should just go back to the station?" Zucha says. "Chief Costello said we should get this footage back to him soon as we can."

I continue holding down the mouse to fast-forward the footage while I turn to face her.

"Nope," I say. "There's something more going on than just whatever's on this footage. Trust me. Something big is going down... and I wanna know what the hell it is."

Zucha puts her hands on her hips and begins to swivel from side to side while looking around my cramped little office. I bet she's thinking about how untidy it is. Course it is. I've been living on my own for months. It smells, too, I bet. Even though I'm immune to the smell by now. I bet it smells damp. But I don't really give a shit. I just want to get to the bottom of this. There has to be something huge going down. So, I turn back to the screen to stare at the concrete alleyway and the two big, black bins.

"Should I make us a coffee or something?" Zucha says.

I nod. And grunt.

"Kitchen's just through there. There might be coffee in the cupboard over the microwave if we're lucky."

As soon as she disappears, I let out a long, silent sigh. I don't think I was breathing properly while she was in here with me. I've never had somebody in this room with me before. This is where I jerk off. I call it the pleasure room. Though I feel anything but pleasure right now. I feel... I dunno... I feel freaked the fuck out 'cause I've no idea what the hell is going on. I lean closer to the screen, because I think I see a shadow in the corner of the shot, but nothing else moves, except the blinking baggy eyes that I catch in the screen's reflection. Damn, I look old. And that cut still looks nasty as hell; the blood has dried, but it's still glowing bright red, rather than darkening as it heals over. I hate my face. It never used to bother me... in fact, I used to really like that I had a big, old ugly bull-like head. It suited who I was. A cop. But my face is startin' to bother me now. I'll be fifty next month. With no wife. No kids. No friends... not really. And I guess that shows all over my ugly head.

"Here y'go," Zucha says, stepping back into my tiny office and plunking an old mug of coffee next to my mouse.

"Cheers," I say, taking my eyes away from the reflection of my ugly-ass face.

"You mind me asking you a question while we keep looking?" she says. She leans her shoulder against the frame of the door and blows into her mug.

"Sure."

"The phone calls you've been getting today... what's that all about? We've been given a mission and just when we're in the middle of it, you have to head off somewhere else. I mean... I like it an' all... I love speeding around in the car. I love the sirens blaring. But suddenly we're doing something and getting close to something and then you have to just take off...."

"Oh," I say, turning back to the screen and squinting at my

reflection again. "It's... uh... it's.... Listen, I'm not entirely sure." I sigh. And then I spin around to face her. "Costello has us on another mission. This isn't just about whatever's on this video footage. It can't be. There's something bigger going down. And I wanna find out what it is."

Her eyes widen over her mug as she takes a sip.

"Wow.... Like, so, uh... that sounds exciting.... Any ideas what it is yet?"

I stare into her eyes and decide for the first time that I'd fuck her. She's not hot or anything. She's got huge fat droopy tits under that shirt, and she walks like a duck 'cause her ass sticks out so far, but I would fuck her.... I miss fucking. It's been way too long.

"I dunno what it is," I say, offering her a smile because she is starting to look excited. "Not yet anyway. But I'm hoping whatever the hell is on this footage will give us some answers."

She scrunches her nose up and I'm certain she's getting cuter by the minute.... Or maybe I'm getting more desperate by the minute. I'm probably only feeling this way 'cause I'm in my pleasure room.

"Hold up... hold up," she says pointing over my shoulder. "Isn't that... yeah, it is... that's Governor Rex Haversham!"

I spin around in my chair. And there he is. Lighting up a cigarette next to one of the big, black bins.

"You're fucking right!"

Her face appears by my shoulder and my eyes move to take her in and I'm tempted to lean in for a kiss because her eyes are all wide and she looks super cute right now. But we don't got time for that, so I flick my eyes back to the screen to see Haversham leaning against the wall, puffing out a cloud of smoke.

"What is that place next door?" I ask her.

She leans away from me, grabs her cell phone from her pocket and begins to tap her finger against the screen.

"It's a bar," she says. "An Irish bar called The Harp."

I lean back in the chair and interlock my fingers behind my head.

"So, this is all about Haversham; what the fuck is he up to?" I say.

We both stare at the screen in silence, watching as Haversham sucks on his cigarette. He seems to be talking to somebody out of the video shot. Then my fucking phone vibrates against my leg and, as soon as the ringtone trills, Zucha stares at me. So, I click the mouse, pausing the footage, before I stand to answer the call.

"Nate," the distorted voice says. "Get your ass to Gray Bridge. You've half an hour. If you're not there by eleven forty-five, I'll drop my finger right on to this button that will release your browser history to the public."

Then the mutha fucker hangs up.

"What's going on now?" Zucha says, her hands on her hips, her eyes squinting. I rub at my face because I can already feel the cut beginning to sting. Then I quickly unplug the USB thumb drive from my computer, pop the lid back on and shove it into the chest pocket of my navy shirt.

"Put the coffee down, Zucha," I say, "we gotta go."

She grins, takes one last sip, and slams the mug on to the desk, right next to my mouse.

"Hey, Nate," she says, her eyes wide with excitement, "can we fire up the sirens?"

AIMEE STREET

A police car zooms past me as I wait at a red traffic light—its sirens blaring, its lights dancing, its wheels screeching. And I immediately wonder if it's him driving: Nathan Bennett. The officer the *Daily Connecticut* headlined a "disgrace." The car whooshed by so fast that I didn't get a chance to see if the face driving it matched the ugly mug in the photograph that accompanied the small article down the bottom of page five of today's newspaper. It doesn't matter. I'm almost here anyway. I'll find him. I'll find out why this scumbag cop is back on the streets.

The traffic light blinks green, and I press on the gas before finally driving the Altima in through the opened blue gates where I park it in one of the slim parking bays next to a cop car. I hate police precincts. Have always hated them. Even before I was a con woman.

I decide I shouldn't take another hit of Ghost Train; not before I've to go in here with all of my guns blazing. I need my wits about me. So, I leave my vaporizer in the car before jogging across the parking lot and pushing my way through the heavy brown door where I immediately notice tears streaming down the face of a middle-aged woman. She's too old to be sobbing like a teenager. But I don't say anything. I just stare down at my shoes instead.

"I'm sorry, Ma'am," the police officer standing behind the

front desk says, "But there's no chance you'll be able to speak with him until he's released."

She dries her eyes with the sleeve of her jacket, then goes to say something but hesitates. She looks at me, then back at the officer behind the desk before huffing out of her nose and storming past me and out the door I had just entered through.

"How can I help you, Ma'am?" the officer asks, eyeballing me just as the door slams shut.

I step forward.

"I'd like to speak with Officer Bennett."

"Officer who?"

"Bennett. Nathan Bennett."

"Oh, he doesn't work here no more."

I dip my brow at him.

"He uh… he does. He returned to work today. Says so in the newspaper."

"Nathan Bennett?" he asks, subtly shaking his head.

"Uh-huh," I reply.

He spins on the spot, pushes open the door behind his desk and disappears beyond it. Through the gap left in the door I see a hive of officers in navy blue shirts pretending to be working. Most of 'em are leaning their asses on desks, sipping from paper cups. I swivel around to take in the posters on the walls behind me; posters of three separate missing people; posters of pixelated CCTV stills of suspects; posters trying to portray how much good the Birmingham Police Department do for the local neighborhoods. One of the posters is of a ginger-haired police officer with the milkiest of skin tones posing with his arm around a Black kid holding a football under his armpit. It's headlined: "White Lives. Black Lives. Blue Lives. All Lives." It makes me laugh. Cops sure are obsessed with color. Specifically, the color blue. As if it's a race of its own. I peer through the gap in the door again; most of those in navy shirts are sipping from paper cups, chatting with colleagues also sipping from paper cups. Maybe drinking coffee is a prerequisite for being a cop. It's probably why every cop who's ever questioned me through the years has always had God-awful stale breath.

I begin to count the heads I can see... only because it seems as if everybody working inside the station is a white male. Except for the brunette girl sitting at her computer, tapping away—and the Latino guy with the dyed black moustache in the far corner. It's when I'm counting my seventeenth white male face that I stutter... then hesitate... then squint. The face maybe quite a distance away, behind another open door on the far wall of the precinct, but it *is* him. Definitely him. That sleaze ball, Governor Haversham. I should sidle up to him and thank him for the generous donation his office made to my fake bank account this morning.

"You're right!" the officer says, stepping into my line of sight and pushing the door open wider before slapping it back closed behind him. "Officer Bennett is back on the job. Nobody told me." He shakes his head and blows out his cheeks. "But he's not here. He's out on the streets."

"Doing what?" I ask.

"Working," he says, nodding again.

"Working at what?"

He squints at me, through the dip in his sunken brow.

"At being a cop, Ma'am," he says. Slowly. Demeaningly.

Fucking cops and their teeny, tiny, skinny white dicks.

"Where is he working?" I ask.

His brow dips even further. Purposely. As he's trying to signal to me that I'm only a young woman and am therefore insignificant to him.

"How the hell should I know?" he says.

"Uh... because you work with him," I say, trying to match his demeaning tone.

He rubs at his chin, still squinting at me.

"Well... that's not how it works 'round here. When you're on the streets, you could be anywhere.... He's out there, somewhere."

He shrugs, waves me toward the door, then sits into his squeaky office chair where he begins to tap his keyboard using just his two index fingers as if a Tyrannosaurus Rex taught him how to type.

"What's Governor Haversham doing here today?" I ask, getting up on my tiptoes and leaning over his high desk.

He glares up at me.

"Miss, do you need to speak with an officer?"

"Yes. I need to speak with Officer Bennett."

"Well, as I said…." He takes a small pen from his ear, then begins to scribble some notes. "Officer Bennett is out on the streets, being a cop."

I walk around the small reception-area, taking in the posters taped to the sky-blue painted walls, wondering what the hell I'm supposed to do next. Maybe I'm not cut out for this journalism bullshit anyway. I don't even have any credentials I could show this cop, to bluff that I need to speak with Officer Bennett as a matter of urgency.

"Actually, officer," I say, "I'd like to speak with the chief."

He stands, pushing back his office chair before rubbing his chin again. He's not hiding his frustration from me. In fact, I think he's reveling in letting me know how pissed off he is with me.

"Ma'am, the chief is busy."

"I hope he is," I say, "he's the chief. Nevertheless, I help pay his wages and I'd like to have a quick word."

He swallows. And then holds his eyes closed.

"Chief Costello is in a very busy meeting and doing important things."

"Officer," I say, "as a citizen of Connecticut, I am asking you to approach the chief and at least ask him if he could spare me a few minutes of his time."

He scratches his chin. Again.

"No, Ma'am," he says.

So, I reach into my pocket, take out my phone and flick the camera on with one scroll of my thumb. Without even hitting record, I point the lens at him.

"Sir, as I said, I am a citizen of Connecticut. All I am asking is for you to approach the chief and ask him if he could spare me a few minutes of his time."

He immediately spins on his heels, pushes open the door and walks through to the office. He leaves less of a gap to stare through this time. But that's fine by me. I stretch up to my tiptoes, reach for the mouse of his computer and wiggle it until I can find its pointer on the screen. When I do, I scroll it straight up to the search bar I noticed when I leaned over his desk a few moments ago. When I click into the search bar, I pause to look through the gap in the door—the scene hasn't changed. White cops sipping coffee while talking to other white cops. Then I reach for his keyboard and move it closer to me and I begin to type.

Bennett

His full name pops up on the screen instantly. And when it does, I look through the gap in the door again before reaching for the mouse. I click on his name and the screen blinks to a dated black screen that shows today's date on the top corner and Bennett's name again, along with the name of another officer—Margaret Zucha. The box under the diary entry is blank. But it notes in the bottom corner that they're driving around in car number forty-three. I click again on his name; at Maggie's name; at the car number... but there's no more information to be found. No details, other than the fact that they're somewhere out there in car forty-three.

I hear footsteps, so I click the "X" in the top corner, then push the mouse and keyboard away before spinning around and pretending to look at the posters again.

"The chief can't come to the desk right now," he says, before the door closes behind him. I don't bother looking back at him.

"Okay, thanks for trying," I say. Then I push open the front door and walk back into the blowing wind with a satisfied grin stretched wide across my face. Maybe I am cut out for this journalism bullshit after all.

BENJI WAYDE

My butt hurts from falling on to the carpet when the big, bald and angry man let go of my sweater. But when I look up and see Grandma with her hands on her hips, I already know she is here to make me safe and so my hands don't need to be this wet and sweaty no more.

"Mr. Pale," Grandma says to the man in the stripey suit, "what the hell is one of your heavies doin' messin' 'round with my grandson?"

And then I know I heard his name before. Mr. Pale. *Mr. Pale....*

"Mrs. Wayde," he says, "this young man was giving us some backtalk about not wanting to leave this house, so we were just helping him on his way is all."

"It's only just gone eleven a.m., Mr. Pale, we have until tonight to get out."

"Uh-huh," he says, shaking his head, "you need to be out by midday. Not midnight."

Grandma looks at me. And I see that her eyes are still yellowy. Then she holds those yellowy eyes closed and I know she is angry and that she wants to shout, "Mother divine!" But she doesn't. She keeps it inside.

"Y'okay, Boy?" she asks me when she opens her eyes again.

"I'm okay, Grandma," I say.

And then the two of the men laugh at me. Again. And when

I'm looking at Mr. Pale laughing that's when I remember the name. He's the man who owns all of St. Michael's House. Grandpa once told me Mr. Pale used to come 'round here to collect his rent money every month, but he doesn't have to no more cuz the money goes straight from Grandma's bank into Mr. Pale's bank without him having to come 'round. Grandpa said he never hated nobody his whole life but if he had to hate somebody, he'd hate Mr. Pale.

"My Grandpa," I say, trying not to stutter, "said he never hated no man his whole life but if he had to hate somebody, he'd hate you."

And then the two men laugh at me again. And Grandma puts her hand on my shoulder and says, "Shh, shh, Boy." Then she turns around to face Mr. Pale and her finger is pointing. "As you know, we've both lost somebody very dear to us, can you please leave us alone to move our belongings in peace? Please?"

I dunno why she's saying "please" to him when he is being nasty to us. She's prob'ly just bein' nice cuz we would have nowhere else to live if Mr. Pale didn't let us live in St. Michael's House.

"You've got one hour to get everything out of this house and over to that apartment over there." He points out our window toward the front rows of apartments, and when he smiles his ugly smile again I just wanna run over to him and slap him. And I've never wanted to slap nobody before. That's how angry I am. Really, really angry. And I don't hate nobody but if I had to hate somebody, I would hate Mr. Pale and his stupid stripey suit and all of his rings on all of his fingers.

"You got it, Mr. Pale," Grandma says. And then she squeezes my shoulder. "One hour. And we'll be outta here."

Mr. Pale nudges at the big, bald, angry man and the two of them leave our living room by slamming the door really loudly. Grandma still has her hand on my shoulder and when I look at her, she holds her yellowy eyes closed again.

"Lord Jesus Christ," she says, "I pray to you to grant me the strength of patience, the strength of character and the strength of spirit to live out my days on earth in peace. Please protect me and

Benji and keep us safe from harm. In your name, I am, Lord Jesus Christ."

Then she opens her eyes again. And they are so yellowy that it don't look right.

"You okay, Grandma?" I say.

She squeezes my shoulder. Harder this time.

"We need to get a move on, Boy. Let's get your clothes from your bedroom closet over to apartment seven as soon as possible. Then if you give me some help with the big TV, we're halfway there."

"I, uh… I, uh…" I say, "I am s'posed to go to Yoga at midday."

Grandma looks at her wristwatch.

"Okay. That gives you a little more than half an hour of helping me. Once you get all your clothes over to apartment seven and then help me with the TV, you can go to Yoga. I can do the rest from there."

"And I, uh… I wanted to watch more of the VHS tapes," I say.

"Oh," Grandma says, "well, you'll have to watch them later. You heard what Mr. Pale said, we need to get a move on."

"B-but I really wanna keep watching," I say. "Momma is in a lovely red dress and has lovely red gloves on and they go all the way up her arms like this," I say, pointing at the top of my arm. Grandma's yellowy eyes look up over her round glasses at me. "And then a boy rang the doorbell and Momma answered it and his name was Pauly and he was in a really nice white suit with a white waistcoat and a black bow tie."

Grandma pushes her glasses up to her hair and covers her face with her two hands.

"Boy, I can't do this right now. Just do as I say. Get your clothes from the closet upstairs, then bring them over to the apartment and leave them lying across one of the beds. You can choose which bed you want in the bedroom, huh? How 'bout that, Boy? You get to choose your bed."

"The one under the window," I say. And Grandma nods her head and squeezes my shoulder again.

"Okay, Boy, you can have the bed under the window. But I don't want you to watch any more of that VHS tape. When you come back from Yoga and we're all settled at the new flat, we'll sit down and talk tonight, huh?"

"Thank you, Grandma," I say. And when she turns around to walk toward the hallway, I think I have to ask one more question. Just one more. Then I'll stay quiet. Then I won't ask any more questions while Grandma is trying to move all of our belongings to flat number seven.

"Grandma," I say. She stops and turns to face me. "The big and bald and angry looking man with Mr. Pale... he said he saw my picture in the newspaper today. Why's my picture in the newspaper today?"

7

LAWNIE CLARKE MAY HAVE ONLY BEEN TWENTY-EIGHT YEARS OLD, BUT she had already formed a legacy for herself as one of the most innovative creatives in American television's short-lived set design history. She had re-designed *The Zdanski Show* set for its last two makeovers at CSN, both in 2019 and then again just before the latest season started—a mere six months before the Meghan Markle debacle. Sarah-Jane instantly adored Lawnie's eye as soon as America's most watched anchor became aware of her designs after she was initially offered the contract of re-designing CSN's *Top Of The Morning* show back in 2018—fresh out of college. The set design attracted a cool one-million new viewers to the show, and suddenly everybody in the TV world was whispering the name Lawnie Clarke. So, there was literally no discussion to be had among the Zdanski team when it came to designing the set for the podcast launch. However, there was immediate surprise among the team when Lawnie finally revealed her vision for the reboot.

"This is the thing about podcasts," Lawnie told the team. "They're intimate. *Really* intimate. So, what I wanna do is... set the whole show up in the most intimate place possible... your own home."

Sarah-Jane was a little taken aback, but she pondered the concept for twenty-four hours before realizing that what Lawnie was pitching was actually quite genius. The moody brown tones, the dim light, that incredible postcard picture-perfect view of lower Manhattan, starting with the stretched-to-the-clouds sight of the Empire State Building before the high-rises expand toward the Freedom Tower in the distance. The perfect silhouette of New York City. The real-life silhouette all other late-night shows could only ever attempt to replicate with fake backdrops.

"Zdanski. Live from her own home," Lawnie repeated on loop as she continued to pitch her concept to the team.

Twenty-four hours later, Sarah-Jane emailed her to agree with her set designer's vision and to set in motion more meetings before everything could be finalized. This was their third meeting since then. And Sarah-Jane had chosen the venue. Søsa Restaurant. Not just for the food. But, to show off the mood lighting.

"Mmmm," Lawnie said. "You're right. This is the greatest sushi."

"Damn right it is," Sarah-Jane replied.

"And you're right about the ambience in here," Lawnie said. "It's the warm golden glow from those blood-orange bulbs under the red-velvet lampshades. It'll look so good in your chocolate-brown kitchen. So intimate. And so beautiful on screen."

Sarah-Jane pointed her chopsticks at Lawnie while she chewed.

"That's why we pay you the big bucks."

Lawnie reached down between her feet to open her designer briefcase, and when her head rose again from underneath the red-velvet circular tablecloth, she spun a sheet of glossy cardboard around to face her client.

"Looks amazing," Sarah-Jane said. "Retro, huh?"

"Exactly," Lawnie replied. "I looked back at all of the sets you had throughout your twenty-five years at CSN and as soon as I saw your very first one, I thought we gotta replicate that for the reboot."

"Hence the neon Zdanski sign?"

"Exactly. I'm gonna get one made in blood-orange and display it across that chocolate-brown wall in your kitchen. So, what I'm proposing here is," she pointed at the cardboard mood board, "that you sit on the end of your kitchen island with that neon sign glowing behind you. Against that chocolate brown wall, and with the soft glow of the mood lighting, your face will stand out. Your face. And your name. That's your entire brand right there in one shot. And it's all gonna be shot in Ultra HD. Girl, you're gonna look more stunning than ever before."

Sarah-Jane pushed out a laugh. She was used to compliments like this, though they had been arriving less frequently than they used to.

"Not bad for a fifty-year-old, huh?" she said. "And what about the guests... they gonna be seated on the far side of the island?"

"Exactly," Lawnie said. "With that stunning view of the New York City skyline behind them. When you go live, between seven and eight p.m. every Wednesday, the sun will be setting and the skyline will be fading into a silhouette in front of America's eyes, with the individual lights inside the high-rise buildings all starting to blink on."

"Genius," Sarah-Jane said.

"It is genius, even if I do say so myself," Lawnie replied, grinning, "mainly because it ain't gonna cost a thing."

The pair of them laughed at the absurdity of it all, especially so as they were both hyper aware that Lawnie Clarke charged ten thousand dollars an hour for her consultancy fees, and this was the tenth hour she had spent on the Zdanski relaunch project thus far... just to propose a set design that would cost little more than a few hundred dollars to create. What was also beneficial was the fact that residents in Sarah-Jane's building had a shared elevator they would take to their floor. But the penthouse had a private elevator at the back of the building straight up from the underground parking garage. It would be perfect to bring guests up and down, without any of the public noticing at all.

"The neon sign is on order. Should arrive within forty-eight hours," Lawnie said. "And I'll speak to the manager of this restaurant to see where he got these bulbs from. If he doesn't know... don't sweat it. I'm Lawnie Clarke. I'll find blood-orange bulbs before you go live for your very first show in five days' time. Trust me." She lifted the glass of Chateau Margaux Sarah-Jane had ordered for her and stretched it across the red-velvet-clothed table. "To you, and your relaunch. It's gonna be quite something. You know what side of America I'm on. I'm on the side that loves me some Sarah-Jane fucking Zdanski."

Sarah-Jane picked up her own wine glass and tapped it against Lawnie's.

"The woman that divides the nation, huh?"

"Well, here's to dividing the nation even further," Lawnie said, before taking a sip. When she set her glass back down, she folded her arms and leaned toward the table. "So, what guests have you got lined up? Who are you launching with?"

Sarah-Jane chewed on her sushi while she pondered the framing of her answer. She adored Lawnie. Trusted her. But she couldn't trust her with everything.

"That's a big secret," she finally said. "The launch is not so much a who, but a what. You'll see when it goes out in five days' time. But until then, honestly, I can't say a word. But I can tell you what guests we have lined up afterward."

"Sure," Lawnie said, always roused by Sarah-Jane's frankness when it came to discussing her experiences of America's most famous names.

"Well, we're kinda hoping our launch makes such a massive splash that it will offer more than enough discussion for two shows. So, our first two shows will all be dedicated to this... this big exclusive news story we're gonna break."

"Oooooh," Lawnie said, before pinching more food between her chopsticks and awaiting the celebrity gossip.

"Show three, we're finalizing discussions with Jennifer Lopez and Ben Affleck to make it their first sit down interview since they got engaged. Or, re-engaged. They're waiting to see what numbers our launch gets on Wednesday. If we pull in over five million, they're good to go."

"And will you pull in five million?"

"Five million's gonna look like dust to us," Sarah-Jane said, winking at her set designer.

"Fuuuck," Lawnie mouthed, slowly, across the table.

"Then show four we've got Judge Ketanji Brown Jackson. She

says she's totally open to a frank and honest conversation with me, so we're really excited about that booking."

"Awesome. You're gonna kill it, Sarah-Jane. I know you are."

"Just wait till you see what we have lined up for the launch... I swear, Lawnie — and this is just between you and me — the story we have, it's huge. It's gonna blow up."

"Get the fuck outta here," Lawnie said, laughing. "So, how is that new producer... whaddya say her name was, Erica?"

"She's great. My social media following has gone up three million since she came on board. She's all about digital media. In fact, she pushed me into doing the whole visual podcast. I wanted to move to ABC News when CSN fired me, but...."

Sarah-Jane trailed off, unable to finish her sentence; unable to admit out loud that she was no longer the most coveted television anchor in the country.

"Well, Erica is right," Lawnie said. "Digital media is where the numbers are at."

"Yep. That's what she keeps telling me."

"And, what about the rest of your team? They all coming with you? Is that Phil guy coming with you?"

Sarah-Jane squinted at Lawnie. The freckled-faced set designer was offering an intriguing subtle smile on the corner of her lips; the same intriguing smile most people sported when they mentioned Phil's name in Sarah-Jane's company. The anchor was always amazed that most everyone questioned Philip Meredith on his appearances alone, and not the fact that he had executively produced the most-watched TV news show in America for the past quarter of a century.

"'Course he is. Phil has literally been with me since day one. I wouldn't be who I am without him."

"From day one you know each other?"

"Yeah... he was my cameraman slash producer at Kansas City PBS back in the day."

"Wow," Lawnie said, before chewing on another bite of sushi.

"But uh... you remember Simon? The guy with blond hair?" Sarah-Jane said. "He was a junior producer with me, and I promoted him to be by my side?"

"Sure."

"Well, he was retained by CSN, for their morning show."

"I love that show," Lawnie said.

"That's because you designed the set."

They grinned across the table at each other.

"You know what I've always wanted to ask you, Sarah-Jane?" Lawnie said, placing her chopsticks to the side of her bowl.

"Go on."

"George Clooney. They say you turned down his advances back when he was at the top in *ER*. Truth or rumor?"

"Truth," Sarah-Jane said without pausing. "The cast of *ER* were like our second guests ever on *The Zdanski Show* back in '97, and afterward George kinda like... well he didn't kinda, he blatantly did. He asked me out for a drink."

"Okay... and?"

Lawnie picked up her chopsticks again while she waited for an answer.

"I said 'no'. I was..." Sarah-Jane shrugged one shoulder, "I was seeing somebody at the time."

"Well, whoever that guy was who you were seeing couldn't have been worth it to turn down Clooney."

Sarah-Jane pushed out a laugh, then swirled her glass of wine, before taking a sip from it.

"He was worth it," she then said, after placing her glass back down. "Anyway... I've still got Phil, still got Erica... and I've still got Howie. For now, at least. Howie's complaining already that there isn't much for him to do. Which is fair enough. There isn't. Producing a live podcast is a small beast compared to producing something for a network."

"Of course. As we have found in our set plans," Lawnie said, before running her tongue over her teeth to dislodge a slither of seaweed.

"So, I don't know if Howie's gonna stay around for long. I've heard through my lawyer that there's an offer of six million coming his way from CSN. Six million to retire. To call it quits. He'll take it. I'm sure he'll take it."

"And then it'll be just what… just three of you? You, Phil, and this Erica girl. Is that enough?"

"Seems it's all we need to run a live podcast," Sarah-Jane replied. Then she took another sip from her expensive wine.

"Y'know," Lawnie said, "if you get your first show right, you might kill it online. You could be bigger than ever. Sarah-Jane Zdanski on our phones. Inside our pockets. With us everywhere we go. It could change everything. The biggest TV star leading us into the future."

Sarah-Jane leaned forward, staring at the freckles dancing around her set designer's face.

"Y'know, I was against it at first. I thought I was selling myself out. That I needed to be a TV star. But…."

"Somebody convinced you?"

"Erica… she's an annoying, overeager little shit. But she's always right. She convinced me that this is definitely the right way moving forward. I know that now. If CSN came crawling back to me, or ABC called me right now to offer me a deal, I'd tell them straight up that I don't need them. I don't…."

She shrugged her shoulder again, and as she did, Lawnie started to say something… then paused. Instead, she ran her finger around the rim of her wine glass while staring into the brightly lit main room of the restaurant, where the non-VIPs were eating their sushi using cheaper, wooden chopsticks.

"What? What are you thinking, Lawnie?" Sarah-Jane asked. "You're a smart girl. And I trust your opinion. What are you thinking right now?"

Lawnie tilted her head slightly when she faced Sarah-Jane, her finger still running over the top of her wine glass.

"It's just… online, it's busy, isn't it? The world and its mother are online."

"I know what you're saying."

"Is there a big risk you might not… like, you may not get the audience?"

Sarah-Jane picked up her red-velvet napkin, dabbed it against the corner of her lips, and then leaned forward.

"We're gonna grab America by the balls on Wednesday," she

said. "Remember you laughed when I said we might get five hundred million views for our debut show? Well… I wasn't joking."

Lawnie squinted, and she leaned back, pinching her tongue between her teeth.

"Are you fucking serious?" she whispered. "Five hundred million?"

"We've got our hands on a story," Sarah-Jane said, leaning even further, "that's gonna shake America to its very fucking core."

BENJI WAYDE

"Okay, Boy… on three," Grandma says. And then she spits on her hands and rubs them together really fast, and she begins to count, "One… two…"

We both lift and we walk with baby steps but fast all the way through the front door.

"Okay, let's put it down, Boy," Grandma says. We rest the TV on the grass outside house number forty-nine and I look all the way to the front of the estate, and I wonder how many times we will need to stop and rest the big TV on the grass before we get to apartment number seven. Then Grandma spits on her hands and rubs them together again before putting them under the TV.

"One… two…" she shouts.

And then we lift. Again. And she starts walking really quickly through the wind and now I am kinda running with baby steps behind her and gripping onto the TV really tight cuz I don't want it to fall.

"Okay, let's put it down, Boy," she shouts again. And we drop the TV onto the grass, and she bends over a little bit with her hands on her knees. "Boy," she says, "don't let those bullies into your head. I told ya, they just making stuff up. You ain't in no newspaper."

Then she spits on her hands again and grabs under the TV.

"One… two…"

And we lift again, and we keep walking over the grass in fast baby steps.

Grandma's already said I was in no newspaper. But I don't know if she be telling the truth, cuz I know Grandma sometimes doesn't tell the truth. Not all the time. Like when she told me we were to stay home from school for a whole week cuz the school was closed but the school wasn't closed. I know it wasn't closed cuz I saw the children walking to school out my bedroom window. Or the time she said she was going away on a holiday for a few days, but I found out she was in St. Bernard's Hospital cuz Grandpa made a mistake by saying to me, "your Grandma looks better today," when he came home from the hospital one day. And like that Christmas Eve when I was fifteen and Grandma told me that Santa wasn't a real person and her and Grandpa and all the parents around the whole wide world just made him up for children. Sometimes Grandma lies. Sometimes everybody lies. I lie, too. I tell Grandma and Grandpa that I am going asleep but really I am playing games in my bedroom. And one time I told Miss Moriarty that my homework was finished but I left my notebook at home when really my notebook was in my school bag under my desk and the homework wasn't done cuz I forgot to do it that day cuz me and Grandpa were having too much fun playing outside on the grass. It made me feel bad to lie to Miss Moriarty and when I went to Mass the next Sunday after that happened, I asked Father Healy if I could do a confession and I told him all about not doing my homework and lying to Miss Moriarty and he said that if I say three Hail Marys then Jesus will forgive me. So, I did six Hail Marys, just to make sure Jesus did forgive me.

"And let's drop it," Grandma says. We rest the TV on the grass again. But we're not far away now. I can see the door of our new apartment straight in front.

"They just... they just lie and lie those guys. That Mr. Pale, he been lyin' to me and your Grandpa ever since we moved in here in 1982. That's all that man does. He lies. And he counts money. That's all. He lies. And he counts money. You don't be mindin' what them men sayin' to you. Those men, they goin' to Hell, Boy. Believe me. Okay.... One... two..."

And then we lift the TV, and we walk like fast baby steps again through the wind and then we put the TV down by the door of apartments number seven, eight and nine and Grandma pushes it open and then we lift it again into the small hallway where the three front doors are. And then Grandma drags it with all her strength into our living room. It looks even tinier with the big TV in it.

"Grandma," I say, "now that the TV is here and all my clothes are here, can I go to Yoga class now?"

Grandma pushes her glasses up to her hair and covers her face with her hand. She's been doing that so many times since Grandpa died. I think she might do it every time she thinks about him not being alive no more.

"Sure thing, Boy," she says. Then she takes her hands from her face and smiles at me. "Be safe walking over there... and remember when you come home, where you're coming home to, huh?"

I smile at her. And then I turn around and walk out of our new flat. When I close the front door tight behind me, I open the bin I saw Grandma throwing the newspaper into earlier and I reach inside and I grab it out. I shove it under my coat and then I jog across the grass really fast. The wind is strong and so I begin to run and run... and run. Really fast. Really, really fast. When I reach our door, I push it open and then get sad again when I see it looking so empty. There's nothing much left in here. Except for my last things I was playing with: The TV with the video player in it, Grandpa's VHS tapes, and my tablet with the smashed screen and my notebook and my pencil. They're all lying on the carpet.

I kneel down in front of the TV with the video player in it, to the spot on the smelly carpet I have been sitting on since the man came and took our sofa earlier and I take the newspaper out from under my coat, and I flatten it out cuz it's all creased. Then I lick my thumb the way Grandpa used to do when he was reading the newspaper... and I open the first page.

NATE BENNETT

She's giddy. Which I guess is nothing new. I'm used to newbies being giddy. I've seen the eyes of new recruits light up lots of times over the years. Hell, I still get that light in my own eyes sometimes. The power light I call it.

"You haven't been in a high-speed chase yet," I shout over the sound of the sirens, "wait till you experience your first one o' them."

"How long you been a cop now?" she shouts back.

I rub my face with my hand, feeling across the sting of my freshest cut. Those cheap-ass fucking razors!

"Coming up near quarter of a century."

"Twenty-five years... wow! Seen it all, I bet?"

"I've seen everything Connecticut has to offer anyway."

"Crazy state, we live in, huh?"

"Yeah... but we get to control the crazy," I say. "That's what made me wanna be a cop in the first place. The power. Why'd you join the force, Zucha?"

"Uh...." She looks unsure... shrugging her shoulders and staring down at her fidgeting fingers on her lap. "Not sure. I used to work in an office... selling insurance. Then I thought, fuck it. I gotta do something better. Something that means something, I guess."

"Ain't nothing more important in this country," I say, "than putting on the uniform." I pinch the collar of her navy shirt, then look down at my own uniform. I've missed wearing it. I couldn't wait to get this uniform back on; to get back out on to these streets. There were so many days when I was serving my suspension that I wasn't sure I'd ever get back out... though I sure couldn't have thought getting back out would be this crazy, this quickly. Haversham lighting up his cigarette in the back-alley pops into my head again. And then I shake my head of the thought....

I reach for the switch, flick off the sirens and then begin to slow down before turning onto the old riverbed that used to run under Gray Bridge.

"Whatcha think we're doing here?" she asks, just as I'm rolling the car to a stop.

I shrug my shoulders. 'Cause I really don't know the answer to her question. Then I push the car door open, against the strong wind.

"We're waiting on a call," I shout over the roof of the car. "That's all I know."

"You think the calls you've been getting are connected to whatever's on that USB thumb drive?"

I push my hands into my trousers pockets. To keep them warm.

"I don't know what to think...."

Then I begin jumping up and down on the spot... not only to keep warm, but to try to rid my head of whatever the fuck it's thinking about.

"Think we'll get into a high-speed chase today?" she asks, just as she begins to jump up and down on the spot on the opposite side of the car, mirroring me.

"We can get into one of them anytime you want," I say.

"Really?"

"Uh-huh."

She sniggers. And then I snigger. This bitch has already caught the bug good.

Suddenly, as I'm grinning back at her, my leg vibrates and

then the phone starts ringing. I turn around on the spot and begin walking away from her as I press the phone to my ear.

"What?"

"Ready for your last act?" the distorted voice says.

"You fucking promise this is the end of it?"

"This *is* the end of it!"

"Then I'm ready," I say.

"Good. You do this, then I'll delete your browser history and you won't ever need to hear from me again."

"Tell me…" I say. "What the fuck is it you want me to do?"

AIMEE STREET

As I'm snatching the car door open, I already have my iPhone gripped just below my chin.

"Hey SIRI," I say. The screen blinks and then the phone pauses before beeping once. "How many police cars are there in the Birmingham Police Department, Connecticut?"

The screen blinks again. Then goes dark for a beat before a multicolored circular light begins to rotate.

"There are three hundred police officers in Birmingham Police Department, Connecticut," the phone informs me.

"How many *cars* are in the Birmingham Police Department?" I ask it, just as I'm climbing into driver's seat of the Nissan.

"I'm sorry. I do not know an answer to this question."

I toss my phone to the passenger seat, and start the ignition.

Three hundred cops. What's that? A car for every two officers? A hundred and fifty cars? And I've to find *one*....

"Fuck," I say, slapping my steering wheel. Getting the car number Nate Bennett is driving around in today is not necessarily the key piece of information I thought it was when I felt I was being a smart-ass sleuth back at the precinct. Though Birmingham isn't that big, is it? Population of what... about fifty thousand? Maybe about three hundred streets in total. Jesus... that means there's one cop car for every two streets in this hood. Maybe my math is fucked on that. Or maybe the police system's as fucked up as folks keep telling us it is.

I turn right, for no reason other than the fact that I have to turn one way or the other at this junction, then I step on the gas, my head swaying from side to side, my pupils darting around for signs of blue-and-white cars. Nothing. There's no way there's a cop car on every second street of Birmingham. That doesn't add up. It can't add up.

Then I hear a siren. In the distance. Growing in volume. I slow down the car, cock my ears to try to tell from which direction the siren is wailing from when it suddenly sounds as if it's coming for me. I glance into the rearview mirror, and, after a pause, the windows of the houses lined to my left flash blue. Suddenly the siren is so loud it could be next to my ears. The blue lights suddenly flash in my face and then... whoosh, a police car zips by me.

So, I step on the gas, following the lights as they pull away from me, determined to keep them in my line of sight. My eyes look down at the speedometer. Ninety-one. Ninety-two. When I glance back up, I notice a red car pulling over ahead, allowing the cops to swerve around it and before it can signal back into its lane, I'm around it too, determined not to lose ground on the flashing lights. But it's not easy. Not in this shitty Altima. As they speed away from me, a green light turns red and it forces me to hit my steering wheel before I slam my foot on the brakes, screeching the car to a skidding halt.

"Fuck-ity, fuck," I spit, staring at the blue lights as they fade away in the distance, waiting on them to disappear totally out of sight. Only they don't disappear. They remain still, flashing in silence. I squint through the windscreen, and when the traffic light finally blinks green, I lightly step on the gas and make my way toward the blue. Both doors on the police car are open; the car abandoned; the back of it on an angle in the center of the road. I slow my Altima as I drive by it, my head turning from side to side, my eyes looking around for a sign of navy-blue shirts. When I see one, walking toward my car, I gently press down on the gas and roll forward faster, hoping the officer doesn't point at me and call me toward him. He doesn't. He just glances back to his abandoned police car. I don't think it's him. Bennett. This officer is white. Definitely white. They all are. But he's got darker hair than Bennett had in the photo I saw in the newspaper. I decide to U-turn, to get a closer look and it's when I notice him getting into the car that I remember all numbers are on the back of each police car. On blue stickers. So, I roll slowly toward the blue lights again and I pass him just as he is lifting a receiver to his mouth. When my car gets past his I twist my neck to make out the numbers on the back of his car.

"Shit!" I say, hitting my steering wheel again.

Car number seventy-seven.

What the fuck am I doing? I'm playing the lottery here. Looking for one car out of a hundred and fifty cars. I've no chance of winning that lottery.

I feel my heart sink as the excitement of being an undercover journalist evaporates. So, I pull the car into the next parking spot and, as soon as I straighten it into the space, I reach into my pocket in search of my vaporizer.

BENJI WAYDE

"Nothing on pages two and three," I say. And then I lick my thumb again and I turn the next page over and look all around it. "Nothing on pages four and five." And then I turn the next page and look all around it and say, "Nothing on pages six and sev—"

And then I sit still, with my thumb touching my tongue and my eyes staring at the picture of me that I have on my Facebook. Except it is in black-and-white and not in color like it is on Facebook. My head begins to feel dizzy, and I don't know what to do and my eyes are blinking. So, I stop them from blinking by holding them tight closed and then opening them again wide. Really, really wide. And I begin to read the big headline next to the black-and-white picture of me out loud, cuz I have to read out loud when I'm reading the newspapers or a book. Otherwise the words don't come to me.

"Security Guard hailed for saving young man's life."

I feel my belly go wobbly and I think maybe I need to vomit into the toilet. But I don't like vomiting into the toilet cuz the last two times I vomited into the toilet I cried cuz it was scary. And Grandma and Grandpa aren't here to make me not feel scared no more like they did those two times.

I stand cuz I don't want to read no more of the newspaper, and I put my hands over my face like Grandma does when she is a bit angry and then I sit back down on the carpet again and take my hands away from my face, and then I stand back up again and put my hands back on my face. My hands are getting sweaty again like they did when Mr. Pale and the big, bald, angry man were in my house. So, I wipe them against my butt and then I sit back down on the carpet again and put my hands back on my face. I can't stay still. I lean a little bit closer to the newspaper and I open up my fingers a little bit on my face and I look at the photograph of me again. And then I start reading the story under the headline, even though I don't want to.

"Timothy O'Brien was being hailed as a hero last night after talking down a local man, Benji Wayde (21), from jumping to his death from the roof of the eight-story high Northfarm Shopping Mall."

Those words are not true. Not true. Not true. Not true. Not true. Not true. Not true. I just wanted to feel the wind in my face. That's all. I was trying to feel closer to Grandpa.

I close the gaps in my fingers, and I try to cry into them, but no tears are coming out and I don't think I want to cry now even though I think I should cry cuz I feel so sad. Really, really sad. And it makes me confused that I am not crying. Then I remember that everybody was being nice to me on Facebook, and I pick up my tablet and tap my finger on Facebook and I read the comments under my post about going to Yoga. Trisha Derbyshire who is the Momma of Charlie Derbyshire who I used to go to school with has written another comment.

Sending all our thoughts and prayers to you Benji. Much love. x

And I think that is the first time anybody wrote the word love to me except Grandma and Grandpa when they give me my birthday card every year. I hold my finger on the "like" button until it turns into the red love heart button, and I let go and it pops a love heart back to Trisha Derbyshire.

Then I grab the newspaper, and I roll it into a ball like Grandma did earlier and I throw it over to the corner of the room and then I slap my hands into my face again cuz I think I should cry now… but there are still no tears coming. Even though I want them to come.

I really, really don't hate anybody. But if I had to hate somebody, I would hate that security guard. He's lyin'. He didn't save my life. He didn't! I just wanted to feel the wind in my face. That's all.

When I take my hands from my face, I look at the top of my tablet to see what the time is. 11:36. Maybe I should not go to Yoga. I feel too sad. But maybe I should go to Yoga cuz I feel too sad. And then I look at the TV with the video player in it, and I press the button with the arrow on the side of it and Momma pops up on screen in her beautiful red dress and her long red gloves, standing in front of house number forty-nine with the boy in the white suit called Pauly. He is standing behind her with his arms around her belly and she is smiling at him and then he kisses her on the nose, and I say, "awww" before the screen goes to Grandma who is wiping a tear from her eye. I think maybe Pauly is my daddy cuz he must have been Momma's boyfriend if they are kissing and cuddling and in love. Pauly! I think my daddy's name is Pauly. And I blink my eye and one tear finally comes out and finally I am crying.

"Mother of divine!" Grandma is shouting. "What in the world are you doin', Boy? You told me you were going to Yoga. Stop watching these old VHS tapes!" She steps over me and she taps at the TV screen, trying to press the buttons at the side of the TV with the video player in it and then suddenly the screen goes all blue and Grandma is still shouting. "I thought you were going to Yoga, Boy. That's where you told me you were going. Not sneaking back here to watch your VHS tapes. You lyin' to me, Boy?"

I stand up and I want to shout but I ain't never really shouted before.

"Y-y-you lied to me, too," I roar. And I point at the newspaper all in a ball in the corner of the room.

I didn't shout really loud, even though I wanted to shout loud. But Grandma hears me anyway over her shouting and she looks at the wrinkly newspaper and then back at me.

Then it goes all quiet. And nobody is shouting no more.

Grandma starts crying and I feel really sad cuz she is crying prob'ly cuz I tried to shout at her and so I give her a big hug.

"I'm so sorry for shouting at you," she says.

"I'm sorry for shouting at you," I say.

Grandma steps back from me and pushes her glasses up to her hair so she can rub her yellowy eyes. Then she puts her hand on my shoulder and squeezes it.

"Don't mind what the newspapers write. They never report anything truthful anyway," she says. "When we're all settled tonight, over in apartment number seven, we'll sit down and talk about it. And this," she says pointing down at the TV with the video player in it.

"Is Pauly my daddy?" I ask.

Grandma laughs a little bit through her nose, and she wipes her nose with her hand and looks up at me.

"I wish Pauly was your daddy, Boy. I wish he was. Your Momma hadda stayed with that boy, she wudda been just fine. Just fine indeed."

Grandma tosses my hair a little bit and I feel a bit sad that Pauly is not my daddy cuz I thought I had really seen who my daddy is for the first time ever.

"I love you, Grandma," I say. And then I hug her again. And she squeezes me tight. Really, really tight.

"Go on, Boy," she whispers in my ear. "Go do your Yoga and when you come back, I'm gonna order us some pizza from Ancelotti's, huh? And we'll sit down in our new home, and we'll talk about your Momma, and we'll talk about Pauly, and we'll talk about the newspapers, and we'll talk about Northfarm Shopping Mall...."

"And Grandpa," I say.

"Yes," she says. "And we'll talk about Grandpa. Now... go on, get goin', Boy—else you gon' be late for Yoga."

MAGGIE ZUCHA

When his phone rings, again, he spins away from me, holding it to his ear before walking further away. It's windy. So, I can't really hear what he's saying. Even though I'm trying to. I'd love to know what's going on. This sure is exciting, though. A secret mission on my first day on the streets. I wonder if it's always this exciting… or whether or not you get used to it like Nate seems to have. Sometimes he seems a little bit excited by it all, 'specially when we're speeding in the car with the sirens blaring, but other times he's just all moody and quiet, and I dunno-what? Like sulky, I guess. Like a sulky teenager.

"Tell me…" I hear him shout, "what the fuck is it you want me to do?"

And it sounds wrong. As if Nate's getting really angry. Even though his back is to me, I can tell he's angry. And I don't know what to think. I wanna know what this secret mission is. And I wanna know what the hell Governor Haversham is doing in that black-and-white footage we were watching until Nate's phone rang again and sent us here. To Gray Bridge—where it doesn't look like anything has ever happened, let alone could happen. I notice him hang up the call and I wait for him to turn back to me. But he doesn't.

"You uh… you okay, Nate?" I shout over to him. He still doesn't move. Doesn't even bother to turn around to face me. So, I walk up behind him and kinda, like, nudge him in the back with my shoulder. "Everything okay, Nate?"

"Follow me, Zucha," he says.

And then he marches forward. And I look back at the car and shout after him, "but the car door's still open, Nate."

He finally turns around to me, and his face looks all pale. And the cut on his cheek is redder and more angry looking than it has been all morning.

"Then close the fuckin' thing," he says.

So, I do. I run over to the cop car, slam the door closed and then I kinda like race after Nate, wondering what the hell is going on with this secret mission. But I don't ask him another question when I catch up to him. 'Cause I already asked twice if he's okay, and he's already not answered twice. So, we just keep walking, me almost jogging to keep up with him, and him huffing out of his nose loudly. I don't think the phone call he got was good. He's gone all quiet. All pale. All sulky. And he's marching. As if he's back in the army and not just a police officer working the streets of Birmingham. I try to match him stride for stride, but my legs aren't as long as his and sometimes I have to skip forward to keep up with him. I want to ask questions. Lots of questions. But I also don't want to ask questions. So, I just keep walking and skipping... walking and skipping. I'll let Nate kinda like focus, or do his thing or whatever. He's been doing this stuff for twenty-five years. This is literally my first day on the streets. So, it's best I just shut up and catch up. So, I skip forward again, until he stops suddenly and stretches his arm right across me.

"Just follow my lead like you've been doin' all day, okay?" he says.

"'Course," I say. And then I look around at all of the concrete around Gray Bridge and I don't know what he's talking about. But I don't say anything. I don't ask any questions while we both stand still with the wind whipping around us.

Then I hear footsteps in the distance before a man comes into view and when I look at Nate, he winks at me. And I don't know what's going on. Until the man gets closer... and closer... and then, just as he is passing us, Nate grabs him by the collar and pins him to the wall.

"You stop right there!" Nate roars into his face, "You have the right to remain silent. Anything you do say may be used against you in a court of law… you filthy fuckin' kak!"

8

HOWIE STOOD IN THE FAR CORNER OF SARAH-JANE'S KITCHEN WITH his hands on his hips, adopting the posture he usually reserved for occasions he felt a need to be dramatic. He had, multiple times, praised Lawnie Clarke's set design vision — or home design vision as it literally was in this instance — so he was somewhat impressed by the finishing touches being put together. Yet he still held an urge to hold his hands to his hips in his own distinct camp, dramatic fashion as he huffed to himself in the shadows.

Sarah-Jane had observed Howie's body language waning over the past few days. But she hadn't given in to his amateur dramatics over the quarter of a century they had been working together and wasn't about to begin now. Even though she understood he had every right to be feeling rather miffed. Howie was used to the fast-paced life of TV production; the speed-walking around corridors; the intense production meetings with TV chiefs; the multiple rehearsals; the pandering to guests; going deep-diving on topics with a team of researchers; bossing around a team of junior producers; barking at camera operators and instructing floor managers. There was never a second for Howie to be standing and doing nothing in the shadows, holding his hands to his hips in dramatic fashion. But this... this environment was different. Totally different. No junior producer was pleading with him to sign off on needless paperwork. No camera operators or floor managers were waiting to be drilled by him on their choreography for Wednesday's live show. No team of researchers were banging on the door of his office, desperate to pitch fresh ideas.

Howie huffed from his dark corner of the kitchen. More audibly this time. But nobody glanced his way. Erica was too busy scrolling through her phone, searching for more statistics that she knew would impress Sarah-Jane. Phil was twirling knobs on the two robotic Ultra HD cameras he had recently purchased. One was set up to face Sarah-Jane, who would be sitting at one end of her marble kitchen island, the chocolate brown wall behind her upon which was now being hung a huge blood-orange neon sign that read the name "Zdanski" in cursive handwriting—almost identical to the sign she had for her first ever season of *The Zdanski Show* on CSN way back in 1997. The second robotic camera that had just been set by Phil, would shoot low across the marble kitchen island, to where the guests would sit—positioned in front of that picture-perfect view of the New York City skyline. The cameras would be run by a remote control no bigger than the palm of Phil's hand by the man himself from the chocolate-colored sofa in the living room of the penthouse—a mere six steps away from where Sarah-Jane would be streaming live on YouTube to America. No camera people were required. Not anymore. In fact, not many people were required at all for the podcast production. Which is exactly why Howie's hands were on his hips, and he was sighing audibly in the shadows.

Despite being close to sixty years of age, Howie was still wearing tight-fitting patterned shirts, tucked neatly into tight blue jeans. His fashion choices hadn't changed much in all the years Sarah-Jane had known him. Some wrinkles had cut a little deeper, certainly so around his eyes, he'd added another chin and his hair was now shaved to stubble given that it had receded so much. But he was no longer wearing the round John Lennon-shaped glasses he had sported for decades after finally being persuaded to undergo laser eye surgery by his estranged wife a few years back. Aside from shaving his hair and having laser eye surgery, Howie

Laine really hadn't evolved much. Not his clothes. Not his amateur dramatics. Not his values. Not his approach to work. Only now the latter *had* to evolve into something entirely different. Into a medium he despised. Which is exactly why his hands were still on his hips.

Aside from his frequent huffing, and the drilling of the neon Zdanski sign into the brown wall, the penthouse was eerily quiet, especially so as they were about to launch a brand-new show in less than forty-eight hours' time. If this was back at CSN, the whole network would be abuzz; phones wouldn't stop ringing; people wouldn't stop stomping around the set; there would be meetings galore taking place in the shadows of the studio and a constant echo of chatter around every corner. There would be an aura of nervous energy. No doubt about it. A nervous energy Howie had always thrived in. The television world. The network world. A world he was beginning to learn no longer existed for him.

"What was your last contract at CSN worth?" Erica said, looking up from her phone at Sarah-Jane, breaking the silent ambience that had been infuriating Howie. Erica was sitting on the far side of the kitchen island—the perfect silhouette of New York City glowing gold from the sunset behind her. Sarah-Jane looked a little taken aback by the question, pausing, and then squinting across the marble kitchen island at her most inexperienced producer.

"Uh… seven and a half mill a year," Sarah-Jane answered. "Why?"

"Well," Erica said, standing up from the stool she had been sitting on and walking her phone the length of the kitchen island toward her boss, "it says here that Joe Rogan got *two hundred million dollars* from Spotify for the rights to air his podcast."

"Two hundred mill?" Sarah-Jane said, grabbing the phone from Erica.

Howie scoffed and huffed so loudly that everybody in the kitchen finally paid him the attention he had been craving by glancing his way almost in unison—including the workman screwing the neon Zdanski sign to the back wall.

"What's up with you, Howie?" Sarah-Jane said, finally pandering to his mood.

Howie removed his hands from his hips and then stepped out from the corner of the kitchen to where the warm glow of one of the newly lit blood-orange bulbs hit his face. "I'm sorry, but these big numbers, they're all bullshit."

Erica tucked her chin into her neck and creased the brow that was hiding behind her thick bangs, making her glasses slip down her narrow nose again. She had known Howie to be a bit of a tough cookie, but he'd never been so outlandishly frank to label her findings "bullshit."

"Whatcha mean bullshit?" Sarah-Jane said, asking exactly what Erica was thinking.

"I mean, it's all algorithms and data and fucking… I dunno what else to call it, it's bullshit."

"But the algorithms are accurate. The data is accurate," Erica said. "It is a fact that Joe Rogan got two hundred million dollars from Spotify for his podcast. A fact that Dax Sheppard gets twenty million for every episode of his podcast."

"It's…." Howie opted to throw his hands in the air, rather than finish his sentence.

"It's what?" Sarah-Jane said, taking a step toward him.

"It's online. *Online*! Anyone can set up a podcast online. Online has killed all the good media we've ever had. It's a blemish on the face of journalism. C'mon, Sarah-Jane. You're too good to be online. You're better than online. Your face belongs on a television screen. Not somebody's cell phone."

"Actually, Grandad," Erica said, taking her first jab at Howie since she began working on the show—something she had been tempted to do for quite some time, "lots of people actually watch online content on their televisions these days. Smart televisions. Where you can download YouTube to watch the podcast. There are lots of ways to watch this podcast or listen to this podcast. At home on your sofa, when you're out jogging, on a train, in bed, in a hotel… wherever you want."

Howie sucked a heavy breath in through his teeth, filling his lungs and puffing out his chest. Then he heavily sighed and turned to his boss, instead of addressing the junior producer who was clearly trying to rile him.

"Online is fucking toxic, Sarah-Jane," Howie spat. "No generation has ever been tired; you know what I mean?" Sarah-Jane pressed her tongue into her cheek as Howie stepped closer to her, the two of them now perfectly lit in the center of the brand-spanking-new *Zdanski* set. "We're having our brains burned by so much information. No wonder depression in humans is growing at an inordinate rate...." He stopped to check himself, then shook the thought from his head and decided to continue, his finger now pointing. "There used to be a time humans didn't wanna go to bed. We wanted to stay awake. Stay alive. Now we all can't wait to get to bed. Every night. Because we're fucking drained. We're having our brains drained by so much bullshit and so much social media," he held both hands out and pretended to strangle thin air. "Y'know what my main problem is..." he continued. The worker screwing in the neon *Zdanski* sign stopped drilling and turned around on his small ladder to witness the speech. "Everybody blames the mainstream media. Oh, it's the mainstream media's fault that the world is fucked up. That's what every idiot in America thinks. That it's the mainstream media's fault. That's bullshit," he spat. "Utter bullshit. The world was working very fucking well thank you very much when it was just mainstream media. Society was civilized. Americans weren't divided. There wasn't a mass shooting every day like there is now. We didn't have reality TV stars becoming president. We didn't have attacks on the Capitol. We didn't have a hundred and fifty fucking men killing themselves in this country every goddamn day. And then... social media comes along. Now everybody hates everything and everyone. They even hate themselves. Look at Britain... they were the most respected nation on the planet before social media came along and began filling their news feeds full of misinformation. They divorced themselves from the European Union for crying out loud. Think that would have happened if it wasn't for social media? Think they'd have that clown Johnson in charge of the UK if it wasn't for social media? Think we'd ever have had Trump in the White House? These folks... these idiots who think it's mainstream media at fault... how can they not see the wood for the trees? It's obvious what media's at fault for the world going crazy these past years. Social media. The world went nuts when social media was born. It fucked everything up. *Everything*."

Howie's face was reddening, so, too, were the whites of his eyes. He was evidently furious; his pointing finger trembling as he ranted.

"Okay," Sarah-Jane said softly, reaching for Howie's shoulder and squeezing it. "I hear you, Howie. I hear you."

"Remember," Howie said, pointing his finger downward as the creases from his eyes glistened, "when all we had to worry about was the President fingering an intern with one of his cigars? Remember when the late shows used to be funny... really funny. Television used to be so great. So great...."

"Exactly," Erica said, "*used* to be."

Howie turned to stare at the junior producer, looking her up and down with a curl at the corner of his lip. She was wearing her Doc Martin boots over her thick green tights and a tartan kilt with a woolen green turtle neck sweater. She still reminded him so much of Velma from Scooby Doo; what with her thick-rimmed black glasses and her red-haired bob framing her fresh, pale face.

"Okay," Phil said, looking up from the camera just as he felt the tension in the kitchen rise. "You two need to park your egos to one side. We've got a show to do. Sarah-Jane, can you sit on your stool? I gotta measure you up."

Sarah-Jane stared at Howie, then at Erica before striding over to her stool at the end of the kitchen island.

"We'll talk later," she whisper-shouted to Howie, then she beamed her beautiful smile toward camera number two. Phil stared at the remote control in his hand, and pushed a button that slowly zoomed in on America's most-watched face with her name glowing behind her in neon blood-orange.

"You look good," Phil said, holding one of his fat thumbs up.

While he was testing the camera shots, Erica and Howie were still standing at the center of the island, lit to perfection, but lost for words.

"And uh, Howie, go sit on the other stool," Phil said, glancing up from his remote control.

Howie nodded, then did as Phil ordered—something he had become accustomed to over the years. Phil pushed a couple of buttons on his handheld pad while eyeballing the small monitor just as Erica walked out of shot, her arms folded. Even with the lines of Howie's brow turned down to a frown, the view of him on Phil's small monitor looked fantastic in ultra HD. The orange glow from the bulbs created a radiant on-screen ambience and the view out of the floor-to-ceiling window behind Howie was striking, what with the buildings fading into silhouettes as the sun began to dip below the earth.

"Okay, and uh," Phil said, pushing his controller again while squinting at his monitor. "Can you two just talk? As if you're having a conversation? I need to test the cross-camera switch."

Sarah-Jane shot her mirror-like green eyes across her marble kitchen island and pursed her lips at her very worried-looking debut guest.

"Talk to me, Howie Laine," she said, opening up her palms atop the marble island. "What's really troubling you?"

"This," he said, leaning on to the marble. "It's not right. Podcasts. They're not regulated. Not like television is. That's why people are just lying on podcasts and making shit up and getting away with it... Jesus, there are podcasts out there preaching all sorts of conspiracy theories and bullshit. And people buy it. They believe it."

"Well," Sarah-Jane said, looking down at her hands, then back at her guest. "I understand your concerns. I shared those exact concerns. I did. I thought, *online*? Online isn't regulated. That's why it has a bad rep. Because anyone can say anything. Truth or lie, right? But it's because podcasts aren't so heavily regulated that we should really embrace this medium. That's what won me over, Howie. I'm sorry. I like the freedom of speech a podcast will allow me. I like that there are all sorts of podcasts out there. I love the bad ones. And the good ones. But... podcasts not being heavily regulated, or not being beholden to advertisers, or billionaire narcissistic owners, that's what won me over. That's why we're here, Howie. For the power. We own everything. Everything we do and everything we say… it's all on us."

Howie paused to scratch at his chin, and as he was soaking up everything Sarah-Jane had just said to him, Phil swiped his finger upward on his joypad, and camera number one swished silently to zoom in on Howie's face.

"I hate it," Howie said. "News going online is killing news. The truth is getting lost among the lies, and the conspiracy theories are as believable as all the above to some people… so…." He sighed. A deep heavy sigh that almost sounded like a sob.

"I hear you, Howie, I do," Sarah-Jane said. "You're a newsman. A great newsman. An eight-time Emmy-winning producing newsman."

"Well, you've won more Emmys than me," he replied.

"I've won more Emmys than most," Sarah-Jane said, tittering. Nobody else tittered. Not Howie sitting opposite her. Not Erica watching from the shadows. Not Phil who was still squinting at the perfectly lit shots on the monitor.

"We should bring this footage to CSN, tell them you have the rights to this and if they give you your show back then you will relaunch with this story," Howie spat out of this mouth as quickly as he could. "They'd kill for this story. Heck, any network would kill for this story. Let's go pitch it to all the networks. You said it yourself, the story is huge. If we get our show back, we could hit the heights again, twenty million viewers would tune in to see this footage."

"Twenty million is peanuts, Howie," Sarah-Jane said. "That's what Erica's being telling us." Howie bent forward to plant his face on the top of the kitchen island, and when his nose touched the cold marble, he sighed deeply, fogging up the shine. "Listen, why don't you pitch yourself around the networks," Sarah-Jane proposed. "Nobody's got a better resume than you."

Howie lifted himself from his face-plant with the groan of an elderly man.

"I'm almost sixty, Sarah-Jane," he said. "No network's looking for the guy who used to be great. They're looking for the next big thing. I'm the last big thing."

Sarah-Jane stepped down from her stool and somberly walked the length of her kitchen island, her lips pursed in sorrow. When she reached her guest, she embraced him with a hug, and then kissed him gently on the forehead with her two hands pressed to his cheeks.

"I think what you need to do is speak to my lawyer, Cody Williamson," she whispered. "He might have something to say to you."

"And cut!" Phil barked from the shadows, holding one of his big, fat thumbs up. "That looked fucking awesome."

AIMEE STREET

When I hold down the play button, there's a moment of silence while I wince in hope... until Richard Carpenter starts strumming his guitar through the car's speakers and it allows me to exhale a cloud of weed while I fist-pump the air with a sense of achievement.

It took ages to hook up my iPhone to the car's speakers, but I finally managed it. The sound is so much crisper than it is coming straight from the phone. I press the button to take the passenger window down all the way and then I readjust my position in the driver's seat, turning so I can stretch my legs across the car to leave my feet dangling out of the opened window. I suck on my vaporizer again just as Karen Carpenter begins to sing about those feelings coming over her, boasting that she's on top of the world. I love this song. Have always loved this song. Probably 'cause I've always strived to feel how Karen feels when she's singing it. That's why I vape weed. To chase feeling on top of the world. I have to chase it because feeling on top of the world doesn't come naturally to me. Not with my looks. Not with this bent nose, and these crooked teeth.

As I'm blowing out another cloud of weed I hear, in the distance, another siren wail and I almost pull my feet back inside the car to get motoring. But I don't bother. I've already given up. Finding one cop car out of a hundred and fifty is not really my idea of how to spend an afternoon. I'd rather sit here, in this rented car, with my feet sticking out the passenger window, my vaporizer buzzing in my hand, and Karen Carpenter gloating about being on top of the world in the most beautiful, melodic voice I've ever heard.

I take one more small hit of my vaporizer then set it aside so I can pick up my phone where I swipe the image of the Carpenter siblings away, ensuring the music still plays, before I tap my finger against the Instagram app. I love Instagram. Almost as much as I hate it. I only follow celebrities; celebrities pretending to be on top of the world, just like Karen Carpenter is pretending she is every time she sings this song. It all made sense to me when I grew up and realized Karen suffered with mental illnesses through all of her successes as a singer songwriter. It was like all of the math problems that strained my brain finally added up. She isn't really on top of the world when she sings this song. She's *acting* like she's on top of the world. Same way these celebrities act when they take photos of themselves splashing around in their swimming pools on the edge of the Hollywood Hills, or when they post a selfie of themselves with some sick girl with a tube running into her nostril. Celebs make me wanna vomit. Yet, I can't help scrolling my way through images of their lives every day.

The only person I follow who isn't a celebrity is Mykel. But he rarely posts anything useful these days. Certainly not since he's been sober. He takes pictures of cups of green tea that he drinks now, or salads that he might eat for lunch. He's trying to tell all sixty-two of his followers that he's coping well with life. Maybe he is. I really don't know. I find it hard to believe he'll ever cope well with life. He has demons inside of him. And they'll come out again when they're ready. They always do. They've been within him ever since I met him as a lost six-year-old little girl, and he was a lost six-year-old little boy.

Thinking of Mykel makes me groan, and my mood takes a nosedive even though Karen Carpenter is still gloating to me in the most beautiful voice I've ever heard. It's annoyed me that Mykel was sober today, yet he still came on to me. I don't think we're ever gonna recover from that. Which is such a shame.

That'll leave me with a number of friends that is too perfectly round: Zero.

To resist the urge to groan again I repeatedly tap at the side of my iPhone, increasing the volume of The Carpenters to the maximum, and then I begin to sing along loudly. Loudly and badly. I'm tone deaf. Always have been.

While I'm singing at the top of my lungs, or screaming, or shouting, the rush of the weed I just inhaled hits and for a moment I feel high. Really high. As if I'm on top of the world, too. I try to cling to the feeling, 'cause I know that these highs are temperamental. Something will come to mind that will drag me back down. Like a memory. Or a reality. So, I close my eyes tight, with Karen still gloating in my ear, and I smile to myself, allowing the cannabis to race through my blood and give me the high I'm always chasing. And as my smile makes my entire face crease, the phone I'm gripping in my hand suddenly vibrates and the sound of The Carpenters pauses, to allow a loud piercing tone to ding through the car speakers. A fucking text message.

I tilt the screen to my face, and tap my finger to light it up.

"Holy fucking shit!" I say, dragging my feet back in from the open window.

BENJI WAYDE

My shoulders are shaking. And they won't stop shaking even though I am trying to make them stop shaking by squeezing my elbows into my sides really tight. And my hands are sweaty. Really sweaty. Sweaty like they were when Mr. Pale was in house number forty-nine, and I thought he and the big, tall, angry, bald man was going to hurt me. But I can't wipe the sweat off my butt like I did back then. Cuz of the handcuffs.

I lift my head and I look up at them and I'm not sure why they have arrested me and put me in handcuffs. The man cop was really scary, and I think he made a mistake and maybe he thinks I am somebody else and he will come over and take off the hand-cuffs and I will get to Yoga before it's too late and the class has already started. The man cop is still on the phone. The woman cop is standing nearby the car, with her hands on her hips. She looks back at me sometimes, and when she does, I just look down at the concrete between my legs. It's sore sitting here, on this concrete and up against the wall of Gray Bridge, but I don't want to move or say anything cuz I don't want the man cop to shout at me again.

She looks back at me, and I look down at the concrete again and I try to think of something else. Like Momma and Pauly on the VHS tapes. And I start wishing Pauly was my daddy and then maybe Momma would still be alive. But if Momma and Pauly had a baby maybe that baby wouldn't be me. Because I am made from Momma and my real daddy. Whoever he is. I wish it was Pauly, though. Momma looked so pretty in her red dress and her long red gloves. Just the prettiest. And then I think of how Grandpa used to always tell me she was just the prettiest which makes me think of how angry Grandpa would be if I told him two cops put me in handcuffs and shouted in my face even though I didn't do nothing wrong. I was just walking past Gray Bridge, to go to Yoga. That's all. Grandpa would prob'ly go to the cop station and shout at the manager if I told him. He did that before. In a grocery store when they wouldn't serve me. Grandpa walked down to the grocery store, and he shouted and shouted at the manager and when he came back home to house number forty-nine, he told me it was okay that I could go back to that grocery store anytime I wanted. But I ain't never go back to that store. I go to the store on the other side of Birmingham... on Emmet Road. The people who work there are nice. They don't say nothing to me.

Grandpa was the best. He was my Grandpa. My daddy. My big brother. And my best friend. All in one little person. It's sad that he's gone. But I'll see him when I get to Heaven cuz I think we'll both be going to Heaven cuz we never did nothing wrong in our lives. I bet Grandpa is looking down from Heaven at me now and I bet he is all angry at these cops cuz they arrested the wrong man. And I smile at him being all angry up in Heaven and suddenly my shoulders stop shaking. And I don't have to squeeze my elbows into my sides no more.

Until I hear shoes coming nearer to me. And they stop. Right in front of me. So, I look up and I see her. The woman cop. Staring down at me.

MAGGIE ZUCHA

I'm not sure where I'm supposed to stand. So, I kinda set myself in the middle somewhere between the suspect and Nate. But that seems to be getting further and further away. Nate's walked back past the car, talking into his phone. So, I'm almost already back at the car, looking between the back of Nate's hair and the suspect sitting with his back up against the wall, hanging his head in shame with his hands cuffed behind him. I did that. Nate pinned him down and said, "Cuff him, Zucha." And I did. I jumped on his back, dragged his arms out from underneath him and I got 'em on real quick this time. Like real quick. In seconds. I thought Nate was gonna say something about how quick I got 'em on, but he was too busy grabbing the suspect up and pushing him forward that he didn't say anything. Then he pinned the suspect up against the wall and was snarling at him until his phone rang and he dropped the suspect to the ground before marching off with the phone pressed to his ear. I didn't know what to do, other than to kinda like stand in the middle between Nate and the suspect. So that's all I am doing. I wasn't sure if I was supposed to question the suspect. But I'm not sure what to ask… what to say. I tried to think of what I learned at cop school. I know we are supposed to assume we are the ones in control. I certainly remember my instructor yelling that at me. I also remember when I had to practice being in control and repeating phrases like, "No, ma'am, it's not your time to talk," and "Sir, you move just one step closer to me, then I'm gonna have to reach for my firearm." But I didn't think I was very good at it. I don't think the instructor did either. He didn't say anything to me, though. He just kinda looked me up and down, and then moved on to the next trainee.

I look back at Nate. He's rubbing his hand through the back of his hair, the phone still pressed to his ear. When I glance back at the suspect his head is still hanging in shame. And I begin to wonder what he did. Why he was arrested. Nate just stopped him, read him the Miranda, and then pushed him up against the wall… before walking away with his phone pressed to his ear.

Suddenly, I decide to just start walking, taking my notepad out from the top pocket of my shirt and pinching the small pen from its spine.

He kinda looks up slowly at me when my feet stop next to his.

"What's your name, sir?"

"B-B-Benji Way-Wayde," he says.

He speaks all weird.

"Address?"

"It's uh-uh uh… it's uh, house number f-forty-nine St. Michael's House, Birmingham, Connecticut."

He looks down while he's telling me his address. But then he suddenly jerks his head up while I'm scribbling it down.

"No," he says, "n-n-no. We moved. We're moving today. Apartment n-n-number seven, St. Michael's House, Birmingham, Connecticut."

"What the hell, dude?" I say.

He hangs his head in shame again, so I bend down, and try to match him face to face. But he just hangs his head even lower and I'm not sure if this guy is playing me for a fool, or if he is a real retard.

"Zucha!" I snap a quick stare over my shoulder and when I do, I fall back onto my butt and roll over onto my stomach. When I look up, Nate is staring down at me, holding a hand over his phone. "Don't ask him any questions. Stay by the fucking car!"

He spins around and walks away, pressing the phone back up to his ear.

I look back up at the suspect and I'm not sure if he grins at me before hanging his head again.

So, I get back to my feet, and brush my shirt down. Then I notice there's even more concrete dust down the front of my trousers. And I bet it's all on my butt, 'cause that's what I first fell onto. But I don't want to rub my butt as I walk away from the suspect, not until I get to the car and can hide behind it and out of sight. When I reach the car, I immediately begin brushing off my ass cheeks. If Nate looks back around and sees me now, he'd think I'm a mad woman. I feel bad. I feel like I've been barked at by the teacher. The teacher I wanted to impress. He looked really angry at me. I just didn't know what to do while he was taking so long on his call. I didn't know whether he'd be more angry at me if I started questioning the suspect, or more angry at me 'cause I was just standing around doing nothing. So, I thought the best thing to do would be to ask the suspect some simple questions. To find out some details for Nate when he got back. And then he might say, "well done, Zucha." But he didn't. He just kinda like snapped at me.

When I'm done brushing off my ass cheeks, I lean my forearms on to the top of the car and I look back at the suspect, wondering if he was putting on an act for me or not. Benji-what-he-say his name was? I feel for my notebook and notice it's not in my pocket. So, I squint back and see that it's over by the suspect, lying on the concrete dust. I walk back and snatch it from the ground, staring at him as I do. To see if he grins up at me again. But he doesn't. He just leaves his head hanging in shame.

When I scoop up the notebook, I turn over to the first page.

Benji Wayde. Lives somewhere over in St. Michael's House. The projects.

There are lots of dealers around there. Lots of trouble. I wonder what sort of trouble this guy's into. I wonder if he's a dealer.

As I'm staring at the top of his hanging head, I hear footsteps come toward me and they make me spin around as quickly as I can to see Nate's face right behind me. It's really pale. And the cut on his cheek looks red. Red and raw.

NATE BENNETT

I brush my fingers through my hair and yank at it. Hard. Then I swipe my hand down through my face and I immediately feel the sting of my cut as if I've just ripped it open for the very first time again.

"Hold on," I say, "you just ask me to randomly arrest the next kak to walk by and now... and now you're telling me I gotta kill this mutha fucker?"

"You can keep asking, Nate. It's the same answer every time. It never changes. *Yes*. That is what I am telling you to do. Of course, you might opt to be a known paedophile the rest of your life...."

My hand shakes as I grip the phone tighter. And my teeth are grinding. This mutha fucker has me over a barrel. I've no way out. No route out at all.

I look back at the kak to see Zucha talking to him and scribbling down some notes. So, I palm the phone and pace over to her.

"Zucha," I whisper-shout. "Don't ask him any questions. Stay by the fucking car."

I spin on my heels and pace past the car, pressing the phone in my shaking hand back to my ear.

"You serious? You just want me to eliminate this guy... here? Now? In broad daylight?"

"How many ways you gonna ask the same question, Nate?

You're in the perfect spot. Gray Bridge. It's the tiniest concrete jungle in Birmingham. Get the job done. It'd hardly be your first time killing a Black man now would it, Nate? What's one more?"

That's exactly what I've been thinking ever since this mutha fucker told me I needed to eliminate this guy. What's one more? One more lazy-ass kak gone from our streets. Not as if I haven't killed a kak before. Course I have. That's what happens when you work the streets. But I can't... not now. Not here. Not with Zucha. That bitch is brand new on the force. She's crazy and all, but there's no way I'd be able to convince her....

I look back over my shoulder at her to see her by the side of the car, brushing off her fat ass cheeks. Then I glance over at the kak sitting on the ground, his back against the wall, his hands cuffed behind him. His head hanging low.

"Who is this kak anyway, why's he gotta be taken out?"

"Did I say your job was to ask me questions, Nate?" the distorted voice says. "Or did I tell you you needed to kill him?"

"Tell me, man. Come on. When I kill a kak... I know who I'm killing. I know why I'm doing it and how I'm doing it. And I know how to cover my ass. But this... come on, man. Talk to me. What's this shit all about? Who the fuck are you? Who the fuck is this kak?"

"Nate, you're gonna have to stop talking, and start listening. It's not your problem what this guy's been up to, or why he needs to be dead. What is your problem, however, is that I have my finger hovering over a button that will ruin you. And my finger is going to fall in five minutes—unless that guy you have in front of you is dead. If he is, this is all over for you. You won't ever hear from me again. But if he's still alive in five minutes, then your browser history will be made public. And you can kiss goodbye to everything and everybody you know, Nate... you gonna save your life? Or his? You've five minutes. Tick tock."

Then the mutha fucker hangs up. And I'm left staring at the blank screen of my phone, and I wanna throw it hard against the concrete beneath me... but I stop myself, and I shove the phone into my pocket instead, before slapping both hands to my face.

"*Holy shiiiit!*" I grunt into them.

The fuck am I gonna do now? Save my life? Or, that fucking kak's life? Why is this even a question? It shouldn't be a question. It can't be a question. Of course it can't. So, I turn, slowly, on my heels, and then I find myself striding toward Zucha, quickening as I go.

"What's going on, Nate?" she says, turning to me as I get closer to her.

"Zucha," I say. And then I cough. Because I have to cough to move the words from the back of my throat. "This kak needs to be eliminated."

AIMEE STREET

The Carpenters are still providing the score with Karen now singing about Rainy Days and Mondays. It's not the cheeriest of songs, but it's a song that suits the mood I've transitioned into since I received that text. As I'm singing along, Richard's guitar and Karen's voice suddenly pause....

"Take the next left in... one-eighth of a mile," the speakers instruct me, and I look at the screen of my phone to see the blue line on the map leading me to the bend that will allow me to take the next left turn. From there, it's not long. Only three more minutes to Gray Bridge.

That's what the text message said.

"Gray Bridge. Get there now! Be discreet"

As soon as I read it, I swept my feet back inside the car, threw my vaporizer onto the passenger seat, turned the key in the ignition and sped off as quickly as I could... all while The Carpenters continued to provide the score.

It's bleak this far out of town. St. Michael's House is the last development in Birmingham before it runs into a barren land of dusty concrete that was once a river providing much of the water to northern Connecticut. But that river has long since dried up. I spot a handmade sign for a Yoga studio pointing into the narrow street I take the left into. But that's all there is around here. A Yoga studio in the middle of the concrete… and I wonder if that's where I'm being sent. To a fucking Yoga class to get my scoop; as if I'm going to catch officer Nathan Bennett doing Downward Dog while he is supposed to be protecting the streets of Birmingham. I slow the car down before I get to Gray Bridge and decide to walk the rest of the way. The text said I should be discreet. So, something must be going on. Something more than a disgraced copper doing Downward Dog in the middle of his shift.

When I get out of the car, I jog lightly toward Gray Bridge and clear the part where the green no longer grows out from the ground… and there's just gray, flaky concrete beneath my feet. It's empty around here. Not a sight, nor sound. My heart begins to race a little. Because this is the type of place you would lead somebody to in order to do something to them. And I immediately stop walking and try to think it all through. The guy who's sent me here, who texted me, he's the same guy who was following me this morning; the same nostril-haired freak who bought me a bottle of water in Starbucks; who rented me the car. I look back for the car… but it's out of my line of sight. Maybe I should run back to it. Get inside and drive myself back to safety. None of this adds up. It doesn't make sense. If I heard that a girl had been killed in Gray Bridge after being led there by a stranger, I'd think she fucking deserved it for being so stupid.

Fuck this.

I gotta get out of here.

So, I pivot on the spot… too afraid to walk any further into the concrete wasteland and it's when I turn that I hear it… a cough, or a splutter. Or, a heaving. As if somebody is about to throw up.

I look all around, at nothing; nothing but gray concrete and the gray sky above it. And then I run my tongue across my crooked teeth while I try to decide what to do.

"Fuck it," I whisper to myself.

And I turn again, tiptoeing quickly across the concrete, and toward the little bridge that leads to nothing but more concrete. As I'm tiptoeing, I cock my ear to listen for more coughing or spluttering or heaving. But it's silent. And my heart races quicker again, and I imagine all the people who will think I deserved to be killed for being so stupid that I followed a stranger's orders to arrive at Gray Bridge alone.

But just then... out of the corner of my eye, I can make out, when I squint into the distance, a cop car. The cop car, I bet, that I've been sent to find. The cop car that has the number forty-three on its rear bumper. And then, as I squint even more, I see a head on the other side of the car. I bet that's him. Nathan Bennett. The dirty cop. So, I take a few more steps forward, and then another head appears next to him. It must be her. Maggie Zucha. What the fuck are these guys up to? Bennett seems to be slapping Zucha on the back. Then I notice her swiping her sleeve across her mouth. So, I tiptoe to the edge of the bridge, hunkering down so they won't see me if they look this way. That's when I hear muffling; the muffling sound of a voice... Chanting? No... praying? I look over the low wall of the bridge to see a Black guy sitting up on the concrete, mumbling about Lord Jesus Christ and his Grandad. When I squint even more, I can make out that his hands are cuffed behind his back.

I glance back at Bennett and Zucha over by the car, then down at the handcuffed guy underneath the bridge and I realize in that moment that what the stranger was saying to me back at Starbucks is right... journalists don't need pens and notepads anymore. Of course they don't. Those days are long gone. Everything my journalism professors have been teaching me, about shorthand and Dictaphones and interview notes, it's all bullshit. Bullshit meant for journalism students of a by-gone era.

I reach inside my pocket and pull out my phone so I can immediately swipe downward to open up my camera. Then I scroll to the video option and stab my finger against the red button...

MAGGIE ZUCHA

"What's eliminated mean?" I say.

I laugh as I say it. But only 'cause I'm nervous. I'm nervous 'cause he looks nervous. And I didn't think Nate would ever look nervous. I thought he was too hard to ever feel nervous. But he does. I can tell. His mouth is hanging open. And his face is so pale that I can see all the pink and purple veins criss-crossing on his forehead.

"What do you think eliminated means?" he says. "Killed. Put to rest. Eliminated."

My stomach rolls over the way it can sometimes when I watch something scary on TV. Only this isn't TV. It's real life. *My* real life.

"Wait. What? Killed. Him? By us?"

"It's the mission, Zucha," he says.

I tilt my ear down on to my shoulder like I've never done before.

"The mission is to kill this guy?" I say, my voice all high-pitched. "I thought we were the good guys... the cops."

He reaches out and places a hand to my shoulder.

"Zucha, this is your lesson. This is why you were partnered with me. You need to learn and understand the reality of what we do out here on the streets."

My stomach rolls over even more. And I'm not sure if I'm

going to be able to hold the vomit down. So, I spread my feet wider apart, just in case it kinda like spews all over my new work shoes if it does come out. Then I place a hand onto my stomach to stop it feeling so wavy and I look over my shoulder at the suspect before glancing back at Nate. He's so pale that the blood on his cheek looks black.

"Hold on. Hold on," I say. I put my other hand on to my stomach too. "You're saying we are the ones who have to eliminate this guy? Seriously?"

"It's our job, Zucha. Prisons are full. The whole court system, it's a mess. You know this, right?"

"I, uh… yeah, I mean…."

"Well, sometimes… every now and then… rather than go through the due process of arresting somebody, charging the mutha fucker, putting him through the legal system, a trial, an imprisonment, it all costs… it all costs a lot. And the prisons are full and we…. Listen, the order's been made. And that's it. We need to get this guy off the streets. He needs to be eliminated."

I blow out a huge exhale while I'm still clutching on to my stomach with both hands and then, for some reason, I begin to spin on the spot in circles as if I don't know what I'm doing— literally because I don't know what I'm doing. I don't know what we're doing. I don't know what's going on. I don't get it. The police kill people instead of arresting them, 'cause of… money? 'Cause there's no room in prisons?

"Have you done this before?" I say. Then I fold both arms on top of my head, while I continue spinning slowly on the spot.

"Course I have." He sucks in through his teeth. "Sometimes, in the heat of the moment," he says, "you might eliminate a guy. Then you try to cover it up to make it look like self-defense and, y'know, you make it look like a warranted elimination. Easy to do once you know how to cover your ass with the paperwork. But it's… y'know…."

He scratches at his face, and I wince 'cause his fingers are so close to his black cut.

"Wait!" I say. And I finally stop spinning on the spot. "Is this why you were suspended? For killing?"

"Fuck no!" he says. And I'm all confused again. "Course I haven't been caught for murder. You kiddin' me? If I was caught killing a kak, I'd be out of the force, wouldn't I? Behind bars for the rest of my life. I'd be a pitiful martyr like Derek fucking Chauvin. No. No. Course not. We don't get caught killing. Take a look around you... there's nobody 'round here. Gray Bridge is empty. We eliminate this kak, then we leave. No one will even know we were here."

"Wait, hold on," I say. "What *were* you suspended for?"

"Just for... you know... being over forceful. Sometimes kaks' complaints go all the way to the top. And when too many get to the top and the local press get hold of the story, the station chief needs to be seen to act. So, Costello had to suspend me indefinitely. But... he called me back. He called me back to train you. He thinks you have all the makings of a great street cop. Someone who gets it. Someone who knows how to really protect these streets."

"Holy fucking shit," I say. And then I start spinning slowly on the spot again, with my arms wrapped over my head. "So, wait... it's Costello who's ordering this guy to be... to be eliminated?" I ask.

He coughs. Then he sniffs.

"Listen, Zucha. I can't say... but this is an order. That's all we need to know. And we don't got long. We gotta do this... and we gotta do it now."

I blow out another exhale.

"This got something to do with the USB thumb drive?"

He nods his head. Once.

"Yeah. I think so. I don't know."

Then he shakes his head a little. And I'm all confused. Again.

"I dunno... Nate."

"For fuck's sake, Zucha," he says. He grabs on to both of my shoulders, to stop me from spinning. "Do you wanna be a cop? You really wanna be a cop or are you another one of them blow ins, huh? Somebody who leaves the force before they even earn their first stripe on the streets? I've seen you in action today, all up in people's faces, calling them 'bitches', and getting rough with them. That's why they put me with you. 'Cause, they know you got the potential to boss these streets. They think you can be a great street cop. You wanna prove you're able to handle the streets, Zucha?"

I press both hands to my stomach again. And then I burp. A loud one. Wet and loud.

"I think... I think I'm gonna be sick," I say.

Nate grabs my arm, and leads me to the other side of the car. And as soon as we're behind it I immediately crouch down like a frog... and I begin to heave. But nothing's coming out... nothing but the sound of my heaving and spitting.

BENJI WAYDE

My butt is sore sitting on this concrete. And cold. Really, really cold. And I don't think I am going to make it to Yoga on time now cuz the cops haven't said anything to me and it's probably midday and the Yoga class has already started. But maybe that's okay. Cuz I can just go back to Grandma when the cops let me go and we can talk about all those things she wants to talk about. Like Momma. And Pauly. And Grandpa. And why my photograph was in the newspaper today. And we can eat pizza. Ancelotti's pizza. My favorite. Even though it costs sixteen dollars and that is a lot of money for Grandma to spend on dinner. That's why I have been trying to get a job. So I can get some money. And I can help Grandma with things for our new home. And maybe I can buy her some Ancelotti's pizza sometimes. Or maybe one day I can get so much money that I can bring Grandma to New York City to eat in one of those big fancy restaurants like Grandpa did for her sixtieth birthday and she was the happiest I ever seen her in all my life. Thinking of Grandma being really happy makes me think of my eulogy for Grandpa cuz the first thing I wrote down is that I love how Grandpa made Grandma happy. Then I look up. To see them. They're still just talking to each other. The man cop finished his phone call a few minutes ago but he still hasn't come over to me to tell me he arrested the wrong man. Instead, they are just talking and talking and talking and talking... and I'm getting cold. Really, really cold.

I look back down at the concrete again and I start to whisper to myself. Just to practice for tomorrow.

"Lord Jesus," I say, cuz I think every time you talk in a church you are supposed to talk to Lord Jesus. "I want to thank you for giving me a Grandpa. A daddy. A big brother. And a best friend. What I loved most about Grandpa was how much he made Grandma feel happy. He used to say, "Here she is, Miss Darlene Wayde the super model" and it always made her smile. One time he brought Grandma to New York City for a special meal in a special restaurant in New York City for her sixtieth birthday. And I remember how Grandpa used to play the music loud and then he would grab Grandma by the hand, and they would dance. All around the kitchen."

I look up. To make sure they can't hear me whispering the eulogy to myself and I see that they are now over by the car and the woman cop is down on her hunkers and the man cop is standing over her. And I wonder if she is being sick. Then the man cop looks over his shoulder at me and I look back down at the concrete, and I continue to whisper the eulogy to myself.

"And Lord Jesus, I want to also tell you that I loved Grandpa because he was really kind. He used to spend some of his money on cola bottles every Friday from the store on Emmet Road near where he worked cuz he knew they were my favorite candies. And there is that time he brought Grandma to New York for her sixtieth birthday. That musta cost him lots and lots of his money. He was always kind with his money. And kind with his hands. Cuz he would help some of the neighbors around St. Michael's House when they needed help with their plumbing cuz he used to be a plumber when he left school for a few years. All the neighbors in St. Michael's House loved Grandpa. They loved him cuz he was really kind. Oh Lord Jesus, please help my Grandpa get to Heaven. Hail Mary, full of grace," I whisper. "The Lord is with thee... blessed are thou amongst women and blessed is the fruit of thy womb..." I hear footsteps coming toward me. And I see shoes. Four shoes. "Jesus."

9

"IT IS APPROPRIATE TO ADVISE VIEWERS THAT THE FOOTAGE ABOUT TO be shown is extremely distressing," Sarah-Jane said, pursing her lips while glaring down the lens of camera number two.

"Okay, and let's just play the footage in real-time for this last rehearsal," Phil barked at Erica.

Erica nodded as she scrolled her finger up the screen of her iPad and, as she did, the footage began to play on the monitor behind camera number two. Sarah-Jane winced, yet again, at the moment the two police officers took off the victim's handcuffs, lulling him into a false sense of security. Then the man cop tripped him up before the woman cop wrestled with him until she was gripping his two hands tightly behind his back. Sarah-Jane rested her chin on her fist and watched, again, as the man cop wrapped his hands around the victim's neck just as he was praying. He flopped around like a fish to try to save his own life. But his wriggling was all in vain. And suddenly it stopped.

"They'll be marching on the streets within minutes of this going out live tonight," she whispered to Phil. Phil was too busy staring at the monitor in his hands—watching as the police officers casually walked back to their car—leaving the body slumped on the concrete behind them. When he looked up from his monitor, he held out three fingers... then two... then just one. Sarah-

Jane glared her marble green eyes down the lens of camera number two, and pursed her lips tightly together.

"The man killed in the video you just saw was named—"

"Might be good for you to wipe your eye here," Phil said, interrupting. "Even if there's no tear… just wipe your eye."

"Yeah, great idea. I shoulda thought of that," Sarah-Jane said. "Count me in again."

So, Phil held up three fingers… then two… and then one….

Sarah-Jane stared down the lens of camera number two and pressed a thumb into the corner of her eye before sniffling. Then she picked up her cue cards for false comfort, because she certainly didn't need to read from them.

"The man killed in the video you just saw was named Benji Wayde," she said, somberly. "Benji was only twenty-one years of age, but he had the mental capacity of a child. He suffered a stroke on the day he was born and as a result had a severe learning disability. You've just watched him being strangled to death at the hands of two police officers serving the Birmingham Police Department in Connecticut. Their names are Nathan Bennett. And Margaret Zucha. Bennett has been on the force for almost a quarter of a century. Zucha is a brand-new recruit, having just graduated a month prior to this heinous murder that happened in broad daylight eight weeks ago in the middle of the day on June sixteenth. This footage was left anonymously on a USB thumb drive in one of the mailboxes at our studio. We are unsure when it was left there. Or, whom it was left by. But what we can confirm is that as soon as we viewed it, and found it was genuine and authentic, we handed it over to the authorities. I can confirm—"

"Hold on," Phil said, stepping into the golden glow of the kitchen.

"Do you think we should go heavier on the fact that Benji was like… I dunno… a simpleton? Should we go all in on him being like a six-year-old… really emphasize how slow he was from the beginning, instead of explaining how or when we got the video?"

Sarah-Jane turned down her lips, still gripping her cue cards.

"Yeah, you're right," Erica shouted from the shadows. "I know this footage says pretty much all that needs to be said when it comes to this story, but every story needs to be sold. Let's not explicitly tell America that he was like a six-year-old, but that he was a twenty-one-year-old who couldn't even read or write. Let's point out the fact that he was *really* slow... make America fall in love with him. Even though all they've done is watch him being killed."

Sarah-Jane glanced up at Phil. And they both nodded at the same time.

"Perfect," Phil said. "I'll write up some new text and I'll load it onto the cue cards."

When he scuttled off, Sarah-Jane swiveled around in her stool to stare into the shadows of her living room.

"Good call," she shouted into the darkness.

"I learn from the best," a voice shouted back, before pausing... "Fox News."

Sarah-Jane huffed a tiny laugh, then turned back to the kitchen island and pressed a finger to the screen of her phone to note the time. Eight more hours until she went live. Eight more hours until America finally watched this footage.

The marketing plan had gone as Sarah-Jane had hoped it would. All that was required was her face, and her name—sent out to every single one of the two hundred million American Facebook profiles in existence. That wasn't the only marketing the new Zdanski reboot had been getting, though it was the only marketing that they were paying for. Once the Facebook ads went out, every TV network, every newspaper and every website in the country were discussing the soon-to-be-launched reboot of *The Zdanski Show*. Especially as the Facebook ads that went out yesterday morning consisted of Sarah-Jane blinking her beautiful bright green eyes down the camera lens and revealing that she would be showing the country footage that would shake it to its very core. It was a minimalist but slick marketing plan, designed to get America talking. And boy was America talking.

She tapped a finger at her Twitter app, then searched for her own initials—a tic she had long since defaulted to every time her phone screen lit up.

. . .

Can't wait to watch #Zdanski tonight. Wonder what she got for us?

Scroll

SJZ better be apologizing to Meghan Markle. Sorry is the only word that needs to come out of that bitch's mouth tonight. #cancelzdanksi

Scroll

The only thing this Zdanski bitch better be showing us tonight is her tits #SJZisasexgoddess

As she was about to scroll again, she heard feet shuffling across the carpet of her living room, before a flamboyant floral pattern emerged out of the shadows.

"You're early," she said, sarcastically.

"Sorry…" Howie replied, offering her a light one-handed hug. "I've spent the morning with your lawyer. Cody Williamson sure is a smart man. Not that likeable… A bit slimy, really, isn't he? But smart. Very fucking smart."

"And?" Sarah-Jane said.

"Cody cut me a deal," Howie whispered. "A huge deal from CSN. So big, I'm gonna be richer than I ever thought I would be. CSN wants to offer me a six million dollar payoff."

"Six million?" Sarah-Jane said in a high-pitched voice before slapping her hand to her mouth.

"But…" Howie said, awkwardly looking down at his feet. "It comes at a cost. They're paying me off. To retire. If I don't go to any other network… or to any other show, I am entitled to the payoff as a thank you."

Sarah-Jane took her hand from her mouth and slowly nodded.

"Do it, Howie. Retire! You've been with me for twenty-five years. You've done it all. Take your family away. Go live whatever life it is you wanna live. You'll go down in television history as one of the best talk show producers ever. It's six mill, for Heaven's sake, Howie. Take it."

"I've already decided," Howie said, nodding. "I'm gonna take it. It's too good to turn down. I never thought I'd retire early...."

Sarah-Jane slapped him on the bicep.

"It's not early. You're almost sixty. You've been in this game far longer than I have."

Howie inhaled deeply, filling his lungs, then he let it whistle out between his lips slowly, as if he was exhaling a cloud from an expensive cigar.

"The game's gotten away from me. You're right. She's right," he said, pointing into the shadows where Erica was seated. "Everything's online now. TV can't compete. Not anymore. And well, I guess I'm an old TV guy."

"A TV god," Sarah-Jane said, slapping a flat palm to her producer's cheek and caressing it.

He leaned in for another hug. A real hug this time. Not a light, barely touching one-handed greeting. But a tight squeeze. A tight squeeze they both held their breath for.

"I'm gonna miss you. So much," Sarah-Jane whispered in his ear.

Then she heard a shuffling of feet behind Howie and when she looked up, Phil was standing there, shoulder-to-shoulder with Erica.

"I'll miss you too," Phil said. He held out a hand for Howie to shake. The first time he'd ever done so in their two and a half decades of working together.

"I, uh... I need to let you guys get on with your final rehearsals," Howie said. "You're gonna kill it tonight. I gotta go home and talk to my wife... tell her we're off to Italy's great lakes."

Sarah-Jane rubbed the side of Howie's arm, just as he looked as if he might be about to cry.

"Driving around in a Maserati in Italy sure sounds like a more exciting life than being here," she said.

Howie smiled, and then nodded. He couldn't speak. Not without risking tears falling from his eyes. So, he touched Sarah-Jane on the knee, then strode out of the warm glow of the kitchen and into the shadows of the long hallway where he could eventually be heard opening the front door of the penthouse before shutting it with a swoosh and a clank behind him.

When the penthouse fell into silence, Phil looked at the two women either side of him.

"And then there were just three," he said.

NATE BENNETT

I catch a glimpse of my reflection in the shine of the windshield just as I'm about to turn the key in the ignition. It makes me pause... to stare at myself. My eyes look dark, like black holes. And that cut on my face is so raw it looks like a surgery wound. I have to blink my black eyes away from my ugly-ass reflection; to snap myself back to reality.

At least she seems okay. Quiet. But okay. She's not freaking out. She's breathing. Steadily. But her fingers are tapping against her knees, and it looks as if she's staring off into the distance.

"You did great, Zucha," I say, nudging my elbow at her. She doesn't move. She just stares straight ahead, her fingers still drumming against her knees.

I turn the keys in the ignition, and pull the car out, leaving the kak lying slumped down in the rearview mirror. I'll see to it that it's an unsolved murder. I'll place a witness or two who will say they saw some other kak from the projects running from Gray Bridge around this time. It'll send the investigation sideways. Nothing I haven't done before. Nothing that isn't part of what it takes to work the streets.

"Don't worry, Zucha," I say, nudging her again. "I'll sweep all of this up. I've got it from here. You... you... Zucha, listen!" I raise my voice, 'cause she still just looks zoned out. "You're gonna be a great street cop. A great street cop!"

She shifts her eyes to glance at me. Back into the real world. So, I relax back in the driver's seat and try to think it all through. I feel for the USB thumb drive in the chest pocket of my shirt. I need to know what this has to do with eliminating that kak. Or, if it has anything to do with it at all. I didn't know that kak's face. He's not a known criminal. Not to me. Not to the Birmingham PD. Maybe he witnessed what's on this footage… That's probably why he needed eliminating.

Zucha holds her hand up to her eyes to see how much she's shaking.

"Hey," I say, "You did great. I knew you'd be a good street cop soon as I met you."

She glances at me again, then back straight ahead. But her fingers stay on her knees. They're not drumming anymore.

"He better be a bad person, Nate," she says.

And I feel relieved that she's talking.

"Zucha," I say, "the force knows who they're eliminating and why they need them eliminated. Don't worry. We did a good thing for the streets of Birmingham today. Me and you. We made these streets safer."

I reach out to her shoulder and squeeze it and then when I notice her fingers begin to drum against her knees again, I flick the switch for the sirens, then press the button to flash the lights before stepping heavier on the gas. She's pushed backed to her seat with the speed and is forced to hold one hand onto the dashboard and the other to the window next to her just for balance. The noise and the lights will help snap her out of it; remind her of her power.

And that makes me think of those who hold the real power. The Governor. And the chief of the dirtiest precinct in the entire state of Connecticut. Costello. I wonder what the fuck they're up to. How deep into this they are. I know Costello is known for bending the rules… hell, he taught me all about the streets. But I never thought he'd go out of his way to order a hit. That's taking it to a whole new level. A level I've never played at before.

AIMEE STREET

I pant short, sharp, quiet breaths into the hand I slapped across my mouth as soon as the cops approached him. I was afraid somebody would hear me breathing. And then they'd come and strangle me until my body stopped flapping around, too.

I inch myself up a little over the small wall of the bridge and stare down at his body slumped onto the concrete. Then I glance toward the police car, just as it pulls away slowly.

"Holy fucking shit," I whisper. "Holy. Fucking. Shit."I turn around and stare down from the bridge again. Yep. He's still there. There's still a Black guy slumped on the concrete fifty feet beneath me. A Black guy I witness being strangled to death by two fucking cops. Two fucking street cops in uniform. In broad daylight. Holy. Fucking. Shit.

My breathing gets all short and sharp again and so I place my hand back to my mouth to keep quiet even though I no longer have to. Not since the two killer cops have driven off; leaving me alone with the dead body beneath me. Maybe I should go down there, make sure this guy's dead. Maybe I should just call an ambulance anyway. Just in case he's not. Or… maybe I should call the cops… but they were the cops. Holy shit! I dunno what to do.

I should probably watch the footage on my phone; to see if I got a good look at Bennett and Zucha while they were strangling this poor fucker to death. I raise my finger over the video on my phone, not sure if I want to press play. I don't need to see it again, do I? I've already witnessed it. In real life. I witnessed a fucking murder!

I swipe out of my camera, and into the dial pad, and my trembling finger taps at the number nine, then one... and for some reason I hold my finger over the one again....

Then I slap my hand to my mouth and this time a cry bursts its way from the back of my eyes and my nose and I'm not sure if I'm crying because I'm so sad for this poor guy... whoever he is... or whether I'm crying 'cause I'm afraid. So, fucking afraid. And so fucking alone.

I decide to pocket my phone, then I get to my feet and begin to jog my way back to the rented car, panting short, sharp breaths and sniffing and swiping away tears and snot as I go.

"Holy. Fucking. Shit!" I whisper to myself. Again.

I snatch open the car door, slide myself into the driver's seat and I lean my forehead on to the top of the steering wheel, making sure I don't touch the horn. I don't wanna make any noises. I can't make any noises. I'm literally at the scene of a murder.

I think it all through; the two of them nonchalantly walking over to him; Zucha releasing the handcuffs; Bennett tripping the poor guy up; Zucha pinning his arms behind his back; Bennett squeezing both of his hands around the guy's neck. As tight as he could. I watched it all unfold on my iPhone screen while my other hand was covering my mouth. And then the poor guy stopped wriggling and they just nonchalantly walked back to their police car. As if they were having a stroll in the park.

I take my forehead off the steering wheel then I lean back into the car seat, pick up my phone and scroll to my messages. The number that was texted to me to get to Gray Bridge... I know who it was. It was him. Obviously. The guy who rented me this car I'm sitting in. The guy who led me here. So, I tap the number and then press the phone to my ear while it rings... and rings... and rings....

"Hello."

"Holy fucking shit," I say. It seems it's all I have said out loud since I became a witness to a murder.

"Aim... what's going on?"

"Holy fucking shit," I say. Again. And then I start talking really fast, "they just walked over and then she held him onto the ground, and he just wrapped his hands around his neck, and he squeezed, and he squeezed and then—"

"Whoa, whoa," he says, "calm down, Aim. Take a breath. And then tell me... tell me what happened."

I take a deep inhale, and then I push the air out through my thin lips making a whistling sound straight into the phone. As the whistling comes, so too do the tears. And I'm crying. Full-on crying. Sobbing and shaking. In a silver rented Nissan fucking Altima in the middle of nowhere.

"They. Killed. Some. Guy." I say, each word shaking out of me.

"What the fuck?" he says. "The cops? The cop you went looking for killed a guy?"

"Y-y-yeah," I say. And then I try to suck up the tears while I wipe the sleeve of my blazer over my wet face. "Two cops. They just walked over to this Black guy and started strangling him... and he's dead. I know he's dead. He's just flat out under Gray Bridge. And they... they just walked away as if nothing happened."

The phone goes silent. All I can hear is the echo my own heavy breathing reverberating back into my ear.

Then he coughs twice, clearing his throat.

"And did you... did you catch it on video?" he asks.

"Yeah. Yeah. I have it all. I caught it all... just like you said. The iPhone is a journalist's best friend... let me send it to you. I'll text you the video."

"No!"

"Huh?"

"Don't send me anything. Let me uh... let me think... lemme think.... Holy shit! You really have it on video?"

"Yeah," I say. "I recorded the whole darn thing."

"Jesus Christ, Aim," he says. "Listen…" And then it goes all silent again, except for the sound of my heavy breathing echoing back into my ear. "Listen… I need you to come meet me. You good for that? Can you come meet me?"

I sob. A heavy sob that makes more tears stream from my eyes.

"Sure," I say, sniffling. "Where do you want me to meet you?"

MAGGIE ZUCHA

I hold my hand out level in front of my face and stare it. Again.

It's barely shaking. Not anymore. Prob'ly 'cause Nate drove all the way here with the sirens blaring and the lights flashing and the wheels spinning. And it distracted me. My hands wouldn't stop shaking before he turned on all that noise. I could feel my fingers on my lap... shivering and wobbling and tipping and tapping. And my head was spinning. Spinning and dancing. Kinda like from one thought to another without even thinking at all.

Nate kept saying to me, "You're gonna be a great street cop, Zucha. You got it. You got what it takes." But my head was spinning so much I didn't even answer him. I just kept seeing it. My arms, wrapped around his waist, pinning his hands behind his back. He was wriggling, like a fish. But I didn't let go. 'Cause Nate said once we commit, we gotta commit. So, we did. We both committed. Until all the wriggling stopped.

"You okay?" Nate says. Again. And suddenly it's all quiet 'cause the lights have stopped flashing around me, and the sirens have stopped wailing, and all I can hear is the sound of the signal ticking 'cause Nate is about the pull into the parking lot of the precinct.

I clear my throat and I nod, and I sit forward.

"Yeah. I'm fine," I say.

"You gonna be a great street cop, Zucha," he says. Again. For about the fiftieth time in the ten minutes it took the car to race back to the precinct. "Now, all we gotta do is go inside, hand this USB thumb drive over to Costello, and be called heroes for getting it to him. We don't talk about anything else... we don't mention the mission."

"Wait," I say. "Wait... wait... wait. Does us killing that guy have something to do with the USB thumb drive? Is that what you said?"

Nate slowly pulls the car into a parking space before answering me, and he reaches out and squeezes my shoulder, sniffs, and turns away from me.

"I don't know," he says. "I know as much as you. That we were given missions and we... y'know... we completed them. The two of them. We retrieved the USB thumb drive. We eliminated the kak. They were our two missions today. But, street cops... y'know... the measure of a true street cop," he turns back to face me, "is that they abide by the saying, "what goes on on the streets, stays on the streets." Street cops don't talk. We're full of action, not full of shit. All me 'n' you gotta do now is go inside, hand the USB thumb drive over to Costello, and we say nothing... that's it. We say nothing. Job done."

I nod my head and when he turns around to open his door and climb out of the car, I hold a hand in front of my face and squint at it. It's still not shaking. I don't know why it's not shaking.

I follow him, climbing out of the car before I jog after him across the parking lot to where he has pulled open the front door for me. We enter the small, square porch of the precinct and when he lets the first door close behind us, he grabs my shoulder and when I spin around, he presses two of his fingers to my chest.

"You nailed it, Zucha. You gonna be a great street cop. But remember, what goes on on the streets, stays on the streets."

He takes his fingers off me, curls one back down and presses the one that's still upright against his lips.

I nod. Again. 'Cause I have a feeling in my stomach that if I do try to speak that vomit will come out instead of words. Then Nate pulls open the second door and we can hear the chatter of the precinct and I have to hold my two hands to my stomach.

"It's true, I see," the man behind the reception desk says, "Nate Bennett is back in uniform."

"Whaddup, Ferguson?" Nate says while he's pulling open the door on the opposite side of the reception area. I don't say hello to Ferguson. And he doesn't say anything to me. He never has. I skip after Nate, along the narrow corridor that leads straight to Chief Costello's office, holding my hand up to my face again as we walk. I think it might be shaking again. But it's hard to tell. 'Cause I'm skipping and walking at the same time. Then he turns around and holds two of his fingers to my chest again, leaning the horrible black cut on his cheek toward my face.

"Aren't you intrigued, Zucha?" he whispers.

I stare at his cut.

"About what?" I say.

"About what's on this fucking thing?"

He leans away from me, holds the USB thumb drive up and twists it around in his fingers. It makes me think all the way back through the day; to him beating up the guy in the office; to me chasing down Roseanna Redford and bringing her on a drive with us; to us watching the start of this USB thumb drive back in Nate's stinking home office; to us stopping that guy at Gray Bridge; to me... with my arms wrapped tightly around his waist, catching his hands behind his back while he wriggled like a fish; to us racing back here in the car, the sirens wailing, the lights flashing, my hands shaking.

"Sure," I say.

He looks up and down the corridor, then puts his hand on my back and leads me through one of the doors along the corridor and into a tiny office that has a tiny desk inside it with a large computer monitor on it.

He pops the lid off the USB thumb drive, and holds down the standby button on the flatscreen monitor on top of the tiny desk, making it rattle.

"Keep an eye," he whispers to me. I look around at the door

behind us and pull it open a little so I can look out, up and down the corridor.

"Clear," I whisper back.

Then I hold my hands to my stomach again. Because it's getting wavy.

When I look back over my shoulder, Nate is shoving the USB thumb drive into the side of the monitor. Then he grabs the mouse and drags it around in circles, tapping his fingers against it. I poke my head out of the door and look up and down the corridor again. It's still clear. So, I close the door quietly and join Nate behind the desk, staring at the black-and-white screen as it fast-forwards through still footage of two big black bins standing in a concrete alleyway.

"You okay?" he says to me as the screen whizzes by in front of us.

"Uh-huh," I say, still holding both hands to my stomach.

"I mean it… you gonna be a great street cop, Zucha."

And then I point at the screen, 'cause I see Governor Haversham.

"There he is," I say.

Nate takes his finger off the mouse and the footage plays in real-time, showing Haversham sucking on a cigarette, resting his back against the wall.

I don't know what's going on. Not just on this screen. But in real-life. In my real-life.

"Who the hell is she?" Nate says, stabbing his fat finger to the screen.

We both lean closer to squint at the young woman with long white hair, draped in a long white coat, under which I can make out long white boots that go all the way up to her knees. I can see the top of them through the gap in her coat when she walks. And I take my hands off my stomach, rest them on the top of the desk and lean closer to the screen. I actually feel like a cop. As if I'm investigating.

I watch her as she grabs Governor Haversham's cigarette from his fingers and flicks it away. Then she pins him up against the concrete wall next to one of the bins. Suddenly she's kinda, like, kissing him all over his chin and his neck while she's wrestling with the buckle of his belt. Then, she's down there, while he leans his head back against the wall, looking up at the night sky with a big grin stretched across his handsome face.

"The fuck?" Nate says. "We out chasing this shit all day, just to save Haversham's ass. He musta realized the suck job he got last night in an alleyway behind the Irish bar he was in mighta been caught on the CCTV from the office next door."

"Wait," I say, my head shaking. "What? What's going on?"

"That's why I was brought in. They knew I could do a job off the books. That I wouldn't need a warrant to see this through." Nate presses his finger to the screen again. "And they couldn't get a warrant 'cause they'd have to explain why. That's all we've been doing today. Saving the Governor's ass."

"This is the secret mission? Wait. Hold on. What the hell's going on, Nate? What's all this gotta do with the guy we kill—"

Nate holds his hand up, stopping me 'cause we can hear voices. Voices coming down the corridor. Nate clicks the mouse, then snatches the USB thumb drive from the monitor and pops the lid back on before tucking it into the chest pocket of his navy shirt.

"Remember," he says, leaning closer to me. "What goes on on the streets, stays on the streets. You get that, don't you, Zucha?"

"Of course," I say, nodding. "What goes on on the streets, stays on the streets."

Then the office door slaps open. And Chief Costello appears, with Governor Haversham and his ugly bodyguard standing over each of his shoulders.

AIMEE STREET

It's so dark under here that I can barely make out the white lines in the parking space I'm trying to reverse the Nissan Altima in between. I tap the brake, and then I pull the key from the ignition and get out into the dark, dingy underground parking lot. And not for the first time today, I don't know whether I'm being brave or just plain stupid.

"Hey," a voice calls out. It echoes around the concrete. And I instantly suck in a sharp breath through the gaps of my crooked teeth before spinning my head around, squinting into the darkness looking for where the voice came from. Nothing. Not even a flicker.

"Hey. Here. Behind you," the voice says.

I turn around, and squinting through the darkness again, I ease myself forward… until I see his heavy figure, holding a door open in the back corner of the parking lot.

"Holy fuck," I say, making my way toward him, racing away from the darkness. He pushes the door open wider with his back and I walk past him into a concrete stairwell. When he stands away, allowing the door to close with a clunk, I exhale a deep breath and as I do, tears come with it—streaming down my cheeks again.

"Hey," he says, brushing the hair from my face. "Hey…." He engulfs me in a big bear hug, squeezing my face into his chest.

I finally take one step back, reach into my pocket for my phone and then I hand it to him while sniffling and swiping the tears away from my cheeks with the cuff of my blazer.

He taps his finger to the screen, pressing play, and then he looks up over the phone at me before blinking his eyes back down to the footage. He moves his head back an inch, squinting more, and I already know that he's just watched the moment the cops begin to walk from their car toward the poor guy handcuffed by the foot of the bridge. Suddenly his face inches closer to the screen... closer again. And then he sucks in air through his teeth while his big, baggy eyes widen... and widen... and then he quickly glances up over the phone at me again.

"Holy fucking shit," he says.

"That's what I keep saying," I tell him. And then I shiver. Maybe from the cold. Maybe from the fright.

"Hey," he says, tapping his finger to the screen, pausing the video. "Let me get you upstairs."

He takes off his jacket, places it over my shoulders and then leads me through another door and into a long gray-brick-walled hallway.

"Where the hell is this?" I say. "Some underground bunker?"

He laughs out through his nostrils, and it makes me picture his horrible dancing nose hairs again. That makes me shiver even more.

"This is where I live," he says.

He turns, into another gray-brick-walled hallway, at the end of which is a large silver door. When we reach it, he presses his finger to a small pad and suddenly a green light blinks on and there's a vibration and a thump behind the silver door before it slides open. He takes a step into a tiny silver elevator while I look around at the gray walls, wondering if I'm gonna be brave or just plain stupid to set foot inside after him. I notice he looks agitated, scratching at his neck. But I've been brave all day. So, fuck it. I step in after him.

"Are we gonna call the police?" I say.

"Jeez, no, no," he replies, still scratching at his neck. "Listen... I'll... Listen," he reaches toward me and sweeps the hair away from my face again, then leans in closer. "I just have to think it all through. Right now, I'm a little...." He puffs out his cheeks while the silver box we're in rattles, then lifts with a swift swoosh.

"I know," I say, "the footage, it's kinda... wow."

"It's not just the footage," he says.

And I squint at him, and look around at the tin box we're rising higher and higher in.

"Where the fuck is it you live?" I ask. "On top of a crane?"

He laughs again out of his nose, and this time I'm close enough to catch them—his nose hairs dancing.

Suddenly, the silver box stops rising and rattling and there's a small hissing sound before the door slides open. I have to blink as I soak in the view in the distance.

"Jesus H. Christ," I say, placing a foot onto the plush chocolate-brown carpet. I don't know whether to stare at the artwork adorning the walls, or the immaculate view out of the floor-to-ceiling windows right in front of me. He tosses his wallet onto a side cabinet and when I take two more steps forward, I find myself among a cozy velvet land of sofas and armchairs, all facing a television screen that stretches the width of the entire back wall.

"You're gonna wanna sit down," he says, turning to face me.

I glance at him. Then past him at the view out of the floor-to-ceiling windows. A view I've only ever seen on TV before. Or, maybe on a postcard. Almost the entirety of lower Manhattan, starting with perfect sight of the top half of The Empire State Building before the high rises beyond it stretch all the way toward the Freedom Tower in the distance

"Well..." I say, "You gonna start by telling me who the fuck you are to afford a place like this?"

He laughs again through his nostrils, but I'm still staring at the skyline to notice his nose hairs dancing this time.

"I, uh... well, I, uh...."

"Honey, that you? You home?" a voice calls from behind the kitchen on the far side of the apartment. My heart races with a panic as the sound of footsteps make their way toward me. And then I gasp. She looks like a waxwork model, striding toward me —one of her perfectly manicured eyebrows rising.

"Who's this, Phil?" she says, looking even more striking in the flesh.

"Sarah-Jane," he says, scratching at his beard again, "I think you're gonna wanna sit down."

She glances at him, then back at me, her eyebrows almost knitting together.

"No... tell me. Tell me now, Phil. Who is she?"

He scratches his beard again. Really awkwardly.

"She's your daughter," he says. "Our daughter."

NATE BENNETT

"Ah, there you two are," Costello says. "We heard you were back in the precinct. Whatcha doing in here?"

"Yes sir, sir, yes sir." Zucha says. And I stare at her, wondering if she genuinely has what it takes to keep it together. Bitch better keep it together.

"Hey, Costello," I say. I take the USB thumb drive from my pocket and twist it around in my fingers.

"Good man," he says, snatching it from me before handing it back over his shoulder to the Governor.

Haversham stares at it for a moment, then looks back up at me.

"You sure this is the only copy?"

I nod.

"Yeah. Well, there were two copies," I say. "One digital copy that we permanently deleted from the office system. And this hard copy on a USB thumb drive that we had to track down. We got it. That is the only one."

Costello slaps the side of my shoulder.

"Great fuckin' work, Nate. And you, Zucha," he says, turning to her. "You keep this guy in check, huh?"

She breathes out a deep, loud exhale and I'm not sure if the next thing that comes out of her mouth is gonna be words or vomit.

"Sir, yes, sir."

"The fuck, Zucha," Costello says, shrugging his shoulder, "what I tell you this morning about all this "sir" stuff? Call me Chief. Or, Costello. You don't gotta suck my dick every time I ask you a question."

He laughs. Then looks back at Haversham who laughs. And then I laugh, too. 'Cause that shit was funny.

"Yes, sir," she says. She glances up at me, and I notice her fingers are starting to tap against her belt.

"Zucha did a great job, today, Costello," I say. "She's a natural. A real street cop. She took no shit. In fact, it was Zucha who got her hands on the USB thumb drive. She did all the hard work today. I'm proud of her. She's gonna make a great street cop."

I punch Zucha on the side of the shoulder and I notice Costello point his lips downward, then he slowly nods his head. That's normally a sign that says he's impressed.

"Good girl," he says. "Your report from cop school didn't exactly glow, Zucha... but as I've always said, you don't know a true cop until they get out on the streets."

He grins and then from over his shoulder Haversham leans closer, staring at us, his eyes shifting between me and Zucha.

"You two okay? You look a bit... I dunno... shady. Does she not speak?" he says to me.

"She's quiet like a mouse. But has the heart of a lion, Governor," I say. He squints at her, then back at me with his Clark Gable eyes.

"Did you two fucking watch this thing?" he says. He holds the USB thumb drive up, twisting it in his fingers.

I find my head shaking at first. Then the words fall out of my mouth.

"No, no, course not," I say.

I look at Zucha. But she says nothing, her fingers still tapping against her leather belt.

"You," Haversham says, pointing at her. "Did you watch this?"

She shifts her feet, then brushes her hands down her shirt before she clears her throat.

"No, sir," she says. "We've just got back to the precinct now. We were gonna come straight to the chief's office but thought we'd just take a breather in here first, to talk about the paperwork we may need to—"

"No fucking paperwork. Not for this," Costello says. "Like I said earlier, this investigation was off the books. That's why we sent you out there, Nate. To make sure this got done without any need for paperwork."

He slaps me on the side of the shoulder again. And then he pats Zucha on top of her head as if she's a puppy dog.

"Okay. No paperwork required," I say. I reach my arm around Zucha and squeeze her closer to me. "But we must celebrate this chick, huh? Popped her cherry on the streets today. First investigation over. And she killed it."

Zucha giggles awkwardly.

"Hold on…" Haversham says, "you two sure there are no more copies of this?"

"Nothing!" Zucha says. "Like officer Bennett said, there was a digital copy that he made sure was deleted, and there was this one copy on the USB that I got back. This footage… whatever it is… it's all yours. And yours only, Governor Haversham. You have our word."

She holds the stare of his heavy brown eyes while I push a relief laugh out silently through my nose.

"Great job, guys," Costello says. "You can both mark that success as the end of your shift."

He goes to open the door, but I tap him on the back, to get his attention.

"What about me, Chief?" I say. "You asked me back to do this job… but am I… am I back on the force for good?"

Costello glances up at Haversham and the Governor looks at me before nodding his head once.

"Yeah… you're back for good," Costello says.

My heart immediately begins to race with excitement. 'Cause I belong on the streets. I'm nobody if I'm not on the streets.

AIMEE STREET

She flattens down the creases on her dress, then sits into the oversized milk chocolate-colored armchair. He's sitting adjacent to her, re-crossing his legs while slouched into the far corner of the dark chocolate-colored sofa. I remain standing. Even though Phil has repeatedly motioned to the seat next to him. I don't want to sit. I can't sit. I can't even move.

She leans her elbow onto the arm of her chair, then rests her chin onto her clenched fist and looks me up and down.

"I shoulda known," I say, opting to speak first. "Y'know why I shoulda known? 'Cause I've always fucking resented you." She raises one of her eyebrows at me, keeping her chin leaning on her clenched fist. "Every time I've watched you on TV, all's I've ever wanted to do is reach inside it and slap you across the face."

Phil uncrosses his legs and leans forward on the sofa.

"Hold on," he says. "Let's not start this all out on the wrong foot...."

"Why's she here?" Sarah-Jane says. "Why today?"

I sigh. And then suddenly I am moving; turning around to take in the artwork hanging on their velvet chocolate-brown wallpaper. This feels way too much like a dream; like an hallucination. This Ghost Train weed sure is a whole new level.

"I got something to show you, Sarah-Jane," he says. And I spin away from the artwork.

"We've got something to show you. *We*," I say, just as he's lifting himself out of the sofa, my phone tucked into his palm, stretching it toward America's sweetheart. My fucking birth mother. I can't believe it. I take in the two of them while they stare at my phone. And it becomes immediately ironic to me that I've felt lucky my whole life; yet in reality America's most beautiful TV anchor is my birth mother, and I didn't inherit any of her looks. Just his—the looks of my birth father who's so gross that he's been making me feel genuinely ill all day.

"Holy fucking shit," Sarah-Jane says.

And that's it. That's something we all share in common. We've all said, "holy fucking shit," the very first time we've watched those two cops strangle that poor dude in broad daylight.

I reach into the pocket of my jacket and grip my vaporizer. When I pull it out, I immediately hold down the standby button, noticing my hand is shivering. When the vaporizer buzzes, I suck a cloud of weed down to my lungs to help me relax, just as Sarah-Jane is slapping a hand over her mouth.

"Holy fucking shit!" she says. Again. Phil glances over the phone at me, just as I'm exhaling a large cloud of weed into his plush penthouse apartment. "This is huge. This is… this is…" she stands, placing her hands on her hips. "This is gonna be the biggest story of the century. Two white cops just walking over to a black guy and strangling him to death. How did we… how the fuck did we get this footage?"

"Aim," Phil says, nodding his head toward me. "Aim did it all. She caught it all."

Sarah-Jane death stares me, then looks back up into his ugly mug.

"But how… her? Our daughter, Phil? What the fuck's going on?"

"Listen," he says, heaving himself to his feet. And suddenly the three of us are standing in a triangle across their chocolate-colored rug that's draped over their chocolate-colored fucking carpet. "Here's the thing…" Phil scratches at his beard. "I was doing my usual thing this morning… going through all the newspapers. And…." He scratches at his beard again. And as he does,

Sarah-Jane gives me another death stare; a side glance of those huge famous green eyes. It makes me stare into his tiny round brown eyes, which makes me roll my tiny round brown eyes around. "I came across this story in the *Daily Connecticut*, about this cop who'd been invited back to the force after being suspended for a string of abuses of power against Black people. Beatings. Framings. Suspicious deaths. This guy was shoulder-deep in shit. knew he was a walking, breathing crime story. I remember thinking... there's a fucking reality TV show if ever there was one. So...." He scratches at his beard again. A weird nervous tic for somebody who looked so unshakeable to me all day. Maybe it's her. Maybe she has the power to reduce anyone to a nervous wreck. "I guess I created a reality show for him," he says. And I immediately stare at the vaporizer in my hand and begin to think this must be the weed. "I started digging around," he continues saying, "hacking into his computer, to see if he left any clues about his abuses of power... any story I could use to manipulate him. And... well, I found a treasure trove. This asshole's been watching kiddies. Thousands of online videos."

"What the fuck?" Sarah-Jane whispers. And then she looks up at me again. "I don't get it. I don't get it," she repeats.

"Well..." Phil readjusts his feet on the rug, then rubs his hands together, "I turned the pages in the newspaper. And there's another headline. Some young guy tried to kill himself last night. He was about to leap his ass off the roof of some shopping mall downtown. Only a security guard grabbed him, saved his life. Well, I... uh, I found him. Found him online. On Facebook. He posted on Facebook that he was going to Yoga at noon today and...."

"Jesus H. Christ," I say. Suddenly my hands are sweating. And I think I need to lie down on the chocolate-colored rug beneath my feet and just fall asleep and hope that when I wake the fuck up, I wake up in my own bed. And Sarah-Jane Zdanski isn't my birth mother. And my birth father isn't actually telling me right now that he ordered a killing... and then used me to catch it all on video.

"I guess I put two and two together and I...."

"You manipulated this?" Sarah-Jane says, tapping her finger against my phone. "This? You manipulated this?"

"I didn't think it would work... I didn't know what would happen," he says. "All I knew was that I had a dirty cop by the balls," he says. "But I wasn't sure how far I could push him. I... I..." he scratches at his beard again, "I tested him... got him to empty his savings. When he did that, I knew I had him. I knew he'd do anything for me once there was the threat of his kiddie porn obsession getting out. So, I led him to... you know... to this other guy. This Benji guy. That's the one who's been killed. Benji Wayde. He lived in the projects at the back ass of Birmingham, Connecticut. He was a no-hoper. Tough life. So tough, he wanted to end it all, didn't he? So...."

My breathing becomes heavier. And I'm certain I'm about to collapse to the rug. So, I try to breathe in through my nose, slowly, and then out through my mouth slowly. But she looks at me — my birth mother — with those big green eyes I didn't fucking genetically inherit. And when those famous eyes meet mine, I turn away and begin walking toward their plush kitchen that's divided from the living room by a marble island that looks as if it's the size of my entire apartment. When I reach the sink, I turn the nozzle on the faucet, and then go in search of a glass, opening one cupboard, then the next... then the next.

"Just above the coffee grinder," my birth mother yells toward me. And I take two steps to my left, open the cupboard above the coffee grinder and grab a heavy whiskey glass. I fill it with cold water, then down it in one gulp while staring at my reflection in the glistening brown backwash tiles of the kitchen. When I blink, I see him—wriggling like a fish.

As soon as I turn the faucet off, I hear her. Whispering. Whispering my name.

"Well..." Phil says, before he pauses to rub his two hands together, "Aim lives just outside Birmingham, Connecticut. So, when I was thinking about who the camera person for my reality TV show could be, I just... I thought of her. She's training to be a journalist, aren't you, Aim?"

I place the empty whiskey glass onto the ridiculously large

chocolate-colored marble top of the kitchen island, then walk toward him so that the three of us are all standing in a triangle on the chocolate-colored rug again.

"Kinda," I say. "Haven't been to a class in weeks. But... but... how did you know all this? How did you know I wanted to be a journalist? How the fuck do you even know who I am?"

Sarah-Jane stares at him.

"I've uh... I've always known who you are, Aim." She exhales a loud sigh and then she shifts her feet and places two of her fingers against each of her temples. "I've never let you out my sight," he continues. "I saw you move into foster home after foster home. I watched you form a friendship with Mykel... that kid you've known since you were both six-year-olds. I saw to it that you stayed on the right path. I made sure you were accepted into Kennedy High School. Made sure you got into journalism college. That apartment you live in didn't exactly fall into your lap."

My memories begin to collapse in my mind, like a domino set.

"You? *You?*" I say. "You're the reason I've always thought I was lucky? Lucky Aim. *You?*"

He scratches at his beard again. Then he nods at me, sheepishly.

"I didn't want you to fall into any traps," he says, "so whenever it looked like you were gonna fall into a trap... I just, y'know... I intervened. I just made sure there was always a safety net for you."

"My whole life, I always felt I was being followed," I say. And suddenly all of my memories come flooding back to life, as if the domino set has reversed itself in my mind. "Holy fucking shit."

"Holy fucking shit is right," Sarah-Jane says. She takes a large step towards Phil, then slaps him on the chest. "You're a genius, Phil. This footage... it's gonna cause riots on the streets of America."

MAGGIE ZUCHA

When we get outside, to the parking lot, I hold my flat hand level to my face again. It's not shaking. Not anymore.

"You did great, Zucha," Nate whispers to me.

And I say, "thank you," cause I believe him. I believe I did a great job. He's happy with me. Costello is happy with me. Governor Haversham is happy with me. And now I know I'm going to be a cop. A real cop. A proper street cop.

Nate leans up against one of the cop cars and covers his face with his hands. He does that a lot. Probably why the cuts on his face never heal.

"Hey, Zucha," he says, "you continue following orders the way you do, you're gonna go down in history as one of Birmingham's finest-ever chick cops. I promise you. I ain't never seen no chick cop with the balls you have."

I nod. It's kinda like a thank you nod. And then I step closer to him, just as that guy wriggling like a fish flashes through my mind again.

"Thanks, Nate," I say.

"You uh... you wanna come back to my place?" he asks. "For lunch. Not on a date or anything like that... just, y'know...."

I exhale a deep sigh as I look up and down the parking lot.

"A date? Me and you?"

"No," he says, leaning away from the car. "That's what I said, it wouldn't be a date. *Not* a date. Just lunch. At my place."

"I think I'm gonna go home, Nate. And just… take a long, hot bath. I feel, I dunno…."

He reaches a hand to the back of my neck and pulls me closer to his face, until our foreheads rest against each other.

"Great idea. Take some time to yourself, Zucha. But if you feel you need to talk to anybody, call me. And me only. You know where I live."

I can taste his breath. It's raw. And warm.

"Sure," I say.

He grips the back of my neck even tighter.

"Whaddya say that when we see Costello in the morning that we ask him if we can be partners permanently, huh?"

I nod my head. Even though my forehead is stuck to his. And I wanna get away. Not 'cause I don't like Nate. I do. I think I do. But just 'cause his breath is so raw. And so, like, warm or something.

"Sure," I say.

"Great. 'Cause me and you… we can be king and queen of these streets. We can rule the fucking streets, baby!"

"Sure," I say. Again. And then he finally lets the back of my neck go and I take one step backward just to get away from the rawness of his warm breath.

"They'll be making a fuckin' TV show about us… Bennett and Zucha."

He laughs.

And I do too. A fake laugh. The type of fake laugh I've learnt to laugh ever since I started as a cop.

"I'd watch that," I say.

Then I slap him on the side of the shoulder, turn on my heels and begin to walk away. 'Cause I really need a bath. I need to wash everything off of me.

"See you tomorrow, Zucha, okay?" he shouts.

"See you tomorrow, Nate."

"And remember…" he shouts even louder. "What goes on on the streets…"

I wave my hand in the air as I walk away from him.
"Stays on the streets," I shout back.

AIMEE STREET

"This is the one," Phil says, stepping closer to her. "This is where we go it alone."

Sarah-Jane blows a raspberry through her lips.

"No. We need to take this to CSN. Get it on air on Wednesday night. It'll be the biggest story in decades. It'll be even bigger than the George Floyd killing. This is premeditated, unmistakable murder in broad daylight. It'll start a revolution. The movement… it'll go stratospheric. They'll be marching on every street in America."

"Exactly," Phil says. "Stratospheric. That is why this is where we go it alone."

She covers her face with both hands and when she removes them, she's not staring back at the great ape like she had been. But at me. Her daughter. The daughter she had forgotten she had. When she moves closer to me and reaches out a hand, I turn away.

"You can touch me when I invite you to touch me," I say.

She bites her bottom lip, and nods at me. Slowly. And up this close, it's paining me how beautiful she is.

"What do you think?" she says to me.

"He's right," I say. She raises one of her perfectly sculpted eyebrows at me. "Who the hell watches TV anymore? Every single network is witnessing a dramatic fall in viewing figures. This story is going to make a huge splash either way. So, do you want CSN to benefit from that coverage. Or, you?"

She squints at me, fidgets with her hands, and then turns to the great ape again.

"But… how?"

"We'll work it out," he says. "You've talked about setting up your own visual podcast for two years now. We've discussed this… your own channel. Where you are the host. The floor manager. The producer. The director. The CEO. The President. The owner. You'd own the whole fucking caboodle. A podcast and a YouTube channel. *The Zdanski Show*… online. For anybody to watch or to listen to. Anywhere in the world. Anywhere they go."

When she covers her eyes with her fingers again, I notice they're trembling. Maybe she is human after all.

"But we'd… we can't. We're contracted to CSN. We can't just set up our own channel."

"We'll wiggle out of the contract," he says.

"We can't do that," she says, removing her hands from her face. "We're tied in for another three years."

I take one step forward.

"What about the interview you've been plugging non-stop this past week," I say.

The two of them twist to stare at me.

"What about it?" Phil says.

"Do it then."

"Do what?" Sarah-Jane says.

"Say something that will force CSN to cancel you."

"What the fuck are you talking about?"

"When you interview Meghan Markle, say something outrageous… something that will get you canceled from CSN."

She squints at me. And then Phil claps his hands together twice and reaches out to grab my bicep.

"You fucking genius," he says. Then he turns back to her, still clutching my arm. "Call Meghan out. Call her a liar. Live on TV. The network will flip you off… void your contract. Half the nation will agree with you. Half will hate you. But everybody will be taking about you. And then… then if we launch our own podcast and a channel through YouTube off the back of that controversy with this... with this..." he points at my phone, "the whole of America will tune in. This will get a hundred million views in a matter of hours. A hundred million sets of eyes on your debut show... it'll be the biggest launch in the history of American media. And we'll own it all... the whole caboodle. You'll be the most-watched star America's ever had."Sarah-Jane holds a hand to her forehead, then she takes two steps backward and collapses down into the chocolate-colored armchair she had first sat in with her chin resting on her fist while she eyeballed me for the very first time. Only this time she's fidgeting with her fingers; fidgeting with them while her head begins to nod up and down... really slowly.

I look at him; at the raw red scratches across the patches of beard on his neck; at his fat bulbous nose with the gross long hairs hanging from them; at his greasy hair; his jowly chins. When he stares back at me, I look away and then suddenly, without warning, she's out of her armchair striding toward me.

"What about her?" she says.

"Aim... well, Aim can come with us," Phil says. "She has no family. No friends. She can start a new life. With us."

"The fuck I will," I say.

"A new life as a producer. On the biggest show in America. On one million dollars a year."

I have to stop myself from gasping. Then I take a step forward, closer to her.

"This is my footage. That's my phone."

"Two million a year."

I glance at him. Then back at her.

"I see three people here," I say. "Thirty-three and a third percent each. I think that's the least you two owe me."

She pushes her tongue into her cheek, then steps closer to me and stretches out a hand.

"Deal," she says.

I stare down at her hand.

"You can touch me when I invite you to touch me," I reply.

"Well, ain't that just perfect," she says. "A cute little family business." She takes another step toward me, so close I begin to scan her perfect face for signs of a blemish… any blemish. I can't find one. "But we'll uh… we'll have to give you a new identity, of course," she says. "A new name. A new look. She picks up a handful of my matted hair from my shoulder, "chop this all off… most of it anyway. Maybe give you a crisp bob, huh? Red. Red hair would suit your pale face."

"Red hair does suit me," I say. "I actually started the day as a redhead."

She squints at my face.

"A new nose. And definitely new teeth. You could be pretty, you know. Being pretty isn't about looks. It's about money, Aim," she says. "And I guess we gotta stop calling you Aim, don't we? What is it we should call you… whatcha want your new name to be?"

10

"Erica!"

Sarah-Jane swiveled in her new hairdresser's chair when she heard heavy Doc Martin boots sweeping their way down her chocolate-brown-carpeted hallway. When Erica turned into what used to be one of the penthouse's spare bedrooms but had recently been turned into a makeup room with three needlessly large vanity mirrors, Mollie moved to one side.

"Whatcha think?" Sarah-Jane asked Erica.

Erica held two thumbs up.

"You did a great job, Mollie," she said.

Mollie flicked her fingers around a curl in Sarah-Jane's curved bob, making it spring, then bounce back into position.

"Ma pleasure. I've missed doon your hair," she said in her thick Glasgow accent.

Sarah-Jane had known Mollie since her very first day at CSN. Mollie McRae was in fact the only real girl friend Sarah-Jane had bonded with in all her years at the network. Not any of the other female anchors. None of the dozen or so female producers. Nor the long list of sexy weather girls. Just her hairdresser. Mollie McRae. Who Sarah-Jane hadn't spoken to for over four years prior to calling her out of the blue earlier this week. Mollie had lost her freelance role at CSN when she was one of the fourteen women to out Walter Fellowes as a serial sex predator. Over the course of the next four months, following the initial allegations, Mollie's hours at the network were cut to nothing. Sarah-Jane had had her hair done by a new, younger freelance hairstylist, and rather than maintain her bond with Mollie, she let their relationship fizzle to nothing—blaming her busy schedule as justifiable reason to turn down multiple text invites for catch-up lunches. Mollie eventually got bored texting… about four years ago, and she had in fact thought she'd seen the last of Sarah-Jane Zdanski in the flesh until that famous name popped up on the screen of her phone earlier this week. Sarah-Jane was starting a new show. A YouTube show. A show she had full autonomy over. And she got to choose who her hairstylist would be for that very show. Mollie McRae. Whom she missed. Dearly. Just not dearly enough for her to make time for them to meet for lunches over the years.

"Well, I missed having you around," Sarah-Jane said as she stood up from her new makeup chair to brush down the creases of the little black dress she had just squeezed herself into before Mollie curled the finishing touches to her perfectly coiffed contemporary bob.

When Sarah-Jane placed her arm across the shoulders of Mollie, she began leading her old friend to the hallway.

"Only ten minutes until I go live," she said.

"I hope the show goes amazing for you. I do. I hope it blows up."

"Thank you, Mollie. So, shall we say same time next week? I'll need you here at around five every Wednesday evening just to touch my hair up."

"Absolutely," Mollie said. "I'm so happy yiv chosen me to do your hair for your new show. Means a lot. Honestly."

She stood in the hallway with her heavy satchel draped over her shoulder as a silence washed its way between the three women now forming a tight triangle.

"Okay, bye then," Erica finally said, ending the silence, "Nice to meet you."

"Oh?" Mollie said, raising one of her eyebrows. "I have tae go, do I? You don't need me, Sarah-Jane? For touch-ups during the commercials?"

Sarah-Jane's shoulders shook while she giggled.

"There are no commercials, silly," she said.

Then she lightly hugged Mollie, making sure not to smudge her freshly applied makeup against the shoulder of the hairdresser's short-sleeved blazer.

Mollie waved a quick hand at Erica, then turned and walked down the long chocolate-colored hallway before pulling open the heavy hall door and walking out, allowing it to close behind her with a sweep and then a heavy clank.

Sarah-Jane turned and walked toward the glowing kitchen, where Phil was fiddling with a knob at the side of one of his shiny new ultra-HD cameras.

"What are the numbers like, Erica?" she called back as she moved into the golden light.

Erica waited until she had reached the glow of the kitchen herself before revealing her latest findings.

"You're not gonna believe this. But there are twenty-four million people online waiting."

"Holy shit," Sarah-Jane said.

Phil seemed impressed enough to look up from the knob he was fiddling with.

"That's a crazy number," Erica said. "Especially as we're still… what…?" She took her iPhone out of the zip pocket of her short houndstooth woolen skirt and tapped a finger against the screen, "eight minutes until we're live. That number's only gonna get bigger. Much bigger with every minute that ticks towards seven p.m. We're gonna go over thirty million for the first show. That's bigger than your very first launch at CSN back in 1997."

Phil looked up from his camera again, then took two steps toward the kitchen island to form another human triangle.

"This is gonna be fucking huge," he said.

"Humongous," Erica replied.

Phil cracked a half-smile on the edges of his dry, choppy lips.

"If we get over thirty million tuning in live to YouTube," Erica said, "imagine how many are gonna watch this footage once word gets out? This podcast will have been shared on hundreds of millions of social media accounts by the time we wake up tomorrow morning."

Phil breathed out a satisfied huff, then turned and walked back into the shadows behind his brand-new cameras.

"Oh," he said from the darkness. "When you mention the two cops, say they were arrested in the early hours of this morning. We've just written "this morning" in the script, but the police confirmed for me a couple hours ago just as Mollie arrived that it was in fact the small hours of the morning when they went to their homes to arrest them. Maggie Zucha was arrested first at about three a.m. and then Nate Bennett half an hour later."

"Goodie," Sarah-Jane said, scribbling the update Phil had given her onto a cue card.

When she placed her pen back down onto the marble top of her kitchen island, she turned to look at Erica, then pushed out a small laugh before stepping toward her.

"All the damn time," she said. She stretched an index finger toward her junior producer's face and pushed the frame of her thick black glasses backward. "That surgeon sure did make that nose extra thin, huh?"

"You can touch me when I invite you to touch me," Erica said, balking away.

"Five minutes," Phil said as he waddled back into the light, "Let's get you mic'd up."

Sarah-Jane stepped up onto her high stool from where she was about to greet tens of millions of Americans, her famous name glowing in neon orange behind her. While Phil fed a tiny plastic piece into her ear with his chunky fingers, Erica walked back into the shadows to fetch her iPad. The iPad had been her greatest companion these past weeks. She relied on the data it gifted her. And data in the digital world is dollars.

"Remember," Phil said. "Sensationalize how slow this Benji guy was. Make America feel really sorry for him. That's the big story here: That this guy was a simpleton. That these two cops killed an innocent, helpless simpleton."

"I will," Sarah-Jane said, touching her ear to readjust the piece.

"No better woman to sell a story than me—no matter how beautiful the story already comes packaged. You know that, Phil."

"You nervous?" Phil decided to ask. Which was unusual. He had never mentioned nerves to Sarah-Jane before—not even ahead of her debut show on CSN some twenty-five years prior.

"Please," Sarah-Jane said, scoffing. "I'm just excited to be going live to tens of millions again. It's been too long."

"Holy fucking shit," Erica said, suddenly appearing in the warm glow of the kitchen again. "There are forty million waiting in the queue. You're about to go live to forty million people."

Phil stared at Sarah-Jane. Then he grabbed her in a tight embrace, laying his jowly chin onto the shoulder of her little black dress. When he pushed a laugh through his nostrils, Erica winced, turning her head away and curling both of her hands into a balled fist.

"Hey, watch my makeup," Sarah-Jane said, pushing Phil away from her shoulder.

He lifted his jowls, then met her nose to nose, just so he could gaze into those bright green marble-like eyes.

"We've done it," he whispered.

Then he kissed her, passionately, sucking her bottom lip in between his, before marching out of the perfectly lit kitchen and into the darkness behind his brand spanking new cameras.

"Ninety seconds," he shouted.

"Shit," Sarah-Jane said. "Erica, can you come help me touch up my lipstick?"

Erica rushed from out of the shadows and grabbed the black lipstick case from Sarah-Jane's grasp before squinting at the mouth Phil had just snogged.

"He's right," Erica said as she touched up the anchor's lips. "This footage doesn't need selling. But we all know you can sell the shit out of anything."

Sarah-Jane kissed her lips, then winked a thank you at Erica.

"I *will* sell the shit out of it. I've been selling the shit out of stories since before you were born. Trust me... by the time we wake up tomorrow morning Benji Wayde is going to be an American hero. And Nate Bennett and Maggie Zucha will be the most despised people in the country. There'll be marches organized. And protests. And riots. And you know what excites me the most? You know what the population of America will be saying over breakfast tomorrow? They're going to be saying "did you watch *The Zdanski Show* last night?"

Their eyes met, and they stared at each other in silence, a small grin forming on the edge of both their lips, until Phil barked, distracting them.

"Ten seconds!"

Erica swept herself out of the glow of the kitchen and into the shadows behind the camera from where she reached for her iPad... noting that there were now almost forty-five million people waiting for Sarah-Jane's face to appear on whatever screen they had positioned themselves in front of.

"Ready?" Phil huffed.

When Sarah-Jane nodded once from her high stool, Phil took one step forward and stretched one of his chunky arms into the glow of the kitchen.

"Okay, we go live in three," he said, showing three fingers... then two... and then just one, before stepping back into the darkness.

Camera number two inched forward with a cool swoosh just as Sarah-Jane glared her beautiful green eyes down its lens.

"Good evening, America," she said. "And welcome to the show..."

...

Watch a short interview with the author of this book in which he discusses:

- *The real-life case that inspired the twist for this novel*
- *The clues to the twists that occur in this novel*
- *What's likely to happen to these characters next*

To watch the video, please just use the link below.

www.subscribepage.com / footagevideo

A Black person is killed every thirty hours by a police officer on the streets of America.

The End.

The Footage That Shook America is the second book of a trilogy. The third book will be released at the end of 2022.

In the meantime, check out David B. Lyons's other trilogy sets.

The Tick-Tock Trilogy
Midday
Whatever Happened to Betsy Blake?
The Suicide Pact

The Trial Trilogy
She Said, Three Said
The Curious Case of Faith & Grace
The Coincidence

ACKNOWLEDGMENTS

This book is dedicated to my cousin, Margaret.
Thank you so much for allowing me to stay in the spare bedroom of your home in Portland, Maine for ninety nights exactly—as many as I was legally allowed to on an open American visa. Those ninety days — spent out of the comfort of my conditioning — totally changed the direction of my life. I have, ever since returning home from that runaway in 2004, only earned a living from the written word. I made a promise to myself during those ninety days of hanging with you that I would never be employed again—that I would never allow somebody else to own my time. I learned that time spent is more valuable than money spent...
I mean, you personally did nothing... so it's not a *huge* thank you. But just... y'know, this is my eighth novel now and I'm kinda running out of people to dedicate them to...
A special thank you also goes to my cover designers on this project. MiblArt are based in Ukraine and worked on the designs for this novel whilst their country was under attack from Russian soldiers. Julia, Nadia, and all of the team at MiblArt, my thoughts continue to be with you during this tumultuous and tragic era.
May peace dawn on your lives real soon. x
Thank you also to Eileen Cline and Kathy Grams for reading early drafts of this novel and helping me to fine tune it.
And to my editorial team of Lisa Geller, Brigit Taylor, and Maureen Vincent-Northam—thank you for your wonderful work.

Printed in Great Britain
by Amazon